Stand

Stand

Book 3 in the Fieldings Series

Kimberley Ash

TEA ROSE

PUBLISHING

Cover Design by Llewellen Designs

Dedication

For the Silenced

Contents

Author's Note and Trigger Warning

This one's a little different. For a start, I have to tell you that Sam and Ty don't get a night of steamy goodtimes the way you might expect from my books. If you can figure out how they could sneak away from the children they're sharing bedrooms with on a three-day road trip, you're a better plotter than I am. Trust me, they have plenty of roaring sex once they get their own room.

Now for the tricky part. This book concerns domestic violence, but not in the way you're thinking. A few years ago, within the space of a week, I heard a radio show about men who had been physically abused by their wives, and separately I talked to a woman whose fiancé had experienced the same thing with his ex. When the world shows me stories, I have to write them.

Abuse within relationships is so horribly prevalent in our world. The vast majority of the victims are women. But women get told they're overreacting or that they should get over it or that they're lying. Or that it's "not that bad." Or worst of all, that they should just put up with it. Women have died because of this, and that infuriates me. Of course, abuse doesn't have to be physical to be debilitating; words can also very effectively destroy someone's life.

So since the general narrative dismisses the woman's experience, I thought, what if a man talks about *his* experience? What kind of man "allows" this to happen? Why does *he* stay? Thus, Ty's story was born. He's a man suffering from years of gaslighting by his ex, to the point that he doesn't think Julia's abuse was "that bad." This story includes incidents of verbal and physical violence she inflicted on Ty, and his children are sometimes witnesses.

I wrote this story partly to give Sam her perfect foil—a man who needs her to save him, but who can save her in turn—and partly to shine a light on spousal abuse and the harmful lies we tell ourselves so we can go about our day.

If you need help or if you'd like to help victims of domestic violence, you can reach out to your local shelter or to the National Domestic Violence Hotline at https://www.thehotline.org/.

PART I

Chapter 1

That was *it*. Sam was getting the hell away from this house, its people, and all its memories.

"Come on, Cairo," she said. Her German shepherd leaped up from his spot under the kitchen table to meet her in the front hall.

"Samantha!" her older sister yelled from behind her. "Get back here! You can't walk away every–"

"Don't call me Samantha!" she yelled back, clipping on Cairo's leash. She should never have come back. Coming back only turned her back into an angry, childish seventeen-year-old who hated her name. Instead of an independent thirty-five-year-old with her own career and her own home and a state on the other side of the country that she missed like crazy.

"Sam!" her younger sister, Megan, called. "It's raining!"

"I won't melt!"

Sam slammed the ancient oak front door of her family home and took the steps down from the porch in one leap, Cairo happily jumping alongside her. The old house seemed to groan in protest. Yeah, yeah. She'd upset the status quo. Again. When Cat called her "Samantha," she was really in trouble.

She took long strides away from the house, down the street she'd grown up on, the trees that had been venerable thirty years ago now creaking with old age and the weight of rain on their summer leaves. The town was late in cutting back the overhanging branches. She let them hit her in the face, punishing herself for her moment of weakness.

"I tell ya, Cai," she grumbled aloud, "I shouldn't have come back at all. Not even for Thea's wedding. Not even to meet Kane's babies." They weren't babies anymore; the oldest was four. She winced.

Cairo matched his long legs to her strides and looked up at her, his brown face grinning happily at the walk. Sam took another tree branch to the face as she looked down at him. She didn't want him to cheer her up. She didn't want to see how thrilled he was with the new smells and new people he'd met.

"I guess you wouldn't have gotten your road trip though, huh, buddy?" she conceded, reaching down to scratch between his ears. He'd loved the three-day drive so much, sniffing the air through the crack in the window, visiting national parks, and sleeping on her bed at pet-friendly hotels. Had it been worth it just for that?

No. "Not for *nothing*. Shoulda packed up the car and gone back home right after the wedding."

Her feet took her down a couple of side streets and through a short back alley to the public footpath in the woods. The slick mud oozing into her sandals soothed her. She knelt down and smeared some on her hands, too. There. That was more like the Sam she knew.

Had her love for exploration started here? The family home's backyard was like many in this cookie-cutter suburb of Boston: small, dominated by the house, a detached garage and a long driveway for the many cars that had come and gone through the years. So she and her four siblings—Catriona, the oldest, the mother hen; Kane, the only boy, handsome and carefree until their father had died; Thea, studious and quiet, laughing at Sam's jokes; and Megan, the baby, running to keep up—had often come to this trail, racing each other through the trees to the stream that ran through the middle of the woods and reflected the seasons.

Sam knew every curve, every eddy, every inch of that stream. She'd learned about erosion from watching it curl around a tree root until the root became exposed and the tree fell across the water. She'd crawled in and out of the old farmer's cottage that had fallen to ruin in the middle of a thicket of brambles, not caring about the scratches when she found an old wooden bucket and rusty ladle. She'd learned about foundations and strata and decomposition alongside how to navigate her sisters' moods and weaknesses. And which of her brother's friends were worth getting to know.

Well, that had been years ago, when their lives were simple.

Before they'd lost their father and then their mother and Sam had lost all faith in men being there when they were needed.

She sat down on one of the slick rocks near the tiny waterfall the town had aggrandized with its own name, and stuck her feet, sandals and all, into the rush of water. When she let Cairo's leash out to its farthest extent, he hopped down to sip from the cool current.

Lifting her heavy hair from the nape of her neck, she raised her face to the rain coming through the trees and tried to blank out her mind.

But Cairo gave his warning bark, and then she heard the voices.

"It's raining. Can we go back now?"

"No. We just got here."

"Ugh. Dad, this is so lame."

"No, it isn't. This is family. This is what we do."

"Lame family."

"Well, it's all you got, so suck it up and look at the falls."

Sam opened her eyes. Two children with faces as uninspired as the weather had appeared on the other side of the narrow stream. Sam had three sixteen-year-old nephews, and the boy looked about their age, though he wore a hoodie that covered half his face. The girl might have been younger; she was in flip-flops, which couldn't have been useful on the rocky path down to the water.

Behind them, their father had a scowl on his face that he quickly rearranged when he saw her. From where she was sitting, he looked tall, taller than her own five foot eleven. The calves she could see below his Bermudas were strong. He either ran or rode a bike on a regular basis.

He looked familiar. The rainy shadows slanting through the trees across his face reminded her of something.

She squinted across the stream. The bike. The blond. "Tyler?"

He took off his sunglasses. The long, thin face of the teenager she'd known had become chiseled cheekbones and a strong jawline, but his ocean-blue eyes were the same.

He didn't recognize her. Not surprising. After years spent outside, she was permanently tan, and her sleek, dark hair had lightened and coarsened in the sun. "It's Sam Fielding," she said awkwardly. "From... school."

His eyes widened at first, but then they narrowed, his lips thinned, and he said, "Oh. Sam," and it sounded as if her name hurt him to say.

Unsurprising, really, given the last time she'd been near him.

Her half smile faltered and died. His kids stopped their desultory exploration of the falls and stared at them. "You know each other?" the boy asked.

"Yep," Tyler said, biting off the word.

From the way their eyes narrowed at her, the kids could sense he wasn't happy. "Uh..." Sam said. "How are you?"

He shot a glance at his kids. Thank God he wasn't about to follow up that scowl with a trip down memory lane. "Fine," he said. Then, after a pause, he added, "Did you move back to town?"

"God, no," she said before she could stop herself. "I mean... no. I live in New Mexico."

The girl's eyes widened just as her father's had. "Cool," she said, then she looked at Tyler. "Like Uncle Noah?"

Sam recalled a kid who'd hung out with Tyler in high school, with the same emo fashion sense, the same reputation for being a great artist but otherwise not worth her time. "You're still friends with Noah Tran?"

He looked away, then back. "Yep."

"Do you live in Taos?" the girl went on. "That's where Noah lives."

Sam couldn't be as reticent as Tyler, not in front of this girl's enthusiasm. "I'm in Albuquerque, but right now I live near the Zuni Pueblo. Do you know what that is?"

"Where the Native Americans lived?"

"Uh-huh." Ignoring the dislike Ty was quite understandably radiating at her, she went on. "Many of them still live there. My company helps them save the ancient sites they were driven out of. Find artifacts, that kind of thing."

"So are you an archaeologist or an anthropologist?" the girl asked, obviously knowing her stuff.

"Both. My doctorate was in archaeology, my bachelor's in anthropology."

"You have a PhD?" Tyler interrupted.

"Yeah." Sam couldn't help herself. She lifted her chin. "Surprised?"

"No. Just..."

"I want to be a psychologist," the girl interrupted. "Or a psychiatrist. I haven't decided."

"You don't have to decide yet," Sam assured her. "That's what college is for."

The girl wore her hair in a fat braid down her back, and now that Sam focused on her, she saw a thick purple stripe on one side of her hair. Sam smiled at her. "Cool hair."

The girl beamed. "Can I pet your dog?" she asked.

"Sure. Do you know how to approach him?"

"Of course." The girl walked into the stream. Her father opened his mouth, but she said, "I'm fine, Dad," before he could speak, and continued to pick her way through the shallow water toward Sam.

Sam had given Cairo the "stay" hand command, and now she aimed a radiating welcome at the girl so Cairo would know she was safe. "Cai, say hello."

The girl held out the back of her hand in a fist and let Cairo come the last few inches to sniff her. Cai did so, then looked at Sam. "Okay," Sam said, and Cai wagged his fuzzy tail and stepped forward, his whole backside swaying at meeting a new friend. He looked scary but was a big old mush, really.

"His name's Cai?" the girl asked.

"Cairo. And I'm Sam. And you are...?"

"Alyssa." Alyssa was on her haunches now, rubbing Cairo's long ears while he panted with joy. "Cairo, like the city?"

"Uh-huh. Nice to meet you."

"He's perfect."

"Thanks. Yes, he is."

"So why are you back?" Tyler asked, reminding her of his presence.

"My sister got married." Guilt twisted in her stomach. Thea would want her to be at home right now, apologizing to Cat. Pretending there was nothing missing in their lives.

"Which sister?"

He remembered she had a bunch of sisters. She'd rather that than the other things he knew about her. "Thea. She was a year ahead of us." The one who'd driven Sam to school for two years, until their father had died and everything had changed.

Tyler looked at her for a moment longer, his pinched expression screaming dislike. *I'm not that girl any more*, she wanted to tell him. *I'm not ashamed of most of it, but I'm different now.* She couldn't say it, not in front of his kids, not in these few startled seconds.

"All right, guys, we should go," he said, turning back to his children.

"We just got here!" complained the boy. His frown made him look just like his father. Their pale skin was even tanned to the same light biscuit.

Even Sam had to hide a smile at the exasperation on Tyler's face as he turned to his son. "You were just saying you wanted to—"

"Sam!" a voice called from behind her. "Sam?"

It was Megan, sent to find her. "Yeah, Meg!" she called back, still looking at Tyler. Cairo leaped away from Alyssa's hands and over to greet his auntie.

Megan came through the trees. She, of course, looked perfect, even for a casual family Sunday lunch. The clothes horse of the family, dressed like she was on her way to a photo shoot. Her white skirt floated beautifully off her slim hips, and she somehow owned rainboots that still looked chic by matching her black embroidered blouse.

"Hey, puppy," she said lovingly to Cairo, then, "Hi!" to the other three, whose bright clothes stood out in the shade of the wet trees. They were all unashamedly staring at her. She gave them the full-wattage Fielding smile. "Nice day, isn't it?" She held a hand up to the rain.

"Hello," Tyler said. He didn't know Megan; she'd still been in middle school when they'd graduated. His son was staring at her, his Adam's apple bobbing up and down. Megan tended to do that to people. Sam gave Tyler credit for not staring too.

What was the protocol here? "This is my sister, Megan," Sam said. "This is Tyler Cavanaugh. We were in high school together."

"Not together," he said and turned away from the women. He put his sunglasses on and raised his voice a little to the kids. "Let's go." This time, they didn't complain. "Nice to meet you," he said over his shoulder to Megan as they began to walk back up the opposite bank. "Bye, Sam," he added with the merest flicker of his eyes toward her. The trio disappeared into the woods.

"What the hell did you do to him?" Megan immediately demanded.

Sam lifted her hair off her neck again. Those last couple of years of high school… well, she didn't think about them. If she did, it was to remember with bravado the nights of drinking, making out with boys she forgot the next day, or her first time with Brennan Caplan and how she'd made him wear two condoms. Which was *not* a good idea.

She liked to think Megan didn't know any of this. "We were in different circles. I met him a couple of times."

"Oh." Megan clearly had other things on her mind. "Okay. Let's go back. Mother Cat's had another glass of wine and Kane's asking her opinion on the company, so she's in a much better mood."

Looking over the stream again before they turned to go home, Sam imagined Tyler as he'd been in high school: bony, wearing glasses, his hair cut in some painfully homegrown way. She flinched a little as she wrapped Cairo's leash around her hand.

"Oh, come on," said Megan, who'd seen her wince. "We're not that bad."

"I wasn't thinking about—" Sam finished the sentence by butting Megan's shoulder with hers. "Yeah, you are."

Megan butted back. "You just say stuff to piss Cat off."

"It's my favorite pastime. And a good reason why I don't visit."

Megan sobered as they came out of the woods and onto the sidewalk. "Did you have to bring up Dad, though?"

Sam folded her arms, the familiar bullheadedness taking over.

"Why not? Is he like an inverse Voldemort or something? He Who Was Too Perfect To Be Named?"

"No," Megan said, her tone even, but Sam already felt like shit. "He was just Dad. But he was the only one we had, Sam."

Megan had been only ten when their father had died. Sam had no business tainting her memories of him with her own anger at his pointless death and the mess he'd left the family in when he'd gone. She put an arm around her little sister's shoulders, which were as tall as her own. "Sorry."

At Cat's house, things were chaotic but normal. The adults pretended nothing had happened. The rain stopped, so the kids recognized fresh meat and dragged Sam and Cairo out into the yard to play catch. The family golden retrievers dropped soggy bones at Cairo's feet and shook the rain off their fur.

After a little while, Kane's daughter came up to show off the half-eaten dinosaur she'd dug out of the sandbox. Sam crouched down and talked to the little girl about T. rexes. Thea's younger son, Benji, and the friend whom he was about to have a sleepover with while Thea was on her honeymoon, joined the group to listen.

Megan came up behind her and nearly knocked her into the sand by hugging her from the back.

"Get off!" Sam said in a muffled voice, her face smooshed into her knees.

"I just wanted to say I'm sooo glad you came home," Meg said into her back.

"Only for Thea," Sam said crossly, but she squeezed the hands that had wrapped themselves around her neck. "And Libby. And maybe you a little bit. Now get the hell off me."

"Get the hell off me!" four-year-old Libby echoed. Seven-year-old Benji and his buddy gulped with shock and delight.

"You're the worst aunt in the world." Meg laughed, easing up on Sam's neck. "Don't talk like your auntie, Libby."

Sam's other nephews had forgotten they were hip and cool sixteen-year-olds and were having a loud game of basketball in the driveway. Jake was now spiking the basketball like it was a football while Paolo or Mateo—her twin nephews would have to stand still for her to be able to figure out who was who—tried to jump on his back.

"Now that you've broken the ice," Meg said, "will you come see us more often?"

Sam looked at her. They had the same dark-brown eyes, same strong eyebrows, same toothy smile. She hadn't been in Meg's life since Meg had left high school. It suddenly occurred to Sam that her baby sister could have used a friend in those years.

"I'll try," she said.

Chapter 2

The kids were quiet on the way home. When Alyssa had to climb over a tree trunk and scratched her thighs, she didn't even squeak. Ty said, "You okay?" She nodded and kept walking ahead of him.

Sam freaking Fielding. Of all people. Sam Fielding, come from God-knew-where, sitting on that rock with her arms up and bent, her hands in her thick, reddish hair, her face turned to the rain like a goddess of the woods or something. In profile, her breasts had been thrust forward, reminding him of their perfection, whether in a sloppy football T-shirt or the tailored green top she'd worn today. She had changed enough that if he'd seen her from a distance, he might not have recognized her. But he'd seen her from twenty feet away, and yeah. He knew it was her. His gut had clenched, his heart flipped over, and his brain froze.

Sam freaking Fielding. Coming on him when his kids had been at their brattiest. Matt, who would ordinarily be the responsible older brother, had just gaped at her like... like Ty had back in the day.

And then. And then! She'd smiled at him! Like they'd been friends or something. That damn Fielding smile they'd all had, even the quiet sister, Thea. The smile that said they owned the world. He should have been glad of that smile, really, because it had reminded him of everything she was, everything she'd done in slow drip-drips of disdain and contempt, every side-eye, every flick of her gorgeous curvy hip, every...

He shook his head to dispel the guilt that pushed at him as they got out into the open near the parking lot. *It was years ago. You gonna be that guy for the rest of your life?*

Only then did he see that Alyssa's leg was bleeding.

"Jeez, Alyssa," he said, irrationally angry with her. "You should have said something!"

He pulled the first aid kid out of his SUV and had her lean against her door while he squirted his water bottle at the back of her leg.

"What are you yelling at her for?" Matt snapped. "God, what a waste of a day." He slammed himself into the back seat and slumped down, pulling his hood over his face.

"I didn't yell." But Ty counted to five anyway. "I'm sorry, honey," he said to Alyssa. "I'm not mad at you. I'm mad that I let you get hurt. Let me see."

Now washed, the back of one leg was okay, but spots of black were embedded in the graze on her other leg. Alyssa sniffed a little. "I'm okay."

She always said that, and he knew it. He should have remembered. Recently, she'd been more vociferous when she was unhappy with something. Before, when the divorce was going through, Alyssa had always been "fine." Today had been a cranky day for all of them.

He gave her a one-armed hug, noting the changes in her height and weight in just a year. Being her dad had been tricky the first year, bliss the next few, and painful the last couple. Now that she was officially a teenager, he knew it was going to get a whole lot worse.

He pulled out the cotton balls and hurt-free antiseptic and was as gentle as he could be while he cleaned her up. "You'd better take a bath when you get home. Soak out the dirt."

"N'kay," Alyssa said. His heart squeezed. He had a spare blanket in the back and had her sit on it while he strapped her in. She was plenty old enough to do it herself, of course, but she let him this time.

The ride home was quiet. They'd just turned onto his street when his phone rang.

He looked at the caller ID on his dashboard. "It's Mom," he said in an even tone. Despite that, he felt the atmosphere behind him thicken with apprehension. You never knew with Julia. "Hello?"

"Hey, guys!" Her voice came through the speakers high and crystalline. Sharp enough to break. Or to hurt. "Are you in the car? Having a good day?"

"Yes, thanks," the children echoed dutifully. Ty felt guilty, again, about Alyssa's legs.

"Oh, good. Well, let me tell you how my day's been. I've had the best time!" Julia said. "My friend Tania—you know, I told you about her, she's so special to me, we met at the supermarket a few weeks ago, I tell you, it's amazing how we connected, you know how you feel when you just know you've found your soul mate? Friend soul mate, of course. Nice try, Ty; bet you'd like that, wouldn't you!"

He cringed openly this time, and the kids did too. God, he could only wish that Julia would find a new partner. Why would she think he'd care what gender that person was?

"Well," Julia went on, "she told me she's buying a timeshare in Florida, right outside Disney World, and she wants me to go in on it with her, isn't that amazing? And it's got two bedrooms, so there's room for the kids, and you could come when it's my turn and we could go to Disney and Universal and just be in the sun and wouldn't that be great? So she wants us to go down and see it, and I thought—"

Here it comes.

"You wouldn't mind if I took the kids, Ty, 'cause it is summer after all and this way you can work uninterrupted 'cause I remember you used to bitch all the time if I tried to talk to you when you were—"

"Julia," he finally interrupted. They had pulled up in front of his house. "Kids, go inside."

"Disney?" Alyssa said.

"Universal?" Matt said.

"Let me talk to your mom." The children got out and walked slowly down the path to the front door.

Julia had started talking again as soon as he stopped. "I know what you're going to say, Ty, but this time it's a good deal. A friend of Tania's bought one, and she got two weeks down there every year, and it cost barely a thousand dollars a week. Can you imagine what a week at the Cape would cost? And this would be Florida!"

"Julia," he said again. "You are not allowed to take the kids out of state. Remember?"

"Only without your say-so, and you have to see this is so great for them! Who wouldn't like it?"

"Florida in August? No one likes it."

"You just don't want me to be with my kids!" she shouted, and her voice went from hyper to hysterical in a second. "You're keeping them from me!"

Ty slumped, trying to ease the pulsing pain that had started again in his lower back. Julia did that to him. At least he'd gotten the kids out of the car before they heard her tone. "I'm not keeping them from you any more than you're allowed to have them. We have an agreement. With a schedule that your lawyer read over with you in my presence and that you signed. Remember?" Stupid question. She didn't remember anything she didn't want to. Same as when she'd decided to leave the family when the novelty of being a mother wore off.

"But this would be barely more than a night!"

"No, Julia. Last time you took them out, you left them at the diner. I'm not letting you take them to God-knows-where in Florida."

She began crying—rich, messy sobs he'd witnessed so many times he could tell within a millimeter where on her perfect cheeks the tears would fall. "You've been telling them I don't love them, haven't you! That's why they don't want to come with me!"

He sighed. "I tell them you love them every day. And they love you." This was true, but she would never believe it. And forgetting to come get her kids from movie theaters or yelling at them if they didn't like the food at a fancy restaurant she insisted on made it hard for Ty to defend her. "I'm going to hang up now. You know this timeshare is a waste of money. You'll see them next weekend. Same as always."

"Yeah, in *your* town, with *you* breathing over our shoulders the whole time! Fuck you, Ty."

As he had finally taught himself, he pressed the button on the steering wheel and ended the call. He turned the car off, pulled the key out of the ignition, and lowered his head to rest on his hands on the steering wheel.

Why hadn't he seen it? How had she so completely snowed him?

Ach, he knew why. She'd looked up at him, big brown eyes all soft and wet, and told him how much she wanted him. Ty, raised on a steady diet of no dad, a poor, busy mom, and school bullies, had felt like a million bucks for the first time in his life. When she'd taken him to that little hotel their first year in college, he'd hardly thought twice about following her lead.

And the result, as he kept reminding himself, was Matt. Then Alyssa. And that made it all worth it. Shrugging off a feeling of being in a vise, he got out of the car and followed the kids into the kitchen.

They were at the freezer, the door open, tubs of ice cream sitting on the countertop. Two pairs of worried eyes locked on him.

"She said to say she loves you," he said. She did love them, in her own way. As long as they didn't get in the way of her social life or her next obsession.

"Is she really buying a house in Florida?" Alyssa asked.

"No. It's a timeshare. You buy a couple of weeks a year. Usually, the good weeks are all taken and you get... well, you get now. And if you think Massachusetts is humid in the summer, you should try Orlando."

Alyssa dug into the vanilla with the biggest spoon in the drawer. "Get a bowl," Ty said automatically, though right now he could hardly care.

"It'd be cool, though," Alyssa went on. "We could go to Harry Potter every day."

"Can she afford it?" Matt asked more shrewdly.

"Probably," Ty said. He closed the freezer door and got bowls out for them all. Julia came from money. Money and two parents who'd cut him and the kids off as soon as Julia had left town. Now she'd come back, and they still hadn't called. Too embarrassed, Ty hoped, knowing how they'd enabled her to avoid her responsibilities. "Load me up there, bub."

Ice cream as compensation for an absent and unstable mother. It was the best he could do.

♦

When the kids were in their rooms for the night, Ty went to his workshop. Squeezed onto a wooden table at the back of the one-car garage, the small collection of tools and blocks of wood hardly deserved the word, but he could feel his blood pressure drop the moment he closed the heavy door from the house.

He pulled his latest project off the shelf, hooked his foot around the stool, and sat. His working glasses were right where he'd left them, as were his leather finger guards and the strap of fine-gauge tools he'd carefully oiled the other day. He regretted, in a way, that he was almost done with this sculpture, a ruby-crowned kinglet for Alyssa to add to her collection. He would have liked to hack away at a new lump of wood with sweeping strokes that tired him out and helped him sleep.

Still, the kinglet's feathers required concentration and control, and Ty loved the feel of the chubby little woodcarving in his hands as he worked. Julia, the kids' worries, and Florida all faded away.

His phone, predictably, rang. He swiped it and hit speaker. "Hey, No."

His best friend, Noah, had a deep voice made deeper from all the experimental "healthy" substances he'd smoked over the years. "Tyler. What's going on?"

Ty picked up the narrow, sharp blade and kept on whittling. "Same old same old."

"You carving?"

"Uh-huh."

Noah snorted. "I tell you, man, you should be down here. You're an artist at heart."

"And a capitalist at mouth. I have kids to feed, remember?"

They'd been having this argument since Noah had moved to Taos five years ago. "Costs a lot less to feed them down here," he pointed out.

"Enough," Ty said, hoping the smile on his face translated to his voice. "You wanna tell my mom her only grandkids are moving two thousand miles away? Quit bugging me. Why d'you call anyway?"

"Just catching up." Ty heard a long drawn-in breath and a held-in cough. Another reason Ty wasn't about to move nearer to Noah's lifestyle.

"How's the gallery?"

"Good. Decent business. Weather's been good. Lots of hikers. You?"

"Usual. Alyssa's graduating middle school in a couple days. Matt was looking for a summer job, but he waited too long and the college kids got them all."

"Send him to me!" Noah said at once. "Does he like horses? I gotta friend who—"

"It's okay." Ty had to put the kibosh on this right away. "His buddy's stepdad is going to get him something in his business. Plumbing."

"*Plumbing*? Jesus, Ty. You trying to punish the kid? When he could be here riding horses and chatting up girls? It is girls, right?"

"So he tells me."

Ty imagined the world Noah lived in. He had to imagine it, because he'd never been there. Noah had left the state just before Ty and Julia had moved back into town from his original workplace near Philadelphia. They'd come back because she was getting more and more erratic; her parents refused to believe there was a problem, and he needed his mom to help out. Julia had hated the idea. Ty hadn't loved it either, given his high school experience with these kids and the town's reaction to his young fatherhood. But his mom was the most stable person he knew, and whatever the town thought of him, he hadn't regretted coming back.

He and Noah had hung together throughout middle school and become inseparable in high school. Noah's Vietnamese heritage had looked the bomb with black eyeliner and his collection of vintage '80s goth band T-shirts. They'd dodged the same bullies, gone to the same concerts, and shared everything about their lives.

When Julia had left, Ty had called Noah first. Ty would always love him for his support during that time. And for these stupid, probably pot-fueled conversations that meant nothing and everything.

"You gotta admit," Noah said, "you're interested."

"I'll think about it," Ty said.

"Think about it *hard*. Alyssa could work the counter at the store. I'd take care of them."

Unfortunately, he coughed again at that moment. Ty wouldn't ask him to swear he wouldn't smoke if he got the kids, because Ty had no intention of sending them so far away. The thought of being away from them for so long made his heart shrivel up inside him. People said their kids were their reason for being, and it was a cliché, but not for Ty. Snowplow parent? Sure. If that were remotely possible with a mom like Julia, Ty would do it.

"Julia been around?" Noah asked.

"Quit reading my mind. Yeah. She called today. Wants to take them to Florida, for fuck's sake."

The blade slipped out of its notch on the wood and almost impaled his finger but for the leather guards. He swore and shook out his hand.

"She couldn't even get through a meal with them, last I heard," Noah said.

"Right. It's just an idea of hers. She'll go off it soon. I just wish she'd—"

He couldn't finish. "Yeah, man. I know," Noah said. "You're doing right by them. You're doing good."

"Thanks." He didn't want Julia to invade his happy place in the garage, so he cast around for something else to talk about.

And fell on Sam Fielding.

"Hey, speaking of difficult women in our lives, guess who I saw in town today?"

Noah laughed. "That doesn't narrow it down a whole lot."

"Remember Sam Fielding?"

"Sam Fielding? Rich kid, all legs, looked down on us mere peasants?"

Ty winced. It sounded worse when Noah said it out loud. But he'd been thinking it. "That Sam Fielding. Yeah."

"Seven Minutes in Heaven Sam Fielding?"

The knife went right into Ty's glove that time. "Ouch. Yeah." He pulled off his glove to inspect the wound. Just a red mark. No permanent damage. Like those seven minutes. Right?

"Made Brennan Caplan wear two condoms?"

He'd forgotten that rumor. "Jeez. Yeah."

"Worked her way through the basketball team?"

"Yes! That Sam Fielding!" God, if that was the kind of gossip that even Noah remembered, Ty could sympathize with the woman for getting the hell out of town like she had. For looking so pissed off that she was back.

"Wow. Did she give you the time of day?"

"Of course she did. This isn't high school anymore." His hand was gripped too tightly around the handle of his blade. He forced himself to relax. Noah was only voicing everything Ty's scrambled brain had thought on first seeing Sam. It was Ty who'd been ruder than he wanted. "Her sister got married."

Belatedly, he realized something. "Thea. Matt's friend Jake's mom. I've talked to her a couple times this year. She's all right." Meaning, she hadn't turned her nose up at him when they'd met on the b-ball sidelines.

"And?"

"And what?" Dammit. He sounded stubborn and childish. He knew what Noah was asking. "Yes, she's still..." *Breathtaking. Beautiful. Heart-stopping.* "Attractive."

"God. What would I say to her if I met her now?" Noah mused.

Not what I did, I hope. "Welp. I doubt I'll see her again." *So quit feeling bad for being such a prick. Hasn't she earned it?*

No, she hadn't. "Their dad died in that explosion, remember?" he added. "They were all kinds of fucked up after that."

"Doesn't give her an excuse to treat us the way she did."

"She ignored us, mostly." *Mostly.*

"There's ignoring and there's ignoring," Noah said wisely.

"She was nice to Matt and Lyss today." Now why had he said that? What did he care about defending this woman?

"Oh-ho. Attractive, you say. *And* nice to your kids? You sure she isn't sticking around town?"

"I'm hanging up now."

"Okay, okay. If you *do* see her again, tell her I said hi. Actually, tell her I said I hope she gets... uh... rickets."

Noah could always make him laugh. "Sure. I'll do that. See ya."

Chapter 3

"Want me to drive you guys to school today?" Sam asked Jake when he came downstairs the next morning. If the buses were on the same schedule as they'd been twenty years ago, he and his cousins were about to miss theirs, and she hadn't even seen Paolo and Mateo yet.

Jake focused on her with difficulty. Six forty-five was way too early for a teenager. His dark hair stuck up at the back, and he obviously hadn't showered. "Yeah?"

Last night she'd remembered a lot of things she'd pushed to the back of her mind. She wanted to check out the high school, wanted to push on that sore tooth that was her guilt for her last two years there. "Sure. Go get showered. I'll make you a smoothie to drink on the way."

He perked up at once. "Could we take my friend too? He lives on the way."

"I don't see why not if you get a move on."

"Cool, thanks, Aunt Sam. I'll text him."

While he showered, she made smoothies. The boys came down, and although they made a face at the sludge-colored smoothies, once they tasted them, they didn't complain. Cat kissed the top of her sons' heads; Sam took her keys; Jake shuffled into his Converses, and they were off.

Sam should probably be having some deep conversation about Jake's feelings about his mom's remarriage, but she just wasn't up to it, and with the twins in the back seat, he might not have wanted to talk anyway. Instead, while Paolo and Mateo seemed to fall back to sleep, she and Jake discussed her work. Jake was into computers and asked a bunch of questions about monitoring equipment and using sonar to find buried artifacts.

Tyler Cavanaugh and his friends had been into computers. Back then, their interest had damned them to the fringes of school society. Sam frowned at a traffic light. She *hated* remembering high school. This was a bad idea.

They pulled up to a townhouse, one in a long row with scant landscaping out front. A small SUV sat in the driveway.

Jake unfolded himself from her front seat and went to ring the bell. A man with blond hair opened the door, looked behind him, and yelled, "Matt!" before squinting out into the sunlight.

Shit.

She contemplated slouching down in the seat, but he'd already looked past Jake and seen her through her open window. "Hi," she called over, knowing the word was inadequate.

Jake waved a lazy hand behind him. "That's my aunt. She's staying with us for a couple of days."

Sam gave a close-mouthed smile and a shrug, as if to say, *hey, I'm just as surprised as you are.*

He turned around and yelled, "Matt!" behind him again. The boy from yesterday appeared, looking even more sleepy and unprepared for school than Jake. The boys started to walk toward the car just as Matt's sister poked her head out the door. With her hair down around her face, her purple stripe was more noticeable. Sam gave her a wave, and she beamed back. Nice kid.

Matt had opened the back door and slid in next to Paolo before she realized that Ty had followed them. Something in his face made her get out and join him on the sidewalk. He was rumpled like his son and just as tall and rangy as yesterday. Yep, no denying the geek had grown up.

"I..." he began and grabbed the back of his neck. "I just wanted to... apologize for being a little... short with you yesterday."

Sam laughed before she could stop herself. "I'm five eleven," she said. "And I have to look up at you. You couldn't be short if you tried."

He didn't smile with her. "You know what I mean."

"Sorry." Sam sobered up. His hostility from yesterday had gone, replaced with an intensity she couldn't translate. "It's fine," she said.

"I'm not... proud of a lot of what happened in high school. Particularly..."

"Well." He got crinkles around his eyes that implied he would smile if it weren't so damn early in the morning. "Neither of us were our best self in high school. Who is? I have apologies to make to you."

"What?" Had she not remembered something from that party? "What did *you* do?"

He opened his mouth, then shook his head as though he wanted to tell her but didn't know how to start.

Sam could see the stubble on his chin and his pulse in his neck, thrumming away slowly.

"Aunt Sam!" Jake yelled out the window.

"Right. Right. Well, bye."

"Bye," he said. "Thanks for taking Matt."

"Sure."

Such stilted language. Yet there was something underneath it all. Something Sam couldn't catch hold of.

Their brief history didn't have to be raked over again. Ty lived a good life now. A safe life, here with his kids. She wondered where his wife was. Partner, whatever.

A mystery for another day. Or never, since she was driving home tomorrow. She gave him one last glance before going back to her SUV. He hadn't taken his eyes off her.

"You guys strapped in?" she said brightly to the boys. And they drove away, leaving Ty behind.

The high school was and wasn't the same. There were more cars than ever, the parking spaces strictly outlined and numbered. She remembered a few fights over spaces, a few smashed lights. She might have encouraged one of them, she remembered with a squirm.

The school looked small, the children even smaller. Surreptitiously, she inspected her passengers. Jake seemed to be one of the "regular" kids with his pants low, Converses the required level of beaten-up, hair the perfect blend of messy and gelled. He had the dark hair and blue eyes of his no-good father, and Sam wasn't surprised when two girls waved hello to him before he'd even straightened up from his seat. He was one of the cool kids, like all the Fieldings had been, even Thea, who'd spent all her time buried in books. Matt was blond and solid and looked like he played sports, she noted approvingly. Paolo and Mateo, peas in a pod, were dark and swarthy like their father. And their mother. And the whole Fielding family.

Sam, with her sun-lightened hair, was the odd one out among her siblings.

All the kids filing into the building were cool. Sam appreciated the ones carrying hockey sticks just as much as the ones draped in sweats, trying not to stand out. It was so easy to see their value now. Why hadn't she seen it when she'd come here? She wanted to go up to each and every one of them and tell them that they were important, that they shouldn't listen to anyone who made them feel less than. Anyone like Sam Fielding in grades eleven and twelve.

She squeezed her eyes shut. Why had she done this to herself? She could have been driving west by now. Not raking over these hot coals, waiting for another fire of guilt to break out.

◆

She spent the day trying to keep out of Cat's way. The woman was a dynamo. After hosting yesterday's lunch, she seemed determined to scrub all evidence of it out of existence. Megan had gone back to her apartment in Boston, so Sam had no buffer. Even the dogs hid. She helped where she could, took Cat's fussing at how she cleaned as calmly as she could, and gratefully got out of there as often as possible to walk Cairo.

Jake came through the door at two fifty-five precisely. Sam knew this because Cat looked at the kitchen clock and said, "Two minutes late."

"Does it matter?" Sam asked. Cat shrugged. If she planned on answering, it was stopped by Jake's face as he walked into the room.

"Aunt Cat," he said, in that tone that immediately made Cat say, "God. What? What happened? Are you okay?"

"I'm okay," he said, but he looked extra morose, even for a teen who had just suffered through another day of school. "But I don't think Matt is."

"What happened?" Sam said. "Cairo, leave him alone." Her dog was sniffing Jake all over, and Jake didn't even put out a hand to pet him. "Here." She snapped her fingers and Cairo came to her side.

"Matt's mom came and picked him up," Jake said.

"Is that bad?" Sam asked.

"He didn't want to go with her." Jake mashed his hands under his armpits, making him look hunched over and old. "She said his dad had said they could go out for ice cream. And... I dunno. Maybe he did. But I texted Matt from the bus, and he hasn't texted back. And he told me about–"

Cat nodded. Sam folded her arms. "What's going on? Why is it bad for his mom to take him out for ice cream?" She'd enjoyed her vision of Tyler Cavanaugh in a steady marriage with two good-looking kids.

"Matt's mom left them," Jake said. "His dad got full custody 'cause she flaked out, but now she's back and she wants them back."

"Lord." Her pleasant vision collapsed. "You say 'wants them back' like that's a bad thing."

"Yeah, but she's been kinda... off," Jake said. "Like, took them to the movies and then left them halfway through because she was bored, and then forgot to come back and get them. And she talks about taking them out of state, and they don't want to go, but she keeps talking about it."

"How long has she been back?" Sam asked.

"A couple months."

Cat looked at the towel in her hands. Her voice was uncharacteristically subdued when she said, "I understand why she doesn't want to stay in town. The rumor mill around here is fierce."

You don't have to tell me.

"If she wants to be back in their lives," Cat went on, "that *is* a good thing. I mean, she didn't give up."

"She *did* give them up, Aunt Cat," Jake said. "Two years ago, remember? She has to get their dad's approval if she wants to take them anywhere now."

"Well, then," Cat said. "I hope you're being a good friend to Matt, because this is real hard on him." Cat looked around at her house. Sam knew she was thinking about the stability it represented. "Count yourself lucky, Jacob."

He rolled his eyes but mumbled, "I do," and Sam believed him. His mom had fought for a long time to bring that kind of steadiness to her boys' lives, and her new husband had added to it. Sam, on the other hand, had run fast and far away from any kind of responsibility she wasn't paid to deal with.

"We have to call his dad," Cat said.

"I know," Jake said. "But I don't know his number."

"The parent directory app will have it," Cat said. "Unless he's unlisted."

"There's always Google," Sam added as Cat opened her phone.

"Or we could call the school," Jake suggested. "But they've all gone home."

"I got it!" Cat thrust her phone into Jake's hands.

Jake just as quickly thrust it back. "Can you call him?" he begged.

"Jake, you're the one who saw what happened." Cat turned into Stern Auntie. "You need to do it."

Jake sighed, and Sam tried not to let her lips twitch. Teenagers gonna teenage. He took the phone, dialed the number, and put it on speaker.

"Tyler Cavanaugh," the voice said. Sam did *not* blush. She did *not*.

"Mr. C, it's Jake Field–McConnell. Fielding."

"Jake? Is Matt with you?"

Of course. He already knew something was up. His son hadn't been on the bus.

"No." Jake swallowed visibly. "I'm sorry, I asked him if he wanted to go, but she—"

"Jake," Cat hissed, "tell him from the beginning."

"Did his mom show up?" Tyler said at the same time.

"Yeah." Jake sounded relieved and scared at the same time. "She said you'd said she could take them out for ice cream. She swore you said it was okay."

"She does that." Tyler's voice was grim.

There was silence. Tyler's mind must be scrambling to take in the information. How bad was this? Would the kids really be in danger from being with their mother? In Sam's experience, mothers were the reliable ones. It was fathers you had to watch out for.

"What can we do?" Cat asked. "It's Catriona, Ty. Jake's aunt."

"He has a lot of those, huh." His tone was deadpan.

"Yeah, I'm here too," Sam had to say. She didn't want him to think she was eavesdropping on this.

"Hi, Sam," Ty said.

"Hello."

Cat gave her a sharp look, and Sam raised her eyebrows at her. *What?*

"Okay," Ty said in a normal voice—as normal as Sam knew, anyway. "I think I know where they've gone. Did you say 'they,' Jake?"

"Uh-huh. She said they had to go quick to pick up Alyssa."

"Shit."

That one word carried years of pain in it.

What did Ty do when he was stressed? Was he pinching the bridge of his nose? Running his hand through that coarse blond hair? Scratching the stubble she'd noted on his cheeks this morning?

She was just wondering.

"Can we help?" she said, echoing Cat. "Do you need me to drive anywhere?"

"I... thank you. I have to call the..." He sounded more distracted now. "Thanks for telling me. I have to go. Jake," he said, "if he calls you..."

"Sure, of course I'll call you," Jake said. He sounded scared.

Sam didn't mean to, but the words burst out of her. "Where do you think she's gone?"

"Florida," he said and hung up.

The three of them stared at each other. "She's not allowed to take them out of state," Jake repeated.

"Do the airports know that?" Cat asked. "Or is she planning on driving them?"

"God. Poor kids." Sam felt choked, panicky. For all that she didn't want her own children, Sam couldn't stand to see others in difficulties. Jake and Benji had been through the mill. She felt guilty every day for how long she'd let Thea struggle with single motherhood before she'd met Liam. But Sam *couldn't* come back here. She just couldn't.

Jake and Benji's dad had come back as well after years away and expected to walk back into their lives. All he'd done was disrupt everyone's happiness and cause trouble. It sounded like Ty's ex was doing the same thing.

"I'm going to take Cairo out," she declared. She needed to move. "Cai, walk."

Cairo skittered over to them from the corner he'd been snoozing in. "Sam," Cat began.

Sam rounded on her. "What? What good am I here? I need to do something useful."

"I wasn't going to—! Never mind. Go."

Chapter 4

Thus dismissed, again, from Cat's presence, Sam left the house and walked Cairo blindly down the road. No direction in mind, no notion of what was around her. She knew all of this town. She would find their way home. Eventually.

She walked so fast that she was through the center of town and onto the streets around Ty's house before she knew it. *Coincidence.* But she knew which house was his. His car was still in the driveway.

What could she do? She didn't know, but she knocked on the door anyway.

Ty opened it. His hair was disheveled and his lips pulled tight. There was a haunted look in his eyes, as if he knew she was bad news whatever she said. "What"—he looked behind her—"What are you doing here?"

"I'm not sure," she said honestly. "Have you heard anything?"

"I'm waiting. The police are in touch with the airport. But if she decides to drive..."

Sam hitched her weight to one foot. Cairo gave the mildest of whimpers, his request to greet the human he didn't know yet.

The distraction helped Ty break out of his stupor. "Hey, buddy," he said and crouched down to Cai's level. Cai didn't need more invitation than that, though Sam knew he would back off the moment she ordered him. She didn't like out-of-control dogs. Or situations.

Ty scratched Cai's neck and behind his ears, and Sam couldn't think of one single thing to say.

From his crouched position, he said in a voice that almost didn't carry, "Alyssa's graduating from middle school tomorrow, for God's sake."

"Is she really going to take them to Florida?"

Still talking as if to Cairo, he said, "My ex, she... she doesn't understand consequences. Once when they were seven and five, she left them at a diner for two hours while she went to find a motel, caught sight of a park, and decided to explore it so she could take them there. By the time Matt remembered my phone number, Alyssa was hysterical. And then when Julia came back this time, she did it *again*."

"Jesus. I'm sorry, Ty."

"Yeah."

A chiming came from his cell phone. He let go of Cairo and looked at it. "Alyssa," he breathed and had to swipe the screen twice, his hands had begun shaking so badly. Sam froze.

"Alyssa, honey, thank God. Where are you? ...I know, it's okay, hon. Don't be sorry, I understand... Where are you? Okay, well, we'll have the police there in two minutes. Which gate? Uh-huh. It's gonna be okay, sweetheart; we'll have you home in a... I know you didn't; it's not your fault. I know she scared you. I'm sorry, Lyss. Okay, let me call security over there. Just stay with Matt. I love you, too."

He didn't hang up, just dropped his hand to his side with the phone still on. "Where are they?" Sam said.

"Logan," he said. "The plane leaves in thirty-five minutes. She took Matt's phone, but she forgot Alyssa got one for her thirteenth birthday." His whole body began shaking. "Alyssa finally got her to let her go to the bathroom."

"Do you want me to call the airport?" He was obviously beside himself.

"No, I..." But he seemed to have forgotten how to use the phone. She took it out of his hand and hung up, then hit the last number dialed button. When they answered, she handed it to him. In short, jerky sentences, he gave them the information he had, listened for a moment, then said, "Okay, I'll be there as quick as I—" and hung up without finishing the sentence.

Ty didn't say anything more to her. He disappeared into the house, came back out with his keys, slammed the door, and walked the few steps to his car. But he was visibly shaking, and guilt or responsibility or pity made Sam follow him.

She watched him get into his SUV and waited ten or fifteen seconds while he tried to get the keys in the ignition. Then she strode over and opened the door. "Move over," she said, intentionally making her voice authoritative, cutting through his panic. "I'll take you."

"No," he said at once.

"Let me drive you." She looked at his handsome face, now marred by eyes darkened with fear.

"I can ask my mom to do it." But his voice was faded, as though the steps necessary to even talk to his mother were beyond him. He looked at the key in his hand as though he'd forgotten what it did.

"Please," she said. "Let me help."

He got out of the car. This close, she discovered that he smelled of wood shavings and dryer sheets, and blond stubble dusted his cheeks and chin. When he slapped his keys into her open hand, she felt rough skin.

No time to ponder this, of course. Sam opened the back hatch, and Cairo easily hopped up into the space. She thought of asking Ty if he minded a dog in his car, but that was the least of his worries.

Sam was soon heading for the highway, Ty holding on to the oh-shit bar above his door as if she were about to drive them into a wall, and constantly checking the phone in his other hand.

He didn't speak until they were on the exit ramp for the highway. She couldn't imagine what thoughts were going through his mind, but he said, "You probably think I'm overreacting."

"No!" She took her eyes off the road to see him looking at her. "No, absolutely not."

He didn't hold her gaze but continued scanning the road. "Julia... gets these ideas in her head." He didn't look at her, instead shifting his attention to Cairo. "They don't usually pan out. She took them to a fancy French restaurant last month and was pissed when they wouldn't eat snails. So she left them there."

"Jesus, Ty."

"Told them they were ungrateful and to go back to me if they liked me that much more than her." His shoulders hunched.

"I'm so sorry." Inadequate response, but it was all she had.

He gave a little snort. "The thing is, *she* never says that. She never thinks she did anything wrong. The world is against her. I can't fight it."

Sam didn't know what to say. They drove in silence for a minute more, but she was well aware of when he began staring at her profile. He was looking at her as though she were some kind of exotic species he'd suddenly found in his car.

"Where did you go after high school?" he asked abruptly.

"UNM. Then a master's in Egypt. But I came back for my doctorate. The pueblos were where I wanted to be."

"Huh." He stared at her even harder. Even for Sam, who had no problem with the way she looked, the scrutiny made her fidget her hands on the steering wheel.

"What?" she said. "What did you think I'd be doing?"

He shrugged, turning his attention to the road. "I don't know. Working for your family business, I guess."

"*Hell* no," burst out of her. The very thought made her throat close up. Office buildings, factory inspections, marketing meetings. Ugh.

That elicited a short laugh from him. "Okay then. I just... didn't think the Fieldings would ever leave Massachusetts."

"You don't have to say 'the Fieldings' like we're the Sopranos or something." He didn't reply, just kept his eyes on the road. For some reason, she got annoyed. "So what do *you* do?" She squinted at him. He'd been one of the emo kids at school. Holed up in the art room or sitting under trees in black on hot days.

"I design office spaces," he said.

Well, that sounded suburban. "Not comic books?"

He looked back at her with a heavy-lidded gaze. "Graphic novels, and no. This pays better."

"So you *did* want to draw—"

"Don't miss the exit!" he interrupted, and Sam had to swerve hard to catch it. Chastened, she focused on her driving. She wasn't here to tease Tyler Cavanaugh. She was here to shut up and drive.

His phone rang. "Tyler Cavanaugh," he said into it. "Okay. Okay, good." He swapped his phone to his other side and put the hand closest to Sam up to his face, covering it from her. "Good." He sounded more strangled with each word. She wished she could give him some privacy. "We're just coming up to the airport. I'll be there in five minutes. Okay. Yep. Thanks. Thank you." The last word was a fervent whisper, even as he took the phone from his ear to hang up.

"Good news?" she said into the silence.

"Yes. They got them." Most of the tension oozed from him, but now he put his hand on the dashboard in front of him, leaning forward as if willing the car to move faster in the airport traffic.

"I'm glad," she said.

He grunted acknowledgment, but she could tell his mind was far from niceties now. Sam dodged around as many cars as she could, and within the promised five minutes she was pulling up to the departures entrance. "Wait!" she said as he opened the door almost before the car had stopped. "I can't leave Cairo. Take my number. I'll wait for you."

Impatiently, he tapped her phone number into his phone. Then he was gone, pushing through a small knot of people going through the doors, their excited chattering a contrast to the strain she'd seen in his face.

Sam parked Ty's car in short-term parking and burned off her nervous energy walking Cai around in circles, checking her phone every thirty seconds. After forty-five minutes, he texted: **We're done.**

That was when Sam remembered she didn't have her wallet. She'd driven all the way here without a license. "Well, shit, Cai," she told him. "So much for being his knight in shining armor."

Thank God she could download the app on her phone and had memorized her credit card. Panic over, she cracked a back window so Cai could stick his nose into the late afternoon heat and pulled around to the drop-off area.

She had to circle a couple of times before she spotted them. Ty had one arm around his daughter. She had both arms around him, and her head was buried in his side. His other arm was around Matt, who stood slumped against him, his blond head leaning against Ty's.

Sam's heart twisted. Ty Cavanaugh was a *dad*. And a good one, from the way Alyssa was holding on to him. Sam could hardly wrap her head around it.

They looked completely wiped out. Alyssa's cheeks were still wet. What had they thought when their mother had driven them onto the highway and into the airport? Their pain was clear on their faces.

Under one of Ty's eyes was an angry red mark that covered his cheekbone. *Where the hell did that come from?*

It was Matt who recognized the car first and instinctively straightened.

"Hi, Matt," she said quietly. "Hi, honey," she added to Alyssa. "I just drove your dad here."

"You brought Cairo!" Alyssa said. Not that the kid was capable of a big grin right now, but she brightened.

"Let's go, peanut," Ty said.

The kids' backpacks were in a pile next to them. As she rounded Alyssa for the backpack, Sam couldn't help but lay her hand briefly on the girl's vulnerable back. Alyssa gave a sigh that shook her whole frame, and Ty's arm tightened around her. To an observer, they looked as if they had recently been bereaved.

It must feel like that. I lost Mom and Dad once; they lose their mom every time they trust that something will be different and she lets them down.

Ty got in the back, sitting between the children as though he needed their bodies pressed against his to reassure him they were safe. The narrow seat made a joke of his long legs, and his head brushed the roof. Both kids reached around to pet Cairo and then, as far as Sam could tell, fell asleep on the drive home. A few times, she caught Ty's eye in the mirror; he didn't smile at her and he looked away every time, but she thought she felt his eyes on her when she wasn't looking. Ty looked shattered, as if the responsibility he carried was literally pressing him into his seat.

He nudged them awake as she pulled into his driveway. The soft murmur of his voice threatened to bring tears to her eyes. He had a nice voice, low and melodious. She wondered if he sang. Megan could sing, and part of her charm was her deep, sexy voice.

Sam blushed a little. *Not the time to think of Ty and sexy simultaneously.*

"I don't want to go to school tomorrow," Alyssa said.

"It's your last day of middle school, Lyss," Ty said. "You don't want to miss it."

The kids got out of the car and began to walk to the front door. Ty shifted along the seat to follow them, but Alyssa had come back. Her blue eyes were big and dark with fear, just as her father's had been an hour before. "Can you check the house?" she said in a low voice that Sam nevertheless heard as she had her window open.

Ty answered by getting out and going with them. Sam got out of the car as well, and she and Cairo hovered by it. She tossed the keys in her hand.

In a few minutes, he came back outside. Wordlessly, she handed him the keys. Again, there was the briefest touch of his fingers on her palm, but she noticed. Noticed the glints of gold in his blue eyes, the thick blond hair now spiky from his running his hands through it so often.

Despite being in a car and an airport for the better part of the last two hours, he smelled as though he'd come back from walking on the beach. He had a long nose to go with the long chin he'd grown into since high school. She could see the small cut under his eye. His broad shoulders filled her line of sight, making Sam, who considered herself well-muscled after years working outdoors, feel small and suddenly very female.

His lips parted. Sam looked up at him. Again, there was that sense of waiting, of something unsaid, just out of reach. Maybe it was just this attraction, one she had no right to, especially if she allowed herself to remember how she'd ignored him and his kind all those years before.

He blinked, twice. Shook his head quickly like a dog with water in its ears and backed up. "Thanks for what you did today," he said. "It was... I should have called their grandmother, like you said."

She hadn't said it—he had, which proved that she'd been right to insist. "It was the least I could do."

"It was more than that. I appreciate it."

The words hovered. Did he hate being beholden to her? She wasn't getting hate from him right now. Had he felt the attraction she had?

Jesus, Sam. Get out of your own head. This week had been the first time in a long time she'd had to please anyone but herself. She liked to think of herself as a thoughtful, helpful person, but two hours with this guy and she was reverting to a selfishness she didn't like.

He looked around them, at the dark night, at his car. "You'll need a ride home."

Okay, good. Practical matters. "I can walk." Although suddenly, she was exhausted. Too much emotion. "Or my sister will come get me."

"Come inside while you wait."

He was just being polite. She couldn't intrude on him when he had to concentrate on his kids right now. And she needed to get away from him. Away from this town. Back to the life she'd created for herself. "We'll be fine here on the porch."

"Well." He hooked his hand behind his neck again. "If you're sure."

"I am very sure. Go." And as though she hadn't said any of that stuff inside her head, she put a hand out and pushed him gently.

Mistake. His chest was as solid as the rest of him. And he looked down at her hand as though he didn't know what it was. Sam removed it, fast. Thank God she was never going to see him again. She hadn't been this wrong-footed around a man in years.

"Bye, Ty," she said, then to break the thick air between them, "Ooh, I'm a poet and I don't even know it."

He shook his head again; she caught a smile he tried to hide. "Bye, Sam. Bye, Cairo."

He turned to the door and this time, he didn't turn back.

Chapter 5

Ty slammed the door harder than necessary and leaned against it, letting out a loud breath.

Sam freaking Fielding.

Everything he'd worked for in the last fifteen years seemed to evaporate when he'd seen her on the other side of that door. Forget all the stability he had now. Forget the lessons he'd learned from jumping into a relationship with the first woman who'd paid attention to him in college. Forget the balance he'd struck between creativity and finances to find a career he loved. Sam had looked at him with those dark-brown eyes and that honey-kissed skin, and despite the fear racing around him that his children were *missing*—how could he have forgotten that, even for a second?—he'd felt like his Adam's apple was suddenly too big.

Sam Fielding had always been sexy as all get-out, and she knew it. Why shouldn't she? She was a member of one of the richest families in town. Her three sisters and brother had been legendary in school. They'd had money and privilege and everything he hadn't. She'd always looked right through him in the hallways. Until she hadn't.

He'd seen the interest in that long, appraising look she'd given him tonight. Or had he? He hadn't been around a woman in two years. He wasn't even thinking of dating again, not ever. Not as long as his kids had to deal with Julia's uncertainty.

Maybe he'd just wanted a distraction from Julia's little adventure. Sam had always scrambled his brains but good. If anyone could distract him, Sam Fielding could.

But she didn't live here, and he had two kids to safeguard. He could be grateful and at the same time not want to capture her long hair in his hands.

Ugh.

He had to remember that she'd just seen him at his most

vulnerable. She'd probably been pitying him, not gazing at him. It was time to go back to real life.

He pulled out his phone. Unfortunately, his lawyer's number was one of his most frequently called. "Lauren," he said when she picked up. "I'm sorry to call you after work, but I'm gonna need you to take out a restraining order against Julia."

He explained what had happened.

Lauren gave a furious growl. "Where is she now?"

"They arrested her. It's a violation of the custody agreement. But she'll be out by tomorrow, if I know her family." Julia's parents had a team of attorneys. Her desertion had made the divorce petition relatively easy, but those lawyers had argued the hell out of every step of the agreement. Ty had credit card debt he wouldn't be able to pay off for ten years thanks to them.

Alyssa didn't know Julia had been arrested tonight. Her fear of her own mother jumping out from behind a bush made Ty rub his hands over his face. He'd tried so hard to keep this unpleasantness from her. Even pretended to look around the house so Alyssa wouldn't find out for a little while. Seriously, how would it help her to know that her mother would spend a night in jail for wanting to see her kids?

"I bet Julia loved that," his attorney said.

"Mmm."

He knew where she was going with this, and sure enough, "Did she hit you again?" she asked.

Ty touched the cut under his eye. "Only a little," he said.

"Tyler," Lauren admonished. "You see now? What happens when you don't talk about it? You know a restraining order usually requires *three* incidents of assault."

He didn't bother answering her. When he'd gotten to the security offices, the kids had been taken into a separate room. But by some stupid twist of miscommunication, he'd been taken to the room where they'd put Julia. He'd walked in, unsuspecting, and she'd socked him in the eye before the guard could pull her away.

Ty had been on edge enough that he managed to tilt his head, so she got him on the bone rather than in his eye, saving him a prize bruising, but her knuckles had still hurt. As they had a few times during his marriage. Lauren knew this. But he'd forced her not to bring it up in the divorce proceedings. Matt and Alyssa didn't need to know that stuff, and Ty was going to be free of her. She'd never permanently scarred him or anything.

Lauren seemed to give up on getting an answer from him. "Fine. The attempted kidnapping should be enough. I'll get the forms in tonight and let you know how it goes in the morning."

"Thanks, Lauren. Sorry about the late call."

"It's not that late. I'm still in the office."

"Well, thanks anyway. Talk to you tomorrow."

He hung up and climbed the stairs to the main floor of the townhouse. Matt was standing at the refrigerator, drinking milk out of the carton. How could he give the kid a hard time? They all had their comforting habits. He'd find Alyssa buried under her bedcovers, a book and a flashlight in her hand, trying like crazy to close out the world. He would go to his tiny workshop in the back of the garage and mess around with his blocks of wood. Matt drank milk.

The defeated slump of his son's shoulders tugged at his heart. "Hey, bud," he said softly.

Matt jumped anyway, holding the carton of milk as if he were surprised to see it in his hand. "It's okay," Ty said. He walked over to the boy and put his arm around the bony shoulders.

Matt hung his head. "I'm sorry, Dad. I shouldn't have gone with her."

This was not a decision Matt should have had to make, to feel that going with his mother might be a mistake but not going with her would be worse. "Don't be ridiculous."

"It was just..." Matt clutched the milk carton to his chest. "She would have gotten Alyssa anyway."

"I know, Matt." Ty shook his shoulder. "You're a good brother. You protected her."

Matt and Alyssa had caught on to Julia's tricks no matter how hard Ty had tried to protect them. Now Matt had to save his sister because Ty had failed to.

When she'd finally gotten in touch after the first time she'd left, Julia had said she just needed a break. Her absence had been a blessing to Ty, but he couldn't have explained that to his heartbroken children. Hell, he'd been heartbroken, too. He'd loved her for years; she'd given him the attention he'd desperately craved. So he'd fought and fought against the reality of Julia's selfishness, of her betrayal, until he couldn't any longer.

Matt was almost as tall as he was now. He just needed to fill out a little and he'd be the image of his dad. Matt had acted out for years, when Julia was with them and afterward, and was still your basic grumpy teenager. But making friends with Jake, who knew the issues involved with an unstable parent, and the circle of kids he knew at school seemed to have steadied him.

God damn Julia into seven levels of hell for intruding on one more safe place.

"You wanna order pizza?" he asked Matt.

Matt's laugh shook Ty's arm off his shoulder. "Is the Pope Catholic?"

"Okay, go ahead. I'll go see Alyssa."

She was where he'd expected, curtains pulled across the summer evening, the room a cave, a haven. Ty wished with all his being that he could make her feel truly safe, that she didn't have to cocoon herself every few weeks, every time Julia did something new.

He sat down next to the lump under the covers and stroked the top of it. "Hi, peanut."

He knew that would get a response. The covers slid off with alacrity. "Dad! I haven't been a peanut for like six years!"

He was happy to see regular exasperation on her face; that was why he'd said it. "Sorry," he said seriously, reaching out to stroke her hair off her face.

Ty could imagine the scene at the airport, though he hadn't asked the kids for any details. The story about ice cream quickly proving itself a lie as they headed for the highway. The increasingly violent orders not to call Ty, to put Matt's phone away. The guilt trips about preferring their dad when she was about to take them to Disney and they'd have the time of their lives and *give me the goddamn phone, Matthew.*

No passport needed at check-in, no baggage except their backpacks, which could have contained a long weekend's worth of clothes. Julia talking nonstop about the place they would stay. Alyssa too afraid to mention that she was graduating middle school the next day, that she was pretty sure she'd be winning an award or two at the ceremony. Matt miserable, feeling he should have known how to change the situation but unable to find the words, knowing at the same time that whatever he said would be overridden.

Julia would have freaked out in the middle of the departure lounge when security found them–public displays of emotion had never been a problem for her. She'd yell at them, at the kids, at everyone around for staring, at the airplane for not arriving sooner so they could have gotten away.

How could Ty stop that memory from damaging them for the rest of their lives?

Alyssa leaned into him. She wasn't the little peanut he'd carried on his shoulders anymore; she was becoming a young woman. If he could just get the kids to college without any more trauma... The restraining order was a last resort, a confirmation that their mom wasn't to be trusted. He wished it could be different. That she could have been different.

"I like Sam," Alyssa said unexpectedly.

"Who?" he said. He knew damn well who. The word had come from Alyssa's mouth and gone straight into his chest, throbbing there in a mass of memories and humiliation and... long legs beneath cutoffs.

"Sam. Come on, Dad–the one who just drove us all home? She's nice."

"Is she?"

"Dad." She lengthened the word and elbowed his ribs.

"Well, she only said two words to you."

"I like her. She doesn't know you, right? But she helped us anyway."

"We do know each other, remember?" Ty found himself saying. "We were at high school together."

"Oh, yeah!" Alyssa's face lit up. "Were you boyfriend-girlfriend?"

"No!" Okay, he'd overreacted to that. And his face was heating up, which would not help his case with his observant child. "No. We were... in different circles."

"Which one was she in?"

Alyssa's eyes were open, clear. Unsuspecting. "The popular crowd," Ty said.

"Wait—you weren't?"

He laughed. "Thanks for thinking I'm cool enough to be popular."

She shrugged. "You're okay."

He had to hug her for that. "Well, being a geek wasn't cool back then. Not like it is now."

She frowned; he could see that she thought his high school days referred to a time impossibly disconnected from now. He'd thought that too.

"Anyway," he said. "Sam was smart as well as popular."

"Yeah! And now she's an archaeologist. That *is* cool!" One of Alyssa's friends had shown Indiana Jones at her last birthday party. "Do you think she'd tell me about it?"

"I don't know if you're going to see her again, honey. Since she lives out of state."

"Oh."

And the faster she went back, the better. Ty did *not* want to meet her on the street.

"Can she come to graduation?" Alyssa said.

Ty disengaged himself from her, stunned. "What?"

"Graduation." Alyssa looked nervous, but the need was shining from her eyes. "Do you think she'd come? I want to introduce her to Mr. P." She didn't seem able to meet his eyes any longer, but dropped hers and found a strand of hair to put into her mouth.

"Mr. P. taught *her*," Ty said, not that it was relevant right now. Gods. Could he please get this woman out of his life? Out of his thoughts? His fantasies? He'd wasted countless hours back in school either damning her for being a bully or reliving her pressing against him.

"Did he? Wow." Mr. P.'s advanced age obviously only now impressed itself upon her.

"And me. I told you that." Anything to take the subject off Sam Fielding.

"Oh, yeah. I forgot. So can I ask her? Or will you?"

Hell no was what he wanted to say. "I don't know, sweetheart," he prevaricated. "She's only in town for a few days; she might be leaving tomorrow, for all we know."

"Can we ask?"

She was so earnest. She wanted this so badly. The poor girl wasn't going to have any special female in her life there—his mother counted, of course, but she had a full-time job and less time for her grandkids than she'd like.

"Sure. I'll call her in the morning."

"Can you call now? It's not late."

He felt as though the day had been forty-eight hours long already, but it was only six o'clock. As if to verify that, the doorbell rang. Presumably the pizza guy, but Ty was jumpy enough to yell, "I'll get it!" toward Alyssa's open door and get to his feet fast. "Okay," he said to her. "Let me just get the pizza."

"Ooh, pizza!" Alyssa jumped off the bed.

The healing powers of pizza, Ty reflected as he and his kids sat at the kitchen counter in greasy cheesy heaven, should not be underestimated. They sounded almost normal. Matt teased Alyssa and Alyssa was snotty to Matt; she begged Ty to let her watch some R-rated movie Matt had seen at a friend's house, and Ty was able to be a regular father and refuse Matt a sip of the Coke he himself shouldn't have been drinking. Like he'd sleep tonight anyway.

But Alyssa wasn't to be diverted for long. As soon as he turned off the faucet after cleaning up, she was by his side. "Is it too late now?" she asked anxiously.

"All right, all right. Matt? You got Jake's number?"

He shouldn't be this bothered by this. Sam Fielding wasn't supposed to bother him like this. If he didn't want to call her directly, if her phone number was burning its way into his memory from the short text he'd sent her earlier, what of it?

"Hi, Jake? It's Mr. Cavanaugh."

Sam had been Matt's age when her father had died. No wonder she'd gone off the rails. No wonder for all of them, he supposed, but Sam had taken more people with her.

"Hi, Mr. Cavanaugh," Jake said. "Uh. Everything okay?"

"Yeah, thanks. Much better now. Listen, is your aunt there?"

"Which one?"

Ah, the ease of a large family. Jake had so many people at his back, he lost track of them. What was that like?

"Samantha."

"Sam," Jake said almost before he'd gotten her full name out, and he laughed. "Don't call her that other name to her face."

"Noted."

"Hold on, I'll get her."

Jake yelled, "Aunt Sam!" And that giant house Ty had ridden his bike past years ago seemed to echo with all the support that family offered, that he and his kids couldn't find.

There was murmuring on the other end of the phone and then her voice. "Yes?" she said. "Did I leave something in your car?"

"No. Hi," he said. *Great, now you sound like a breathless schoolboy.* "Alyssa wants to talk to you." And he handed over the phone. *Coward.*

Alyssa looked terrified. There was a second where she mimed a no, shaking her hands in front of the phone. Ty held it out more firmly. Alyssa sent him a look as though he were making her walk the plank and took the phone. "Sam?"

♦

Was she in some kind of *Groundhog Day* scenario where Ty

Cavanaugh showed up in her life over and over until she addressed the elephant that sat right between them?

"Hi, Alyssa," she said. "How are you doing, honey?"

"I'm good. So, um, when are you going back to New Mexico?"

"Tomorrow." She wasn't sure where this was going.

"'Cause, uh." There was a silence on the other end of the line, then Alyssa said in a rush so the words flowed together, "'Cause I'm graduating tomorrow and I wondered if you could come because I'd like to see you and so would Mr. P. and you don't have to but I'd like you to." She ran out of breath. "Yeah."

Sam was so surprised, she couldn't answer for a second. Alyssa had met her all of three times for a total of maybe an hour. Now this sweet kid, who'd been handed an ass of a mother, wanted *her* at her graduation?

Graduation. The memory washed over her in seconds, chilling her blood and weakening her legs. It was Megan's middle school graduation, and their mother had just died. For the first time, the "children" were on their own. Cat had just had the twins; Thea was pregnant with Jake and looked much older than her twenty years. Kane was working eighty-hour weeks to build the company back up after Robert's death. Sam was graduating from high school the following night and was desperate to get the ceremonies over with so she could focus on college and getting the hell out of Dodge.

They'd made the biggest effort any of them ever had, to make it a good night for Meg. Her friends monopolized her, keeping her moving, laughing, so that while she was in the line to receive her "diploma," she had a smile on her face. But when she reached the principal, she looked not at him but out into the audience at each of her siblings, and her face had fallen. Right there on the stage, she'd burst into tears.

Cat had risen to her feet, but Kane had reached Megan first, almost carrying her off the stage. Some of her friends were crying for her, which Sam had always appreciated. Sam, Cat, and Thea had to sit through the rest of the ceremony so as not to disturb the other parents, but it made Sam even sadder, which made her angrier, and after her own graduation the next day, she'd gone over to Dan Kowalczyk's house and not come back for two days. She'd refused to allow her siblings to go to her own graduation.

The silence on the phone must have spooked Alyssa. Sam heard defeat in her voice as she added, "You know, not a big deal, but…"

What else could she say? It was twenty years ago. "What time?"

"Six thirty. But if you're flying out then…"

"I'll change my plans."

"Really?"

It was worth it to hear the joy and relief in Alyssa's voice. So Sam had to spend another couple of hours at a school stuffed to the brim with memories. Who cared when this adorable kid with purple hair wanted *her* to be there? "I'd be honored," she said sincerely. "Thank you for inviting me."

"Yes!" Alyssa yelped and followed it up with a "Wheee!" that pierced the eardrums.

There was more noise, the squeal thankfully abated, and then Ty's voice was back on the line. "You don't have to," he said.

The contrast between Alyssa's light voice and his low tones warmed Sam's cheeks and made her think of those gold flecks in his eyes.

Hey. Back to the conversation. "I want to," she insisted. They'd be in a crowd, right? She wouldn't have to talk to him a whole lot. Or even look at him.

Or maybe looking at him would be a nice way to distract her from all the rest of it.

"Great," he said. But he didn't sound particularly enthusiastic. "We'll pick you up at six. I–" He paused. "I'll pay for whatever the flight change costs."

"Don't be ridiculous. She's a good kid." She didn't need to tell him that she'd driven here.

"Yeah. She is."

"So. If she wants me there, I'll be there."

"Sam…"

"Uh-huh?" She liked the way he said her name. Way too much. Her throat went dry.

A silence billowed around them.

"Nothing," he said at last. "Thanks again. Again."

Sam laughed at that. "You're welcome again, again."

Chapter 6

"Hell of a first date," Megan said.

"It's *not* a date," Sam reminded her. "I'm there for his kid and that's it. Now shut up and dress me."

She had to give Megan credit. The dress she'd found in Cat's closet was appropriate without being motherly, and the shoes weren't so high they made Sam teeter. The turquoise made her tan glow and went well with the silver jewelry she'd bought in the pueblo. Megan twisted her hair up behind her head; Sam kept putting her hands up to lift the nonexistent mass off her neck, but she had to admit she looked more sophisticated this way.

The doorbell rang at exactly six o'clock. Megan gave her a thumbs-up from the kitchen doorway. She stuck her tongue out at her sister. Meg was way too happy, and it wasn't because Sam was helping out Alyssa.

Sam answered the door to find Alyssa there instead of Ty. "Wow," Sam said. "You look fantastic!"

"Thanks!" Alyssa was bouncing up and down in fancy silver shoes that contrasted beautifully with her purple one-shouldered dress. She had a small silver clutch in one hand and her hair was straight around her face. She would have looked perfect except for...

Alyssa's sweetheart face was marred by muddy brown stripes across her cheekbones and on either side of her forehead.

"Can I–?" Sam didn't know how to say it without insulting her. But a rapid mental scan of the inhabitants of Alyssa's house–all male, all clueless–made up her mind for her. "Can I make a teeny suggestion?"

Alyssa's smile faltered. "It's the makeup, isn't it? I don't know what I'm doing. I watched a YouTube video about contouring, but–"

"Oh God, you don't need contouring!" Sam exclaimed. "Quick, come in here. Meg!"

Since Meg had been about five feet away behind the kitchen wall, she was there in a second and summed up the situation with an instant, "Oh my."

"Okay, okay, look, she doesn't have anyone to help. We have to be out at the car in two minutes. Help!"

Before Alyssa knew it, Megan had pulled her into the powder room, made a makeup bag appear from nowhere, washed her face, and applied a more age-appropriate palette. Sam hung back while Meg went to work.

When she was done, a light application of mascara and eyeliner turned Alyssa's blue eyes luminous, and her natural round cheeks were shown off with a little blush and highlighter. A neutral lipstick gave just the right amount of shine.

Alyssa looked at herself in the powder room mirror. Sam saw tears start in her eyes. "Hey, no crying," she warned. "That mascara'll run."

Alyssa closed her eyes over the tears and hugged Sam and Megan both together. "Anytime," Meg said, and she looked a little tearful herself. "I mean it, hon. Anytime."

With a giant Fielding smile, Megan ushered Sam and Alyssa out the front door, Sam grabbing a silvery-gray wrap on her way.

Ty was starting up the path toward them, his face like thunder. "We have to get–" He saw Alyssa and stopped dead. In fact, he took a step backward.

Alyssa looked up at him uncertainly. "Isn't it better?" she said. "Megan did it. Sam's sister."

He schooled his face into the slight frown he usually used with Sam. "Well, yeah," he said. "Not that you didn't look... I mean, you looked fine to me but now..."

Alyssa grinned and hopped past him, opening the back door to the car.

Sam stayed where she was. She wanted to take a step back too. Ty was in what she would have called Dad clothes: khakis, blue shirt, navy jacket. But with his hair cut preppy-style and the scruff of blond on his chin, he looked as though he'd stepped out of a Ralph Lauren ad.

"I guess I need to thank you," he said. "Again."

"No problem," she said, trying to tear her mind away from the slimness of his waist. "My sisters are better than me at that kind of thing."

It wasn't that she didn't know about where to put what, makeup-wise. It was just that she didn't care enough. When you were sweating out a couple of pints a day in the desert, you didn't bother with things like mascara.

But for occasions like this, she made a bit of an effort, and so she stood erect while he took her in.

"You look... good, too," he said.

Yeah, she knew she did. But it was nice of him to notice. "So do you. Anything I should know before we get going?"

His stare drifted over her shoulder, then came back. "About what?"

"Their mother. Alyssa seemed pretty good, but I don't want to put my foot in it."

"Oh." His eyes darkened. "I guess, just... don't bring her up until they do."

"My sister gave the impression that you get talked about a lot 'round here."

He laughed, though there was no humor in it. "Yeah. Small town." He seemed to go over the idea in his mind. "Did Matt talk to Jake today?"

"Probably," she answered honestly. Jake had asked her how it had gone when she'd gotten home, and he'd apologized all over again. She could bet he'd gone straight upstairs to text his friend.

Ty groaned. "Yeah. Then I bet everyone knows. Not that Jake would—"

"Dad!" Alyssa yelled out of the car window. "We're gonna be late!"

"Sorry!" Sam called and hurried over to the car. Before she could get there, though, Ty got in front of her and opened her door. Like a real gentleman. If she'd been paying attention to that kind of thing, of course. She nodded her thanks.

"Geez, you two and having long conversations outside cars," Matt muttered while she put on her seat belt.

"It wasn't even a minute," Ty pointed out, pulling onto the narrow street.

Matt humphed. He was behind Sam, his long legs somehow still seeming to take up too much space in the SUV. He was a mini-Ty today, but Sam was pleased to see a leather string around his neck with what looked like a plugged nickel threaded on it. That and his spiky hair made him look very rock-n-roll, despite the polo-playing dude on his shirt.

It was one of those June evenings that promised sultry nights a few days away. The car windows were open, and the breeze swirled around Sam's bare legs. She turned around to wink at Alyssa, who had leaned as far forward between the front seats as her belt would let her.

"So," she said. "You said you live in the Pueblos?"

"Just outside," Sam clarified. "I rent an apartment in Albuquerque, but we set up camp wherever we're asked to dig."

"You live in tents?" Alyssa's eyes widened.

"No." Sam laughed. "In trailers. Hot and cold water and everything."

"Doesn't Uncle Noah live in a pueblo?" Matt asked his father.

"He lives near one," Ty said. "In Taos," he added, glancing at Sam and just as quickly glancing away.

"Oh, Taos," Sam said. "It's beautiful there. I've only seen it in passing. Is Noah an artist?"

"You could say that," Ty said, his tone dour.

"He runs an art gallery?" Alyssa said. "And he sells his own paintings? So yeah, he's an artist. He's so cool."

"You've only met him twice," Matt scoffed.

"Yeah," Alyssa insisted. "And each time he was cool. He made your necklace, doofus, so don't look at me with that tone of voice."

Sam cracked up, and to her delight Ty did too. Caught in their joint amusement, she let her eyes meet his again. And this time Ty swallowed.

Oh yes. Nice to know that no matter what else had happened this week, Sam had managed to make Ty Cavanaugh nervous. It was better than him being all grateful for something anyone would have done for him. Wouldn't they?

Someone beeped their horn behind him; apparently the light had gone green. Did she catch a hint of a blush on his cheeks before she, too, turned away? And was her own face heating up? Impossible. *Remember who you're here for.*

"So you're not working in Taos?" Alyssa went on, hopefully oblivious to the little moment her father and Sam had just shared.

"No. We're helping the Zuni nation. Farther south. They made me this bracelet." She held up her wrist, where a thick, beaten-silver cuff was set off with a small sunburst of turquoise beads.

"Ooh. Can you get me one?"

"Alyssa!" Ty interjected.

"I'll see what I can do," Sam promised her. No way would she let this kid down. "We'll call it my promotion ceremony present to you."

"Cool! Are you married?"

"Whoa." She'd gotten whiplash from the abrupt change of subject.

"Mind your own business!" Matt yelped as Ty said, "Alyssa!" again, this time with more horror in his voice.

"What?" Alyssa asked, blue eyes wide with genuine innocence. "Is it a secret or something? I mean, you said your sister got married. I just wondered if you were too."

Sam twisted around in her seat and held up her left hand this time. "Nope. Not married. Don't plan to be either."

"Do you have a boyfriend?"

"Oh God," Ty moaned next to her. "You do *not* have to answer that."

"It's fine. I don't have a boyfriend. Not right now. Anyway, I'm too busy for that kind of thing these days. I barely have time to shower before I fall into bed at night."

She didn't *mean* to look at Ty's throat after she'd said that, but she somehow did, and he swallowed again.

She couldn't do anything about this... attraction between them, but boy, was it fun to contemplate. She defied anyone to remain unmoved when this Ralph Lauren ad reacted to her the way he did. Smiling to herself, she faced front again.

They joined the line of cars pulling into the high school parking lot. "Maybe we could come see you one day, when we visit Uncle Noah," Alyssa said. "You promised, Dad."

"I did," he said. A policeman in a reflective jacket pointed them into a parking space. "But not in the summer. It's too hot."

"Fall is nice," Sam said, opening her own door. Ty went to the back of the SUV and opened it before handing Alyssa a dark-blue graduation gown and cap.

"But I'll be back at school in the fall!" Alyssa complained.

"Okay, okay," Ty said. "Don't worry about it now. Come on, let's get you graduated." He put his arm around his daughter's shoulders and led them safely through the cars to the sidewalk, where an older woman with short, light-brown hair squealed and held out her arms. Alyssa ran over to her. They were about the same size.

"Hey, sweetheart!" the woman said, sweeping Alyssa in for a hug.

"Hi, Grandma!"

"Look at you! You'll be a high schooler in about one hour!"

"I know!"

"I'm so proud of you!"

"Thanks. Hey, come meet Sam."

Sam wasn't ready for Ty's mother, even though he'd said she'd be there. How much had she heard about Sam in high school? Or about Sam and Ty? Not that there was anything to hear.

"Hello, Sam," Ty's mother said with a carefree smile, and they shook hands. Nope, didn't remember her. Or even recognize her. Also, Sam realized, his mom didn't know what had happened with Julia the night before. Unless she was a freaking fantastic actress.

Mrs. Cavanaugh flicked her gaze from Sam to Ty. "Tyler," she said. "You didn't tell me you were bringing a guest."

"I'm not," he said as Sam said, "He's not," and Alyssa said, "He didn't."

Mrs. Cavanaugh laughed. Alyssa added, "I asked her. She helped us out yesterday when—"

And she quit talking very fast.

The change in mood turned Ty's mom's curious smile into a frown. "When what, sweetie?"

"I'll tell you later, Mom," Ty said. "Hey, Lyss, Gabriella and Kayleigh are over there. You go on ahead." He disengaged her gently from her grandmother. "We'll see you after."

Ty pulled his mother away from the flowing river of parents and students and began to talk to her in a low voice. Sam hung back with Matt, who rolled his eyes in relief when he saw his own friends. He made a beeline for them, leaving Sam alone.

She didn't really mind. In fact, the longer she stayed alone and anonymous in this crowd, the better. She wanted to breathe her way through the memories and keep herself calm without interruption.

The white chairs arranged on the football field in front of one of the goals, the bunting on the stage, and the enthusiasm of the teens began to work on her. Even after the stress of yesterday and her worry about the kids since, there were some things in life too exciting to ignore, and surviving middle school was one of them.

Parents chatted with relief at the lack of humidity, and girls in strapless white dresses were grateful for the warmth. The ground was firm underfoot as Sam stepped onto the grass to let another family go by.

After they'd passed, Ty was looking at her again, his mother behind him. Her eyes were wide, and their conversation wasn't over.

"But, Tyler," she was saying, keeping her voice low, "what are you going to *do* about her?"

"I got a restraining order," he replied through stiff lips. "And now I just want Alyssa to enjoy her night. I'll worry about Julia tomorrow."

"But what if she—?"

"Mom," he said firmly, turning around. "Not today, okay? I don't want her to ruin today."

I'd like to see her try it in front of all these people. Mrs. Cavanaugh didn't look convinced, but she let Ty lead them to a row of seats.

He gave quick waves to a few people and shook hands with a couple more. Sam found herself walking between Ty and his mother.

Now Sam felt exposed. If anyone in this crowd recognized her, they would probably have the same reaction Ty had the other day: shock and a vague but bad memory. To distract herself, she examined the stage. They had a new logo strung up among the lights, but the stage carried the same school colors, the same drapery, even the same podium, she'd swear. The day of Megan's graduation swept over her again and she took in a quick breath.

"You okay there, Indy?"

Ty's hand was on her bare arm. The calluses on his fingertips burned her skin, brought her back to the present. She'd stopped in the middle of the row.

No point in sadness. No point in that knot in her throat when she thought of all the years Megan had lived without any parents, let alone Sam herself and her other siblings. Sam could just take the lesson that she must never rely on a man and move on.

Taking another breath, she was able to meet Ty's eye. "Indy. Funny."

He smiled. It was only on one side, but it was one more thing that made him inconveniently attractive. It had stopped being fun, this hint of longing in her.

Sam really needed to get out of this town. The mixture of sadness, guilt, and attraction was messing with her head.

Just as she was about to sit down, someone said, "Sam?"

She looked around.

"Sam!" the voice shouted, and she had a vague impression of oceans parting as a woman fought her way through the other parents to get to her. It took a moment to place the heavily pregnant body and plump face that finally came to rest in the row in front of her. "Oh my God, it *is* you!" the woman screamed and grabbed her to her chest.

The hug was the reminder. "Janine," she said, hoping she sounded happy to see her. By design she'd lost touch with her high school friends once she'd gotten away to college. Janine had been one of her partners in crime.

One of, if she were honest with herself, the mean girls. They hadn't set out to be that way, or at least Sam hadn't. What had begun as sarcasm and gentle digs had gotten laughs, made her interesting, cemented her popularity as long as she only directed her barbs in a certain direction. She didn't think she'd been that bad. But seeing Janine's face now and remembering Ty's face on Sunday brought back a dozen small infractions of common human decency, and it was hard to smile at her.

"Where have you been!" Janine was saying. "Why didn't you stay in touch? Did you hear?" and she turned to the side, though the pregnancy was blindingly obvious without the gesture. "Twins!"

"Oh, that's great. Is your... partner here?"

"Yes, he's just getting us a seat." Janine waved over into the crowd. "So quick, tell me everything! Where are you living? Why are you here? I thought Thea's kid was already in high school?"

That was when she noticed who Sam was standing next to. Ty's hand was still on Sam's arm. Her eyes and mouth went comically round. "Tyler?"

Ty didn't say a single word. His mouth was a straight line. Sam cringed again, which must have shown on her face, because his look became glacial.

Janine's attitude had brought back the dynamic Sam had been trying to forget—she and Janine on the inside, Ty left out, ignored, derided. His hand left her.

"Ty's daughter invited me to come," Sam said, standing tall. To protect Ty? That was ridiculous.

"Did she? But how do you...?" The cogs whirred behind Janine's eyes. The small-town gossip mill, encouraged and sometimes started by women like this.

"We just met," Sam said.

Janine's eyes got even wider. "Oh! Well! Ty Cavanaugh, huh?"

"That's right," he said. His eyes were flint as he glared at Janine.

"Well… well. Good for you," Janine said. "You've been divorced how long now?"

"We're not dating!" Sam said too quickly. "Not that–" *Dammit.* She'd just added to that gossip mill. "My nephew and his son are friends," she added. She couldn't say Ty was "just a friend." She didn't know what the hell he was.

But she knew she had to throw Janine off the scent somehow. "I live in New Mexico now. I'm going home tomorrow. Who are you here for?"

Janine and Ty hadn't broken eye contact. "My niece. You know, David's kid."

"David's married?" Her older brother had been a notorious asshole. They'd had their own family issues–an overbearing father and a mother who drank. There had always been an excuse for their behavior, always a reason to take it out on the next dweeb in line. David had used his fists instead of doing things Sam's way. Her ability to pretend people weren't there had been Oscar-worthy.

"Divorced," Janine said cheerfully. "Aren't we all! Bill's my second." She looked terribly proud of herself and even winked at Ty. Sam could feel the tension running through him.

"Ladies and gentlemen, if you could take your seats," said the school principal at the microphone. *Thank God.*

"Well, you just have to give me your number so we can catch up while you're here! High school was so much fun with you, Sam!" Janine twisted her hand into Sam's and out again, then sailed back to her husband and her seat before Sam could remind her that she was leaving town in a few hours.

Ty snorted and sat down.

Sam had to say something. "Look, I'm not like her."

Those flint eyes looked up at her. He said nothing, which was worse.

"I mean, yes." She sat down with a thump next to him. "I know. I know what I was like. I know that's not… not something you get a pass on. I've been meaning to say that I–"

But she broke off, partly because the teachers were filing onto the stage and the music had started up again and partly because she knew that an apology at this point was a joke. Despite the mild air, her cheeks burned.

The long-forgotten phrases came back to her as she focused on the ceremony. Alyssa walked up to the stage while the principal told the assembled crowd that she'd won prizes in social studies and math this year. Sam wanted to say something to Ty, to congratulate him, but he'd become so unapproachable since Janine's arrival, he might as well have been on the other side of the field. Matt's crowd at the back whooped and hollered though, and Sam's heart warmed to see the grateful and happy smile Alyssa directed toward him. The memory of Megan's day receded. This was a good day, and Sam had been permitted to take part in it. Alyssa wasn't the only grateful one.

But then Alyssa's smile disappeared, and she stopped on the top step leading down. Another voice, clear over the politely quiet parents, said, "Hey! Alyssa-Belle! I'm here, honey! Look, look, it's me, it's Mom!"

Ty was on his feet with the first syllable. Everyone in the vicinity looked to the back of the crowd and then at him. Ty's mother breathed, "Oh *no*," and craned her neck to look behind her.

The principal gamely carried on calling out names while Ty walked with a bent back to the end of his row and up the aisle. Alyssa, Sam saw, looked about to break. Her classmates moved aside so that instead of taking her place in the front with them, she became hidden in the sea of caps and gowns.

Sam sat there for a moment longer, but she couldn't stand it; she had to help him. His mother wasn't moving, and everyone else was just observing, commenting. The Cavanaughs were a cautionary tale in this town, she could see. No one actually stepped forward.

She ducked down and made her own way out of the row. "Where are you going?" Mrs. Cavanaugh hissed, but Sam didn't bother telling her. Before she'd even made it to the aisle, she heard a woman's strident voice cutting through the list of names. The principal faltered but again continued on.

"Don't tell me!" she was saying. "Don't you say a fucking word!

She's my daughter!" Now she threw her hands out to the watching, silent crowd. "Do you believe this? Put a restraining order on me! Doesn't even invite me to my own daughter's graduation! You *want* her to hate me! You've been doing this for years! Pushing them from me!"

Sam heard Ty's quiet murmur, and just as she got to the back of the crowd, a loud *smack* echoed over the field.

The principal stopped altogether. Everyone was looking to the back now. Sam could see Matt's blond head over all the rest and pushed her way through to him. "No, Matt," she said, not even sure why. She didn't want him to see this.

"You've always done this!" came the voice again, then a soft thump and a gasp from the onlookers.

"Julia, for God's sake," Ty said, and now she could see them. Julia had backed him up against one of the folding chairs in the back row, which had pushed away, effectively trapping him in a U-shape of chair legs and people trying to get out of the way. Julia was hitting any part of him she could reach, screeching now about how no goddamn restraining order was going to stop her from seeing her kids. Ty put his hands up as far as his chest but for some reason was not protecting his face. The small abrasion under his eye was bleeding.

Sam took half a second to listen to the crowd around them. Some were telling Julia to stop, but some were grinning at the show. Phone screens were glinting in the late sunlight. Sam's anger filled her up. *Those assholes should be doing something.*

Julia slapped Ty's head again; he ducked, but she still landed a good whack on his ear. His hair was disheveled. Sam had an inexplicable urge to smooth it down for him, to get him back to that Ralph Lauren guy from the beginning of the evening, who had just wanted to enjoy being proud of his daughter like any other dad.

Three things happened at once. Julia threw a punch at Ty's head, a cop arrived, and Matt threw himself in front of his father and took the punch on the cheekbone. There was a sickening crunch, and he fell backward into the mess of chairs and people.

Julia screamed, an animal sound of outrage, not grief. Ty yelled Matt's name and dropped to the ground to disentangle him from the chairs. Sam found herself in the middle of the circle, behind Julia, her arms around the woman's biceps, pulling her arms back and linking her own hands together so Julia couldn't hit anyone else.

Julia bucked, bending her knees and jumping up again to try to dislodge her, and as Sam's chin cracked against Julia's shoulder for the third time, she wondered what the hell had happened to her life. She'd just come to town for a wedding.

Someone was trying to pull her away, but she hung on tight. Only when the authoritative voice said, "Ma'am, if you don't let her go, I'm going to have to arrest you too," did she realize it was the cop and released her hands. Her arms were shaking, her chin throbbing. She braced herself, expecting Julia to go for her now that she was free, but the cop had the woman in cuffs before Sam had even stepped away. Julia instead was using her energy to scream at Ty, "Look what you made me do! I'm going to fucking *kill* you!"

Another cop came, parting the crowd, and the two of them took Julia away between them, her screaming curses all the way. Matt was sitting up now, leaning heavily against his father, hiding his face with one long-fingered hand—probably so the crowd wouldn't see that he was crying. Just like his father had done the other day.

Her heart suddenly felt too big for her chest.

An EMT crew arrived with a stretcher, and although Matt shook his head, Ty spoke quietly to him, and he finally agreed to get on it. Ty began to walk away with him, then looked over the crowd to the stage, where everything had stopped. The principal was still at the microphone, the students still waiting at the foot of the steps to cross the stage. From this distance, it was impossible to see Alyssa.

Sam moved up behind Ty. "I'll find her. I'll bring her," she said.

Ty just said, "Right. Home. Not the hospital." He threw her his car keys and hurried after the stretcher.

Chapter 7

An enterprising and compassionate teacher—the Mr. P., it turned out, whom Sam remembered and whom Alyssa loved so much—had taken Alyssa into the school building and was sitting with her in an empty classroom. Ty's mother was holding Alyssa's hand. Alyssa gave great keening sobs that went right through Sam's heart.

Surely, this was it. Surely, nothing else could be as bad as this for these children. Surely, Julia would now see that she needed serious help and would take some time away from the children for their sakes.

"Samantha!" Mr. P.—Mr. Pazzano—said when she came in, letting her hair fall out of Megan's chignon. Julia had ruined it anyway.

"Hi, Mr. P.," she said, giving him a sad smile. She'd been one of his favorites, too, back then, staying after class to ask question after question about ancient civilizations until he got her an ID card to study at the local university library. Twenty years later, he had less hair and more middle but still had that air of excitement that made him such a good teacher. Sam had shushed people who'd called him Mr. Crazy when they learned what *pazzo* meant in Italian.

Alyssa looked up at her from his shoulder. Megan's mascara hadn't stood a chance. If Sam hadn't loved the girl before, she did now. She felt another surge of anger against the woman who had done this to such a sweet girl. Screw Cat and her sympathy for Julia. The woman was dangerous, and she was fucking up three peoples' lives.

Alyssa hiccupped and gulped herself into some form of control. "Is she gone?" she asked.

"Yes." Sam gently wiped away the smeared mascara under Alyssa's eyes. "Your dad wants me to take you home. Is that okay?"

Alyssa closed her eyes wearily and nodded, slumping back against Mr. P.'s ample torso. He said, "Maybe some tissues?" and gestured to the teacher's desk, where Sam found some and gave them to Alyssa.

"I can take her home," Mrs. Cavanaugh said. And she was right, of course. What business did Sam have taking charge of Ty's kids?

She nodded, but Alyssa looked up from her tissues. "Oh, no. I mean, Grandma, can Sam drive me home? I mean, Sam, can I go to your place until—until Dad and Matt are done? I wanna see Cairo."

"I don't know," Sam said. "Maybe your grandma should—"

"Come home with me, sweetheart," Mrs. Cavanaugh said, stroking Alyssa's leg. "We'll watch a movie."

"No, I want to hang out with *Cairo!*" More tears fell down Alyssa's cheeks. She was beyond politeness and family hierarchies.

"You're welcome to come too," Sam said to Mrs. Cavanaugh, hoping an apology was clear in her voice. "My sisters would love to see Alyssa again."

"You Fieldings still live up on Pemberton?"

"My oldest sister does. But they're not Fieldings anymore."

Mrs. Cavanaugh narrowed her eyes. "And what are you doing getting mixed up with my son again? You're a friend of that Janine Esposito? Or Julia?"

"No. Grandma, no." Alyssa grabbed her hand. "She helped us. Please, let her take me home?"

"I... I don't understand." The older woman looked from Sam to Alyssa.

"She gave Dad a ride to the airport last night to come get us," Alyssa said. "She's cool, Grandma."

Sam would have appreciated the compliment if it didn't mean Mrs. Cavanaugh being pushed out of the picture.

"We're happy to take her," she reiterated. "And you, too."

"Are you sure?" Mrs. Cavanaugh said to Alyssa, ignoring Sam.

"Yes."

"All right, then," Mrs. Cavanaugh said in a voice that told everyone it wasn't. "I guess I'll go to the hospital."

"Text your dad," Sam said immediately to Alyssa. "Make sure it's okay with him."

"Thanks, Grandma!" Alyssa stood and threw herself into her grandmother's arms.

"Text your dad first," Sam insisted.

Alyssa backed off and pulled her phone out of the small clutch she'd brought with her. While she texted, Mrs. Cavanaugh stared at Sam. Stared this time, not glared.

"Will someone explain this to me?" she said.

"I will as soon as I understand it myself," Sam admitted.

"Why did *you* drive them yesterday?"

Sam shook her head. "I'm not sure." She thought back to Ty's hand shaking on his keys. "Because I was in the right place at the right time, I guess."

"He says it's fine!" Alyssa said triumphantly. "And he says you can go to the hospital, Grandma."

"Well, of course I can." Mrs. Cavanaugh sniffed. But then she relaxed. "Okay, then. You have my number if you need me?" Alyssa nodded and hugged her again. "You'll take care of her," she ordered Sam.

"I promise," Sam said solemnly.

Mrs. Cavanaugh gave Alyssa one more squeeze, and she was gone.

Mr. P., whom everyone had forgotten, got up from his seat with a low cracking of his knees. "It's good to see you again, Sam," he said. "You doing okay?"

"Oh, yeah." Sam gave him a sunny Fielding smile that hurt her face. "I'm fine."

"Looks like you got a bruise there," he said, pointing to her jaw. Sam put her hand up—and just as quickly pulled it away. She was going to deal with that later, too. Maybe when she was back in New Mexico, in a reality that she missed having a hold of.

"I'll be okay," she said. "You ready to go, hon?"

For the second time in two days, Sam drove Ty's SUV. Again, Sam was amazed at Alyssa's resilience. Her cheeks were still red from crying, but she now looked as though she was going to a long-anticipated sleepover.

Megan was still at Cat's house, making dinner, while Cat watched with a glass of wine. They were overjoyed to see Alyssa again, as was Cairo. Sam told them that Ty would be along in a little while and left it at that. They stared at Sam's jawline, but she gave a quick shake of her head, and they took the hint. They ate and joked, a normal family, and Sam loved watching Alyssa bloom in front of them. She peppered Sam with questions about her job and teased Sam's other nephews. Obviously, she was used to sixteen-year-old boys.

Everyone was surprised when the doorbell rang. "Dad!" Alyssa sang, but Sam said, "Wait!" and went to the door herself to check. Paranoid, probably, but she felt she should.

It was definitely Ty on the other side of the door. He looked like he could barely hold himself up.

"Hey," she said. Had she ever wanted to take a man in her arms—platonically—so bad?

Before she could say anything else, Megan came through. "Hey, Ty! Oof!"

Megan's sunny tone took a hit when she saw the state of Ty's face. He looked worse than Sam, with butterfly closures on one side of his face and a bandage on the other. Cairo whined.

Megan recovered quickly. "Thanks for lending us your girl!" she went on. "She's awesome!"

He frowned at Sam. Obviously, he didn't appreciate Megan's cheer. "I didn't tell them anything," she said in a hurried whisper. "And neither did Alyssa."

"Dad!" Alyssa yelled and flung herself into his arms. Ty had to pick her up. Her legs dangled off the floor, almost hitting Cairo, who'd also decided to say hi.

"I'm so sorry, peanut," he said into her hair.

"Is Matt all right?" she asked.

"What happened?" Megan said, all her good mood gone.

"Come on into the kitchen," Cat said from the hall. "You could use a beer. Is Matt with you?"

"Yeah," Ty said. He moved only an inch from Alyssa's hair to answer her. "He's waiting by the car." He looked at Sam, who belatedly remembered she had his keys.

Cat pursed her lips at Ty's injuries, but only nodded. She knew already! God, the gossip in this town. How did Cat know that when

Sam and Alyssa had been here in the house with her the whole time? "I'll get him. He can hang out with the boys. Let's get you some food."

"I'd better do it," Ty said. "He's pretty hopped up on painkillers."

He put Alyssa down with a heavy sigh. Sam touched the girl's shoulder, and Alyssa snuggled immediately into her side. Sam held her as tight as she knew how. If she could be any kind of lighthouse for this kid, she would.

"You okay?" she asked Ty quietly.

He stood in the large foyer, glancing at each of them in turn, then at the old, rubbed wooden fixtures and the antique lights. "Yeah," was all he said. "Could have been worse."

But he didn't look at her while he said it, just turned and left the house. Megan left the front door open, and in a few seconds he was back, ushering Matt slowly up the stairs onto the porch.

Matt's left eye was swollen shut and several brilliant shades of purple. His other eye was an even paler blue than usual and didn't focus on anything for long.

Jake, Paolo, and Mateo approached with remarkable care from the family room where they'd been playing video games. "Dude," Jake said.

"Mm," Matt replied.

"Don't make him talk," Ty said.

The boys looked horrified. Not talk? Not bust on each other in that easy way Sam had heard from other rooms all week? Not yell when they scored points or baskets or blew up video cars?

"Not too much," Ty added. "His whole face feels like a football, he said."

"Mm," Matt agreed.

"You hungry, Matt?" Cat asked, her mother cat side coming out. "I'll make you a smoothie so you don't have to chew." She somehow drew Matt from his father, bringing him into the kitchen and sitting him on a chair with arms to hold him upright. Alyssa went with her, and Megan looked at Sam, at Ty, and disappeared. Cairo followed the smell of food. Apparently, he knew Sam was safe.

"Is she in jail?" Sam asked in a low voice.

"Yep." His lips tightened. "Where she was until this morning. But, of course, her attorneys got her out. Then this afternoon, she got served the restraining order and... she didn't like it."

He swayed in the middle of the room. "Here." Sam pulled out a chair that had never served any useful purpose in the foyer and made him sit—fall—into it. "I'm gonna make you a plate. When's the last time you ate?"

He shook his head. "Who cares? I couldn't... I couldn't stop her." He rubbed his hand over his face. "In a million years, I never would've thought she could... I would never have let them see her if I'd thought for one *second* she'd—"

Sam couldn't loom over him like this. She sat on the floor instead, folding her legs under her so she could be closer to him. So he'd hear her without her having to raise her voice. "I don't think she would, in ordinary circumstances," she said. "She was furious when it happened because she couldn't believe she'd done it. It was an accident."

He paused with his face still covered. She wanted to pull his hand away and kiss his palms. Tell him it was going to be all right. That Matt was going to be all right.

Where had that tenderness come from? Sam Fielding made damn sure she never got close enough to anyone to feel like this.

There were more important things to deal with, and she didn't want her sisters overhearing. "The other hits, though. She knew what she was doing with those. They've happened before. Right?"

He didn't move for a second, then nodded. "Only to me though. Only ever to me."

"Ty. That's fucking awful."

That made him shake with a single laugh. "I shouldn't have married her, huh?"

"This started before you married her?"

"No. I just mean... you know when you look back and you see all the mistakes you made?" He took his hand away and his eyes met hers. "Yeah. I think you do know."

"I know a hell of a lot more than you on the subject," she pointed out. "Are you really going to blame yourself for what she did today? If I were the one sitting there and you were here, would you tell *me* that I caused that abuse?"

The word made him wince. "It's not the same thing when it's the man."

"I don't see why not."

"I never felt in danger," he said. "I knew where it would go. It never went that far." He looked up at the ceiling. "And God, if Matt had just..."

"He's a good kid."

"He's gonna need therapy for the rest of his life for this."

"Maybe. Don't we all?"

He laughed again. "Dammit, Sam. I'm trying to feel sorry for myself here."

"And so you should. But not because you have two great kids. So come on. Cat will want to feed you up and then tell you how to live your lives, and you don't want to deprive her of the opportunity."

She unfolded herself from the floor and took his hands to pull him up. Those calluses brushed against her sensitive fingers again, but she set her teeth and ignored them. Ty let her pull him to standing.

"One more thing," he said, not letting go of her hands. "The police said we should take photographs of your face—your bruises. For the record." Sam let go of one hand to touch the sensitive skin, made more so by his glance.

"This is so weird," was all she could think to say.

"Tell me about it." He looked as though he wanted to smile, but his face just wouldn't do it. "My lawyer told me to do this ages ago but..." He let go of her other hand and scraped his hand through his hair. "I thought it was better not to. Shows what I knew."

"Hey." She wagged a finger at him. "We just talked about this. This is her fault. Not yours. Let's get you something to eat."

She led the way into the kitchen.

"Come here," Cat ordered, taking charge of him so Sam could stay at a safe distance. "Sit down next to your boy and eat this."

"I made it!" Megan pointed out.

"Don't tell him that," Sam said. "We want him to eat it."

Megan poked her, and Sam flapped her hands at her. The chopped salad had plenty of chicken in it and the perfect amount of dressing, but Sam's rule was, never miss an opportunity to bust on your sibling. It felt as comforting as scratching the top of Cairo's head.

"It's great," Ty said, his mouth full. "Thanks."

"Your smoothie okay, Matt?" Cat asked.

"Hey," Paolo said, coming in from the family room. "Matt and Mateo. I just realized."

"Dork," his twin said. "Mom, can we have a smoothie too?"

"You just had—oh, never mind." Cat picked up the plastic jug from the drying rack. "Alyssa? Or would you rather have ice cream? Or a float?"

Alyssa, on the other side of the table from her father and brother, had been watching Matt like a hawk, but now she said, "Can I have a float, Dad?"

Ty swallowed. "If it's not too much trouble," he said.

"If it's not too much trouble," Alyssa parroted, giving Cat a big-eyed, please-let-it-not-be-too-much-trouble stare.

"It's not too much trouble. Boys, get out of here. You're taking up too much space."

"We wanted to see if Matt wanted to watch a movie," Jake said. "He doesn't have to talk to do that."

Matt shrugged and winced.

Alyssa said, "Matt... Mateo. That's funny."

"I don't know how we'll tell them apart," Megan said airily, looking at Matt's blond head and then over to Mateo's dark Italian looks.

Matt smirked, then winced again and put a hand up to his eye.

"No jokes!" Cat decreed. "What movie?" she asked her sons.

"Uh, *Terminator*?"

"Ooh, can I watch too?" Alyssa begged her father.

"No." Ty put down his fork. "You know you can't. And I don't know if Matt should either. With all the..." He mimed tearing off the skin from one side of his face.

"I'll be fine," Matt said. Well, he said, "Ll b'fn," but Sam got it. The kid needed escapism. And at least *Terminator* had a kickass female lead in it.

"That's one of my favorite movies," she said approvingly. "The last one was even better."

"Yeah," Cat unexpectedly added. "You think you're Sarah Connor, don't you, Sam?"

Megan cackled. Ty looked stunned. Mateo and Paolo giggled, and Sam put her hands on her hips. Just because she dug khaki colors and could rock a tank top didn't mean she thought she was the most badass female character around, did it?

"Is she a hero?" Alyssa said, "because Sam totally *is* her, then! She stopped my mom from hitting my brother again!"

The joking atmosphere got sucked right out of the room. "Oh, honey," Megan said, with a mountain of compassion and love behind the words. But she couldn't stop the memory from overwhelming Alyssa, who burst into tears.

The Fielding boys scattered, but there were so many women trying to get to Alyssa that Ty almost couldn't get through. "Come on, baby," he said, putting his arm around her shoulders. "Let's sit outside a little while."

"The back porch is good," Cat said, opening the door. "I'll bring out your float, honey."

They left the house, Alyssa's sobs echoing back into the kitchen.

Chapter 8

They all slept there that night. Jake insisted Matt take his bed while he stretched out on the floor. Alyssa begged to stay in Sam's room, promising that she'd sleep on the floor, too, but Sam said, "It's a queen-sized bed, so unless you sleep like a starfish, there's room for both of us."

"You never know," Ty said.

What else could he do? Drag his kids back to their sad little townhouse? This family—of all the freaking families in this town—was overwhelming in their kindness.

Ty himself was going to go home. No one could pretend *he* was having a sleepover with his friends. But Cat, being Cat, ordered him around until he agreed to take the couch. "You don't have to do this," he protested when she started in on how many pillows she'd give him and how many more were in which closet.

"Like we'd let you drive home in this condition," Cat said, nodding at his face. She seemed to have no compunction about the insult.

Her husband nodded from the door to the family room. "Please allow us to help," he said more politely in his soft Italian accent. "We have luck, and you could use some. Also some pajamas, I think?"

Ty looked down at the blankets Cat was placing at one end of the couch, despite it being a cool night. He was still in his graduation ceremony clothes. Everything in him wanted to hide from these well-meaning folks, who were so kind when he'd fucked up so badly. When all their luck made his skin hurt. But he said, "Yeah, thanks. Maybe just a T-shirt." Antonio was several inches shorter than he. He'd bet he'd look ridiculous in the man's pajama pants. He'd do better in Sam's pants.

His cheeks heated.

Goddammit. You can't keep your mind on your problems for a hot second.

But the unbidden thought made him smile, which was better than crying and brightened Cat and Antonio's faces. They retrieved some clothes for him, handed him a new toothbrush, and left him alone. Their happy couplehood was obvious and made his heart twist.

If anyone had told his seventeen-year-old self that he'd be spending the night in Sam Fielding's house, he'd have waited for the blow, because a fantastical statement like that would have to be followed by a punch or a stamp on his foot or a gleeful, sarcastic laugh at the hope he couldn't hide. Yet here he was, given free run of the house, encouraged to *please, please, eat whatever you find; we'll keep the boys out of here in the morning so you can sleep.* He hadn't been offered food so often in his entire life.

He kept his boxer briefs on and pulled on Antonio's shirt. Sure enough, it was snug. Relying on his ability to keep himself covered and his alarm to wake him up early enough, he lay down in just the shorts. He'd never sleep anyway. The couch was deep and long. Rather than smelling like boy, which he'd expected, the blankets were fresh and the pillows cool. But he definitely wouldn't sleep tonight, with Matt in pain upstairs.

The next thing he knew, the sun was coming through the crack in the drapes over the patio doors, and voices, hurriedly shushed, sounded from the next room.

Ty had no freaking idea where he was.

His first sleepy, absurd thought was that Julia had succeeded in kidnapping all three of them. His heart rate soared before he pieced together the previous day. No. She was in jail now. Really in jail. She couldn't take them anywhere—not that she'd ever had any intention of getting Ty back. His kids were upstairs in this beautiful old house with woodwork that his fingers itched to copy; he'd been told he was welcome here, and he could smell coffee.

A knock sounded on the door—the house was old and the rooms were separated in ways that would make HGTV cry. He sat up, clutching the blankets to his front. "C'min," he said, his voice as groggy as his brain.

The door opened a crack. Alyssa's head came around it. "Hey, Lyss," he said, happy to see her. "Did you sleep okay?"

"Yeah," she said, running over and leaping onto the couch by his side. He took the blanket he'd covered himself with and wrapped it around her instead, like the cocoons she made for herself at home. "Sam snores a little."

Ty's laugh cracked out of him so fast he was surprised at the sound. "Oh no!"

"Not like Matt," Alyssa was quick to clarify, which made Ty laugh again.

"Well, that sounds good," Sam's voice said from behind him, and Ty had no time to cover up his bare chest as she walked into the room bearing a tray containing a mug of what he sure hoped was coffee and two pieces of toast.

"Stay," Sam added. Ty obeyed, even if his chest was still exposed. But then he caught the gleam of Cairo's black and tan coat behind her.

"I told them to give you Nutella," Alyssa said, bouncing on her seat while Ty tried to grab the blanket out from under her. "I only had it once, and Cat has it *all the time!* Try it, Dad, go on!"

"Okay, okay." Sam was in front of him now, and he couldn't pull on the blanket any more without looking like a total dweeb. So eff it. Sam had seen plenty of men's chests, he was sure. She sure wasn't looking at his, anyway, he found when he dared to look at her face instead of the tray she put on the coffee table. Now how did he feel about that?

"Your breakfast, sir," she said. Maybe it had been hot in the kitchen, because her cheeks were pink. Kickass Sam Fielding wasn't about to get embarrassed from his physique. Right?

"Thanks." He took the mug first and drank the coffee black. It was strong and rich.

Kind of like the Fieldings.

He'd known about the rich part, but last night had taught him of their strength. No wonder Sam had owned the joint back in school and walked around like she owned it now. Even without her parents, her siblings had her back and she had theirs. Which made it even more surreal that she'd brought him into the group last night, given him—and more importantly, his kids—the solace a close-knit family could offer.

"What's the plan for today?" Sam asked, turning away from him and striding over to the covered patio doors. She made to pull the drapes back, but hesitated. Her head turned and he thought he saw her glance at him just a little.

Okay, so maybe she didn't want to see his chest. Or she was avoiding him because she wanted to look at his chest.

Either way, it was time Ty found his shirt. He grabbed it from the easy chair he'd thrown his clothes on last night and pulled it on. Once three or four buttons were done, he said, "You can go ahead and let in the light. What time is it, anyway?"

"Seven o'clock." Sam did as he asked, by which time he'd gotten his pants on, too. There. Now she looked at him. He liked it when she did that. "We didn't want to let you sleep in too late in case you had to go to work."

"Oh, Daddy, don't go to work today!" Alyssa's happiness evaporated. "Stay here with me. With us!"

"Honey, we've imposed on these guys long enough," he told her. "I have to go log in at work, and you have to..."

What did Alyssa have to do? School was done. She had a couple of weeks of downtime before she started at a summer camp. Those days that should have been so carefree now yawned in front of him. With nothing to do, what else could Alyssa think about than what she was missing?

"She's welcome to stay here," Sam said. She hadn't moved from the patio door, which looked out over the small backyard and the two-car garage that was open and spilled out bikes and hockey sticks and held up a basketball hoop. "Matt, too. I'm guessing he won't be going to school today?"

"I don't—I don't know. I'll go check on him. I do have to check in with my office and call my—my attorney." He wasn't used to this new world, where hiding that he had an attorney from Alyssa was a moot point.

Sam was wearing an oversized T-shirt that read *Tree-hugging dirt worshipper* and a skirt in some kind of stretchy material that stopped above her knees. Ty didn't want to notice that she wasn't wearing a bra. Nope. Didn't want to notice that. He had shit—stuff to do.

"Well, you can do all that, and we'll take care of Alyssa. That okay with you, Lyss?"

Damn. She was calling his kid by the name he called her. And Alyssa didn't stop her, the traitor. Her face lit up like the sunrise, and she said, "Yeah!" in a voice of breathy wonder.

"That's that, then."

Ty stood. "I'll bring her back some clothes for the day."

"Sure." Sam's voice was light, but something was behind it. "And for Matt, too?"

"Yeah."

Matt. Who needed his meds. Ty put down his mug, ignored the toast with the Nutella Alyssa loved so much, even though his stomach grumbled, and went upstairs to the room Jake had shown him to last night.

Matt was there, still in bed, his face—what Ty could see of it—tight and swollen. "Hey, bud. How'd you sleep?"

Matt's brows came together, and he shook his head.

"You in pain?" His boy nodded. Ty wasn't hungry anymore. His stomach hurt for his son's trauma. "Okay, meds. I'm sorry I didn't give you them before."

There was a glass of water on Jake's dresser, and Matt winced when he opened his mouth the tiniest bit to take the pills, winced again when he swallowed, and winced a third time when he lay back down on the wrong side of his head.

Forget gratitude for giving him his kids. Ty was going to kill Julia.

"Okay. How about something hot to drink? It'll feel good." Matt raised his eyebrows. "Well, it might. You wanna stay here or come home with me? Alyssa's staying."

Matt closed his eyes and opened them, looking past Ty to Jake, who'd come in behind him.

"I'll stay with him, Mr. C.," Jake said.

"You have school," Ty protested. "You don't want to miss your last day."

Jake shrugged. "We don't care. It's only a half day anyway."

This family was turning itself upside down just for him and his kids. Jake and Matt had been friends for less than a year. Jake was a good kid. "Thanks, Jake," he said. "I really appreciate that. You okay with that, bud?" he asked Matt.

Matt nodded, closed and opened his eyes again, then closed them. Ty hoped the painkillers would kick in fast.

◆

Sent off by Cat to his own house with an egg and cheese sandwich, a thermos of coffee, and several instructions to get clothes and other items for his children for a couple of days, Ty got to work quickly. He checked in with his head office, told them he'd have to take a few days off, and forwarded his latest project notes to his colleagues. Then he talked to his lawyer for an hour, hating how fast the clock moved and how much he'd have to pay Lauren for her time.

Then he called Noah.

"Jesus H.," Noah said when Ty told him what had happened.

Something about hearing his friend's horror made Ty head to the workshop. He needed calm and something to do with his hands while he convinced Noah that he was somehow going to make this all right.

"Where is she now?"

"In jail. She broke the conditions of her bail from yesterday, so they probably will keep her in. And if they can persuade the judge that she's a flight risk, she'll be there for a while."

He slipped on his glasses and picked up Alyssa's bird. The last time he'd held it, he'd been planning her graduation day.

"Ah, shit," he said.

"What?"

"Alyssa missed her graduation party. The whole grade was going to the pond. I forgot all about it. And, of course, she didn't say anything."

I'm fine, she always said. Protecting him from worrying about her. Letting him off the hook. He held the small round bird in his fist and squeezed.

"You'll put together another party for her. It's only middle school. Her friends aren't going off to college or anything."

"It's never the same."

Noah made a sound that could have been agreement. "So what's next?"

"Arraignment and bail hearing. That should be today. If Julia doesn't get bail, she'll be in jail until pre-trial." He put down the bird so he could squeeze the back of his neck instead. "It all just happened. My attorney didn't have much to tell me except that she hadn't gone to court yet."

"God." Ty could imagine Noah shaking his head. "I can't believe these words are coming out of your mouth about your ex. How are the kids doing now?"

"Matt's on pain medication, but they said there weren't any broken bones. Alyssa's–" He stopped short. He couldn't tell Noah how Alyssa was without confessing where they'd spent last night. "Fine."

"What about you? Work and stuff?"

"I took a week off. I don't know when I might have to go to court."

"Shit." Ty listened into the pause. For once, he didn't hear the sharp intake of a joint being smoked. It was eight o'clock in the morning in Taos. Maybe that was early, even for Noah. "Okay, listen, man," Noah went on. "You really oughta send them down here to me. Hear me out."

For the first time, Ty said, "I'm hearing."

"Oh." Noah's surprise at the lack of argument could have been funny. "Okay, then. Seriously. Put them on a plane and send them down. I'll pick them up in Santa Fe."

"That's miles from you." One of the reasons Ty had never done it.

"We have vehicles down here, you know. And I'm a sober driver."

"And you know what a pain in the ass the flight is. Changing in Denver?"

"Dallas," Noah admitted.

"Whatever. One of the D's. I can't just put them on a plane. Not with the shape Matt's in." He picked up the wooden bird and examined its tiny carved eye, as though needing it for courage. "But."

Noah whooped.

"Maybe I'll bring them down myself later. Once things have settled down. When I know her court date." God knew he had the vacation time. He never went anywhere. He didn't even have a travel app on his phone.

"I'm holding you to that," Noah replied enthusiastically. "I'll look up flights."

"I don't know when we can come!" Ty pointed out, laughing in spite of himself.

"I'll live in hope," Noah promised. "Keep me posted, okay? And, dude?"

"What?"

"You're doing a good job. This isn't your fault."

He'd said that the other day. Ty had relaxed. And look what had happened.

"Thanks," he said anyway. "I'll let you know how it goes."

"Do that."

♦

He made himself another cup of coffee, which didn't taste as good as the Fieldings', packed up a change of clothes for the kids, and locked up the house. His back pinched a little from sleeping on a couch. Tonight, they'd be back home.

His street was busier than usual. Two cars were parked a little way down from his driveway. Funny thing was, when he pulled up at Cat's house, he could have sworn he recognized one of them, pulling into a parking space a few feet south.

Sam came out to meet him. The house had a deep front porch that was cool in the increasing June heat. She wore khaki cutoffs again and a tighter tie-dyed sleeveless top. All his thoughts of guilt and embarrassment flew out of his head. He could focus only on the little bit of pale-green bra strap slipping down her shoulder.

"Everything okay?" he said, hoping his voice didn't sound as dry as his throat felt.

"Yeah," she replied. "Your kids are fine. Matt's asleep, and Alyssa's baking with Cat. I think Cat's enjoying having a female around the house."

"Apart from you."

She raised an eyebrow. "I don't count."

She sure the hell counted as female to his libido. Not knowing what to say, he looked at the cozy seating area set up on the porch.

"Cat made lemonade," she said, waving her hand at the table set with a pitcher and glasses, along with a bowl of watermelon chunks under a fly cover. "She must really like you."

"I'm very likable," he said, choosing a seat that wouldn't be close to wherever she sat.

"So Thea tells me." Sam chose the gliding love seat, so he got to watch her feet tense and relax as she made the seat move.

"You've spoken to her? Isn't she on her honeymoon?"

"Yep. But she checked in on the boys while you were out. Jake told her you guys were staying." She grimaced. "Sorry."

He shrugged. "It happened in front of half the school. It's not like I can keep it a secret."

She nodded, and there was a pause. A couple of cars drove by, slowing down on the narrow, car-lined street. Ty leaned forward to pour the lemonade. Sam leaned forward at the same time and nearly tipped into his arms as the love seat swung out behind her. "Werp!" she said, trying to regain her balance.

He laughed, and by instinct—because what would anyone else do?—he grabbed her arm so she could steady herself against him.

God, she was strong! She had ropes of muscles in her forearm, and as she flexed he saw her bicep popping too. He swallowed. The woman was impossible to ignore.

And she'd used those muscles to hold back his ex-wife yesterday. She'd helped him, with no other motive.

"Thanks," she said, flipping her hair to the other side of her head so his hand could naturally let go of her arm. "I was going to pour the lemonade for you, but maybe you should do the honors."

"Sure." He could see the dark spread of bruising on her jaw. She'd gotten that protecting his kids. Oh, and her hair smelled incredible, even from this distance. He breathed in, hoping to calm himself with lemonade and watermelon scents, but he just got Sam. Kinda salty, kinda sweet, all kinds of sexy Sam.

He needed to get his kids and get out of here.

"So what's next?" she asked after he handed her a glass. She leaned back in the love seat and tucked her bare feet under her.

"With Julia? I think this time she'll stay in jail." He frowned into his own glass. "It's not what I wanted. The kids don't need to see that."

"But they've already seen it. You should probably address where they are now, not where you wish they were."

He raised an eyebrow. "Thanks for the pep talk."

She held up innocent hands. "I'm not trying to ding you! I see them. Maybe a little more clearly since I only just met them. You know Matt feels responsible for Alyssa. I don't know what the answer is, Ty, but I like working with reality rather than what we wish for."

She looked straight ahead of her and bit her lip. Could he push her to share a little of her life? She knew enough about his to last him a lifetime. And for the first time, he'd heard vulnerability in that sentence. He'd feel better thinking about someone else's problems for a change. "You sound like you're speaking from experience."

She shrugged and looked at the windows next to them and at the front door. All were closed, but she still lowered her voice. "When my dad died, everyone treated him like he'd been a saint. But he'd left the company in massive debt, and he died because he was screwing with a process he should have left alone." She frowned at the old wooden floor planks. "My mom was left with almost no money in the bank. Our trust funds, which his family had built for generations, were worthless. Kane nearly got himself killed bringing the company back, and Thea got mixed up with Jake and Benji's dad. *That* was our reality."

"And you found your own outlet for your anger," he said carefully.

"You mean, sleeping around in high school?" She shook her head. "Don't try slut-shaming me, Mr. Cavanaugh. I knew exactly what I was doing. Every single time."

"I wasn't going to do that!"

She didn't believe him, because she fixed him with her deep, hot-brown eyes. "I like sex. I'm not going to apologize for it. I was over the age of consent, and I liked being in control."

He held up his hands, one with his glass still in it. "I didn't mean that! I meant... well, you brought it up before. The mean girl stuff."

Two days ago, he'd met her and seen only the mean girl. Now he couldn't recognize that girl in the strong, selfless woman before him.

"Oh, that." She puffed a breath up to keep her hair off her forehead. "Yeah. Can we not talk about that?" Then she shook her head. "Scratch that. I know I don't get away with ignoring it forever. I guess I'm going to have to find some of those kids. Apologize, for what it's worth." She looked at him again. "Starting with you."

"You already did," he pointed out.

"I got interrupted."

"But I get it." To show he'd forgiven her—because hell, he had, and in the blink of a second as well—he took the cover off the watermelon and handed it to her. "You were hurting. You were a kid." She gave an unbelieving snort and took a piece of melon. He did *not* watch her pop it in her mouth. "And if I'm gonna think about it, you'd been brought up to be that mean girl. Right?"

She wriggled in her seat. "Because the Fieldings were the big shits in town? Even though everything inside was hollow?"

"Not hollow. It sounds like you had a lot of love growing up, as well as all the rest. You're equating money with stability."

"Money helps a whole hell of a lot. Your upbringing must have taught you that."

"Yeah, we didn't have much money after my dad left. Or before. He was a product of his upbringing, too. His dad left his mom. So yeah. The Fieldings were kings and queens around here. And there were the Cavanaughs, stuck in all your minds as the poor folk."

She grimaced. "You sound pretty chill about it now."

"Figuring out why I did some of the things I did helped make sense of them. And I learned that it's often not people's fault."

"Don't forgive me for what I did then, Ty. I knew better. I had plenty of examples of how not to be a bitch. I chose to ignore them."

He leaned forward. "But you know it now. That makes you a whole different person. And you're sitting there with bruises on your face that *my* ex-wife put there. I think that gives you a free pass on anything that went down in high school."

She put her hand to her jaw. "I wish I'd gotten to her sooner. Your face is a mess. And Matt!"

"Yeah. But it wasn't your job to help us, and you did it anyway."

The switch from memories of twenty years ago and Julia's actions yesterday almost gave him a headache. In a million years, he never thought he'd be sitting here, comforting Sam about her life in high school. Let alone acknowledging that he'd be a lot more hurt if she hadn't intervened.

"Anyone would have, for God's sake. Surely?"

"Well, they didn't. You did." He smiled at her. "Thanks. Again, again, again."

Her bright Fielding smile broke through her intensity. It was like looking at the sun. Ty's heart gave a disturbing tug. "You're welcome, welcome, welcome."

They were pretty close now, their bodies leaning over the table. Sam's lips were slick with watermelon juice. God help him.

He'd been this close to her once before. It had been dark then, and secluded. And she hadn't mentioned it once in all these days they'd been thrown together. But he'd remembered every second of those minutes, and his body reacted to her now. Back then she'd smelled like rum and Coke and pot. Now she was fresh and bright, so bright she hurt his eyes. He could see the lines fanning out from her eyes and the tan marks under her bra strap. He could have stared at her for hours and not be tired of learning every single little thing about her skin.

Did he lean farther forward, or did she? He only knew that his hand had come out to cup her shoulder, which was warm and smooth, and he could feel that bra strap under his fingers. She was so effortlessly sexy. She couldn't even eat fruit without making him want to—

Later, he'd swear she kissed him, but it really didn't matter. All he knew was that he'd been dying to lick that watermelon off her lips, and now he was. Her mouth was as plump and inviting as it looked. She gave a little sigh, and Ty used it as permission to move his hand to touch her hair, which was thick and strong; he thought he could feel all the individual strands against his newly sensitive fingertips.

Her hands were on his waist. Maybe they were holding him up. He didn't know. He could only continue to lean forward and kiss the most intoxicating woman he'd ever known, to feel her breath against his wet mouth and taste her lips again and again and again, not opening his mouth because this couldn't be real but desperate for the dream to continue, to take whatever she could give him, for this second only. And then this one. And this one...

A car's exhaust fumes made their way into his fuzzy brain, imposing on the glorious scent of Sam's skin. He opened his eyes, hating to come back to his surroundings.

An electronic click sounded right below them.

He broke away and looked to his left, beyond the porch railing. A man in a plain white T-shirt and nondescript jeans was holding a camera up to them and had obviously just taken a photo.

"Hey!" Ty yelled, but the man clicked the camera again, then bolted back to his car.

"What the hell?" Sam was out of his arms and halfway down the steps before he could follow her, but the car had already driven off. "Who was that? Press?"

The Fieldings had history—bad history—with the press, but Ty knew that wasn't it. He tried to gather his scattered thoughts. From kissing Sam to this? "She's gotten someone to follow me."

"What?" At least Sam looked as jarred as he did. Her hair was staticky and stood out all over where his hands had been in it, and her cheeks were flushed. "Oh, Julia?" she went on, effectively stopping his inventory of her face. "God, that sucked. I feel so exposed." She hugged her waist. "What good does it do to follow you? She's already in jail! There were a hundred witnesses to what happened yesterday. You didn't do anything wrong."

He went back up the steps to the front door. He hated how shaky his legs felt. He could *not* let down his guard again. "I don't know anymore. Her decision-making is... clinically bad. And her parents back her up. They've got the money to pay a PI. Not that I've got anything to investigate. For Christ's sake."

He opened the door. He'd had a few moments of healing there on the porch. Kissing Sam had been an A-1 level of stupid, though as long as she'd been willing—and she had been, he knew that much—who cared if they kissed? Despite the stinging wound under his eye, he might have considered himself happy in that moment.

So much for that idea.

"I'm going to go check on Matt," he said.

"Okay." Her voice was lower, showing that vulnerability again. Ugh, he wanted to wrap his arms around her and keep her away from peeping photographers and manic ex-wives and everything.

But she was Sam Fielding, and she wouldn't appreciate his machismo. He'd do better if *she* was the one looking out for *him*.

No. You don't get to have that. Not until the kids are safe.

He turned away from her and entered the cool, dark house.

Chapter 9

Sam stayed on the porch until she heard footsteps above her, going into Jake's room where Matt still lay. Then she collapsed onto the nearest chair, whose old wicker groaned at her sudden weight.

She should *not* have done that. Or did he do it? Who'd kissed who?

Whom, Cat's voice sounded in her head.

God. Cat. And the rest of that house. And Ty's kids! How could she have forgotten, just because he'd looked so good and been so open with her, that he was part of a world she could not enter?

Her fingers went to her lips, which still throbbed from his slow, thorough kisses. Not like last time. Closed mouth, as though they had all the time in the world to discover more. And Sam, who had *always* been the aggressor, had let him take the lead because she trusted that he knew what was better for them than she did. None of this was good for either of them.

She covered her eyes with one hand. How was she going to look at him now? Scratch that. How was she going to look at everyone else in the house? Alyssa and Matt, or Jake and the twins? Typical Sam, Cat would say—and so would Megan, when Cat told her. How could Sam tell them that she'd been staying away from thoughts of Ty's body for almost every one of the hours she'd known him? That she knew full well how not to react to a good-looking guy, no matter the signals he'd sent her way? She'd known he'd found her attractive in spite of himself, and she wasn't about to force anyone to do anything.

So with all that, who had kissed whom?

Thank God she was going home tomorrow. She had to be at work next Monday. That gave her five days to do a three-day drive—if she drove all day. She'd hoped to do more stopovers this time and have a couple of days to get set up at home before driving down to the camp. Given the circumstances, however, she should probably get a few miles in this afternoon.

But she hated the thought of leaving Alyssa with her dour father and injured brother, no matter how slow and addictive Ty's kisses had been and how badly she should get away from him.

Another vehicle, a dark-red truck with a noisy exhaust, drove by, making her jump. Shit. That photographer had taken a picture of them kissing. Why? Ty was divorced. He had every right to kiss whomever (*see, Cat?*) he liked.

That poor, poor family. Sam was finally pulled out of her own confusion to consider their future. What else could go wrong for them? How long would Julia keep this up? Apparently, she had quite some power, even from jail. Or were her parents on Ty's case? And for what? What had Ty ever done but be a conscientious, faithful, fucking incredible father?

Oof. Where had that come from?

She shook out her hair from the sweat that the June lunch hour—or Ty's heat—had caused to gather on her neck. *You don't have to have designs on him to think he's a good father.*

That wasn't why, and Sam tried to be honest with herself at all times. It was the spark she'd gotten whenever he touched her. It was how very different he was from that kid she'd ignored in high school, and yet how much of that kid had remained in his thoughtfulness, his careful observation of his surroundings, his gorgeous light-blue eyes?

Dammit, Samantha.

To distract herself, she picked up the tray of drinks and fruit and walked around to the back of the house, where the patio door was open with only the screen to keep the bugs out.

Alyssa's voice drifted outside. "He's cranky, Dad. Don't go up there yet."

Sam lurked instead of walking in. Unfortunately, Cairo sensed her and came to the screen door, wagging his tail. She shushed him and kept out of sight. The group inside the house seemed to assume he was looking out at a squirrel or something in the backyard.

"I have to, Lyss," Ty said. "He needs his meds. They'll help."

"He told us to stop baking 'cause it smelled too good and it hurts to eat."

"I should have thought of that," Cat said.

"It's okay," Ty said. When he wasn't in front of her, Sam could concentrate on the sound of his voice. She liked it. It was low and velvety. A voice you could sink into.

She shook her head. *Not. The. Time.*

"We'll go home this afternoon, anyway," Ty was saying.

"Already?" Cat said.

"Oh *no*, Dad!" Alyssa said at the same time.

"We can't impose any longer," he repeated. "Look, go take Matt this glass of juice, and I'll be up in a second."

Alyssa grumbled, but when Ty spoke again, Sam assumed that his daughter had left the kitchen.

"Someone's following me and taking pictures," he said, his voice low.

"Oh *no!*" Cat said, echoing Alyssa. "Why? *She's* the one who did wrong!"

"Her family's always supported her—as they should, I guess."

How like Ty to be generous to the family trying to destroy his!

"And they might be trying to find out something about me that will get her out of jail."

"What? What the hell would you have done in the twenty-four hours since she did this?"

"Nothing. Yet. I guess."

Sam heard the guilt in his voice. The same guilt churned in her gut. He'd given in to her kiss, like before, and now it might cost him.

"Ty," Cat said. Sam recognized the mom voice. "You have to get out in front of this. How do you know it's her family and not the press?"

"Because the press would have contacted me by now. They wouldn't need to sneak around on a story the whole town saw."

Half the town, Sam whispered.

"Okay, well, then get a restraining order on them, too. Or something. Go call your lawyer. Right now."

There was a pause. Sam had been outside so long that if she walked in, they'd know she'd been listening. So she stayed where she was.

"I don't want to complicate things," he said at last.

"*She's* the one complicating things!" Cat exclaimed. "You need a full army on your side. Starting with your attorney."

He paused again. "Thanks. Maybe I will."

Sam put two and two together. Hell if she cared if they knew she'd been eavesdropping. "We'll call Kane," she said, stepping through the screen door into view. They both jumped. Cairo yipped and then butted her hip in rebuke.

"God, Sam!" Cat yelped. "You scared the hell out of me!"

"Sorry." She shifted the tray to one hand and buried her fingers in the fur on top of Cairo's head. "But Ty needs more help than his attorney can provide."

"No, I don't," he said. He didn't make eye contact with her, which was just fine. She was more concerned about the stiff expression on his face. His jaw was set, and she knew why. He couldn't afford to start up a whole other investigation as well as this one. But like he'd said, the Fieldings had money if nothing else, and Sam was going to use it.

"Yes, you do. And that guy took a photo of me, too. I can have a team of lawyers on his ass—uh, case—in a half hour. For my own privacy, let alone yours."

He raised his brows—yep, he saw right through her. "You don't have to do this," he said, his voice dry.

She raised her eyebrows. "What if they're trying to sully my reputation in this town?"

He wasn't able to resist that. He laughed. Sam loved to hear it.

"Sorry," he said. "I'm not laughing at—"

"Yeah, you are. And that's okay. Look." She moved closer to him, abandoning her resolve of minutes before. "You need help. We already know that no one else around here has actually given you any. Now they've involved me in this, and I'm going to use that to our advantage. Like she does. We'll fight fire with fire."

He was shaking his head. "Julia's already in jail. She can't do anything else to us. *They* can't."

His phone rang. Sam put the tray down on the kitchen island while he answered it. Since Cat didn't move away to give him privacy, she didn't either.

"Hello?" he said. "What? You have *got* to be kidding—that's bullshit! How can she—? Never mind. Yeah, I know."

He hooked his hand behind his neck and turned his back. Belatedly, Cat grabbed Sam's arm and headed for the door to the front hall, but Sam heard him as she went.

"She's not even a—I've known her like two days. Yes, we went to high school. God, if you count that, I'd be dating the entire town!"

Cat's eyes were saucers, and she covered her mouth. "He's talking about you!" she hissed.

"Duh," Sam whispered. Her guilty stomach churned harder. "Shut up. I can't hear."

The swinging door from the kitchen opened. Ty was still on the phone, and he stared at Sam as he said, "Has she served papers yet? Okay. Then I still have full custody. Right? Right. I'll call you."

And he took the phone away from his ear. Sam heard a voice cut off as he hit the off button.

The three of them were silent for a moment. Finally, Sam said, "I made it worse, didn't I?"

Ty's shoulders dropped. "No."

"Why would dating Sam be such a bad thing?" Cat said. "Children-wise, I mean."

Sam rolled her eyes. "My reputation. Women like Janine who could produce dozens of stories of what I did in high school."

Cat put her hands to her ears. "I don't want to know!"

"Believe me, I'm not going to tell you," Sam assured her. "But look, Ty. One instance with me on a porch can't *possibly* be grounds to take the kids from you. Can it?"

"*What* instance?" Cat demanded. Thankfully, Ty didn't enlighten her.

"She only has to file the papers and I'll have to stay to fight them.

Where they can continue to photograph me until it gets sorted out in court." His eyes flickered to her.

"I'm going home tomorrow," she told him. Without her around, he couldn't be seen as an irresponsible dad who was thinking with his... mouth. Could he?

Something flickered across his eyes. "Tomorrow? Alyssa won't like that," he said simply.

"I'll miss her too," she said, looking him full in the face so he'd know she meant it.

He pulled his hand down his face. His hair was sticking straight up—from her hands in it?—and as she looked up at it, his cheeks went pink, despite the situation.

"I have to figure something out," he said. "Like now."

"Absolutely," Cat said. Sam had forgotten she was there. "And Sam's right. We're involved now. If they took a picture of Sam, too, we have every right to call our lawyer. I'll talk to Kane. If you agree, of course."

Ty's ocean-blue eyes looked not at Cat, but at Sam. Could he be thinking of what *she* would prefer in this situation? All she wanted was his and his children's safety. "Let us help," she said.

Cat cut her a sharp look. Had her voice been too intimate? Too breathy? Whatever. Ty shrugged and nodded, and that was what was important.

"I gotta give Matt his pills," he said. "And think."

"Sure." Sam and Cat moved toward the kitchen as one, giving Ty free access to the staircase.

"Just remember," Cat said when he was on the first step. "You're family now. All of you."

Fuck, Sam hoped not. She didn't want to kiss family. Not that she wanted to kiss him again. And again and again.

"Thanks," he said. "That means a lot." He looked at the huge carved stair rail under his hand, shook his head once, and walked upstairs and out of sight.

Cat put her hands on her hips. "*What* instance?"

"I have to go pack."

"Sam."

"Look." But Cat was looking. In that Mother Cat way that meant she was going to get the truth. "It was just a little kiss, okay?"

"Samantha!"

"Jesus, keep your voice down! And quit calling me that."

"Why? It's your name."

"You want me to call you Cathy for the rest of your life?"

"That's not my—" Cat shut her mouth fast. "You're dodging the point."

This was always how their conversations went, and Sam couldn't help but respond in the same childish way. "Which is?"

"That you—" Cat pulled her into their father's study, now Antonio's, and closed the door. "That you're *kissing* that man when he's got all this shit going on around him! What were you thinking?"

"I wasn't!" she burst out before she could stop herself. Cat opened her mouth. "Wait!" Sam said. "I don't need a lecture from you on me mindlessly falling on men's penises my whole life."

Cat's mouth stayed open and her eyes widened in horror. "I would *never*—!"

"Good. Because I haven't, and I don't. I don't care what Thea's told you. Or the rumor mill." She was mad now. Just the plain old sisterly mad that she settled into so easily. "I don't need advice on my love life from you, who found the right guy right out of the gate and has never had to worry about him for a single second."

"Sam."

No. Sam liked the sympathy in her sister's voice even less than her Mother Cat tone. "Don't analyze me. I'm fine. I—" Why was her throat threatening to close? She knew herself. Knew what she wanted and what she didn't. "I made a mistake." *We did.* "I have no intention of getting to know Ty any more than I already do. I'm going home this afternoon and that will be that. Satisfied?"

Cat folded her arms and appraised her. "All right. Just—wait." Her hands fell to her sides. The change in demeanor was so funny, Sam smiled. "This afternoon? That soon?"

"I was supposed to leave yesterday!"

"Yeah, but..."

"Cat, you can't have it both ways. Either you want me out of here or you don't."

Cat's eyes went black, and she leaned back against the heavy oak desk. "You think that's what I want?"

Sam folded her arms this time. Saying the words hurt, but they were also what *she* wanted. To be rid of her siblings' moods and requirements and obligations. To be on the road, free. Single.

Weren't they?

When she didn't answer, Cat said, "You're one of us, Sam. No matter how hard you fight against it. I wish you didn't think we're so terrible you keep running away. We love you, you know."

Ugh. She'd played the love card. Love didn't mean you were good around each other. "I love you, too, you idiot. But I'm not good for this family and you know it. I'm better off back where I belong. Which is why you don't have to worry about me and Ty Cavanaugh."

Cat shook her head. "You don't get it at all." She stood and brushed past Sam on her way to the door. "I'll never stop worrying about you."

Chapter 10

Ty stood in the hallway outside Matt's room. He'd heard Jake go in earlier and needed a minute to compose himself before he saw them. His life was officially out of control.

"Hey," he said. Matt was sitting up in bed, watching Jake, who was messing with a computer at his desk–Thea's desk, maybe, way in the past. The memories of the Fieldings pressed into the walls here. Like everything else today, Ty couldn't believe he was here.

"Hey," Jake said cheerfully. Matt grunted.

"Take these," Ty said, handing his son the water and a couple of pills. "How's the pain?"

Matt grunted again. His face looked more swollen than before–after Julia had hit him, the chairs had done the rest of the work–but there was a light to his eyes Ty was pleased to see. Thank God for Jake and the twins, acting as normal as they could and keeping Matt entertained.

Ty sat on the end of the bed, and Matt moved his feet so Ty could lean against the wall with his feet stretched in front of him. For a few seconds, Ty just sat there. He had to get a handle on this, had to make decisions. Had to protect his family.

"Ah," Jake said. "Got it." He backed away from the screen, and Ty recognized the pixelated scenes from an early version of Warcraft.

"Warcraft!" he exclaimed. "I used to play this."

"You wanna play?" Jake handed him a controller. "It's a version for PS5."

Before Ty could protest, Jake handed another controller to Matt.

"No," Ty said. "You guys play."

"'Sokay," Jake said easily. "I'll go get Aunt Cat to make Matt a milkshake." He paused. "Unless you don't know how the controller works?"

Matt made another grunting sound, though this one sounded less testy. "He knows," he said through closed lips.

Sure, he knew. Games were one of the ways he'd connected with the kids as they grew. He appreciated that Jake had chosen a collaborative game rather than, say, Mortal Kombat. He didn't want Matt making any sudden moves with his arms.

"Cool." Jake grabbed the controller back from Matt and got them to the title screen. "I'll be right back."

The big screen was clearly visible to the two of them. "Okay if I play?" Ty asked. Matt shrugged, which Ty assumed meant yes. He hoped the painkillers would kick in, but he also knew they weren't as strong as yesterday's. "You go first," he said, choosing the two-player mode.

So there he was, the weight of his world ignored, worried only about building farms and holding back orcs. He and Matt played mostly in silence, Matt communicating with nods and hand gestures when he had to. He got frustrated now and again and shouted something, which made Ty laugh and tell him not to talk, then Matt would glare at him.

Sometime during the game, Jake brought in milkshakes for them all and Alyssa joined them, curling up on Matt's bed and leaning on her dad. She asked the occasional question but mostly seemed content to be with her brother and father.

Ty had no idea what was going on in the rest of the house, and he didn't care. Only when they heard the front door open and slam closed and a deep man's voice shouted, "I'm gone five minutes and everything goes haywire?" were they pulled out of the game. Ty looked at his phone—three hours had gone by! His neck was sore, and Alyssa had fallen asleep in a soft pile alongside him. So he didn't rush out of the room to meet this new member of the family when Jake said, "That's Uncle Kane!" and jumped up from his position on the floor. "You wanna meet him?"

"Not yet. I'll be right down."

The answer had come to him as easily as Alyssa had fallen asleep.

"Hey," he said after Jake had left. "What do you think about going to visit with Uncle Noah?"

Matt stared at him, and it was a while before he answered. "For how long?"

"As long as you like. He offered to take you for the whole summer. But maybe just until I can..."

Until he could what? Make Julia see reason? Chase off private investigators? Quash the rumors that would surely get out about him and Sam?

"I was gonna work for Jake's stepdad," Matt said, keeping his mouth and face as still as possible.

"Yeah. You could do that. But..." How much should he tell him? Sam had advocated for honesty. Matt deserved that.

"I think it'd be healthier for you both if you got out of here for a little while. You're not going to be able to work with your eye like that, anyway. It's pretty where Noah is. You can go for walks. Clean the gallery for him. Kind of... detox."

Matt's gaze didn't leave his face. "What was that yelling before?" He nodded to the window.

"Oh. You heard. Well. That was a private investigator, taking a photo of me sitting on the porch with Sam." Okay, Matt didn't have to know everything. "Looks like your mom's trying to find something on me so she can get out of jail and make me the bad guy."

Matt snorted. "That's stupid."

"I'm glad you think so." Ty smiled. "But I don't want anyone following you two around, waiting to get to me. If we go to New Mexico, you guys could stay there for a while until I get this sorted out. And they won't follow us there."

"They might."

"Well, they wouldn't learn anything." Ty cringed inwardly. What could Julia make of Noah's innocuous but problematic habit?

"New Mexico?" He hadn't realized Alyssa had woken up. "With Sam?"

"What? No." But it was too late. Alyssa had brought up a new layer of emotions Ty did *not* need to deal with right now. He got off the bed, hoping the kids wouldn't see his cheeks, which felt like they were flushed crimson.

"She lives there, too," Alyssa said sensibly.

"I know. But I'm talking about Uncle Noah. He's always asking for you guys to stay there."

"We're going?" Alyssa's eyes widened. "Sweet!"

"To get away from Mom," Matt said.

"Matt," Ty interrupted, "don't say it like that."

"'Strue though," his son said, his voice leaden. "You wanna get away from Mom, Lyss?"

"Oh." Alyssa went from excited to sad in one breath. "Isn't she—isn't she in jail now?"

"Yeah." Ty had tried not to talk about it with her. He rubbed both hands over his face. "I'm sorry, hon." How would a thirteen-year-old girl take this new fact of her life?

"I'm not." Alyssa's face was as set as Matt's voice. "She hurt Matt. I don't want to see her again."

Ty let out a sigh. "I get that, Lyss. Maybe you'll change your mind one day." The words "she's still your mom" died in his throat. He couldn't continue to force his kids to allow this toxic relationship into their lives. He should have kept them from Julia when she'd come back to town. "So you'd be okay with going to Noah's for a little while? Until things settle here?"

"Yeah." Alyssa nodded. Matt nodded too.

"Guess I'd better call him, then," Ty said. "We could leave tonight." Good thing he'd taken the week off from work. Until the kids were settled down there, he wouldn't leave them alone.

♦

Sam's brother was a pain in the ass in many ways—most of them similar to Cat's controlling nature—but she couldn't deny she was glad to see him pound his way through the front door and into the family room where she'd set up her laptop to figure out her journey home.

"What's all this about a stalker and you nearly getting arrested and some kid getting hurt?" Kane blustered as he came over to give her a hug.

"Okay, none of those things happened," she said sensibly. "Well, almost none of them. Okay, they all happened, but it's not my fault!"

She sounded like her teenage self, faced with Kane's black stare. Thank God he'd been too busy to learn what she'd been like as a teen. He'd have locked her up in a convent by now.

"Calm down, Kane," Cat said, coming in and hugging him in turn. "It's complicated."

"It's not that big a deal," Sam said, though she squeezed her arms around her middle at the memory of the photographer catching her kissing Ty. Her cheeks heated. "It's one of Jake's friends. His family's kind of going through some stuff, and I was there at the right time."

"What's the matter with your face?" Kane said, not even slightly soothed. "That doesn't look like the right time to me."

She touched her jawline. If she didn't move her face, she could pretty much forget about the bruising. Ty and Matt had gotten it much worse. "I'm fine. Anyway, I'm going home tomorrow." She couldn't get Cat's disappointment out of her mind. And she wanted to say goodbye to Alyssa properly.

"You're going home *tonight*," Kane thundered. "And none of this driving crap. I'm putting you on a plane and watching it take you away from this."

She shook her head. "Thank you, dear overbearing brother, but I'm not putting Cairo in a luggage hold. It's also not necessary. I'm not the one in trouble here."

Wrong words. "So it *is* trouble?" he said.

"Will you sit down for a second and stop yelling?" Cat said, pointing at the couch. "I'll bring in some lemonade, and Sam, start from the beginning."

She was just finishing up the story when Ty came downstairs, followed by Alyssa. Sam jumped up. Which was embarrassing. "Hey," she said, looking at Ty but hoping it sounded like she'd meant Alyssa.

"Hey!" Alyssa replied anyway. "We're going to New Mexico! Can we go with you?"

"What?" Sam responded as Ty said, "No, Lyss. That's not what we agreed."

"But she's going anyway!" Alyssa said. "It makes sense! We could fly out with her!"

"I'm sorry," Ty said, looking at Sam, who felt as though a wildebeest had just stampeded over her chest.

"It's fine," she said at the same time Kane announced, "Since you don't look in much better shape than Sam, I'm gonna assume you're Tyler?"

Ty pulled himself out of the emotions going on behind his eyes long enough to shake Kane's hand and introduce himself and Alyssa properly.

"Good to meet you," Kane said, looking at Alyssa. "You okay? Sounds like you've had a rough time."

Alyssa glanced at Sam, then back at him. "I'm fine," she said. Ty's shoulders hunched. "You look just like Sam."

Kane's face split into a grin. "Thanks. I assume that's a compliment."

Alyssa's fair skin blushed scarlet. "Yes."

"Thanks, hon," Sam said. "This is my pain-in-the-butt brother. He takes care of us like Matt does you."

"Not that you let me take care of you," Kane said.

She pushed him. "I don't need taking care of."

"Now you do," he said, bristling again.

"No." They all turned to Ty. Sam thought she saw his Adam's apple bob at the attention. "We've taken enough of your help. We're going to head out as soon as I pack up the kids' stuff."

"Already?" Cat said. "But those guys outside—"

"Are they still there?" Ty said.

"I parked the car between them and the house," Kane said with satisfaction. "My driver'll see them off."

"Your driver?" Sam asked, diverted. "Hark you, Mr. Billionaire."

"Shut up." Kane poked her. "I was at work when Cat called. Ellen made me hire him, given the hours I keep. And if I'm a billionaire, so are you, dumbass. Oops."

For the first time, he looked unsure, but Alyssa and Sam both laughed. "He *is* just like Matt!" Alyssa exclaimed.

"Well, we still have to go," Ty said. "Even more so if Sam is leaving tomorrow."

"You're welcome here as yourselves, not just because of Sam," Cat interjected. "Matt's Jake's friend, so we'll do whatever we have to to help him."

"I appreciate that," he said. "But we're going to stay with my friend out of state for a little while until things die down."

"Noah?" Sam said.

"Yeah!" Alyssa replied. "In New Mexico! So you see, we could go with you!"

Ty was already shaking his head. Sam hated to let the kid down. "You wouldn't want to go with me," she said, sitting down on a chair arm so she could talk to the girl face-to-face. "I'm driving. It takes three days."

"You *drove*?" Ty said, forcing her attention up to him. "Why? Are you afraid to fly?"

"No. I like driving, and so does Cairo." The dog, who was still on alert with all the shouting, cocked his head at his name. "I... haven't been back up here for a while"–she pointedly ignored Cat's "humph" of disapproval–"and I was out of the US for a bunch of years, so I drive a lot. I see more of the country that way."

"You drove. For three days. By yourself." Ty shook his head this time.

"With Cairo," she corrected.

"Do you have sisters, Ty?" Kane said.

"No."

"Good. Don't get them. See these gray hairs?" He pointed to his temples. "Sam's given me at least half of them."

"Don't be a doofus," she said. "I told you, I can take care of myself. And it's not like I go looking for problems. I stay at decent hotels, keep my car in shape. I'm not out of my mind."

She stopped and chewed her lip. She couldn't help but look at

Ty, expecting a frown at the allusion to Julia. But he smiled—smiled! Probably at her embarrassment.

"Indiana Jones with AAA membership," he said. Now she wanted to poke him. But she couldn't touch him.

"So can we drive with her?" Alyssa said, oblivious to the charge running between the two adults. "Let's do it, Dad! We could see the country too. We've never been *anywhere*."

"Sweetheart, *no*," Ty said kindly.

"*Please*, Dad!" Alyssa said, and her eyes filled. "I don't want to fly! I don't want to go back to the airport. I want to drive with Sam. She makes me feel safe."

"Oh, honey." Sam couldn't resist the tears. She leaned over and hugged the girl. "I'm glad I make you feel safe, but a flight is just as safe as driving."

"No! I don't like the airport. Please don't make me go back there!"

"It's not up to—"

"Sam," Ty cut in. Could he tell she was softening? What difference did it make to her if the kids came with her? She could drop them off with Noah and continue on to Albuquerque.

"The distance from Albuquerque to Taos is a pain," she said.

"Can I talk to you for a minute?" he said, widening his eyes at her. In other words, *talk to me or you'll regret it*.

"Sure," she said, though she didn't think being alone with him was a good idea.

"Don't talk her out of it!" Alyssa said in an anguished voice.

"You have to let them make the decision," Cat said, taking the girl in her arms as Sam and Ty—and Cairo, who'd had enough of Sam coming and going without him—left the family room and moved to Antonio's study.

Ty closed the door. Sam swallowed.

"Listen," he said. "It doesn't matter now—except for me to apologize—but you have to know why we can't go on a whole crazy car journey together."

"Why not?" His urgency almost scared her.

"Because of those seven minutes in Heaven, and even if you've forgotten it, I haven't."

Chapter 11

Senior year. A bit of a blur if she were honest. The only time she focused was when she was applying to colleges, because she might have been angry, but she wasn't stupid. Everything would get better in college. She would be able to put the last few shitty years behind her. She wouldn't miss her mother as badly because there would be no reminders of her in college; she wouldn't have Cat's reproachful stares and meaningful conversations about not being *easy* to deal with at school. Not that Cat ever said that, of course, but she might as well have. Anyway, Sam'd be nineteen and on her own, and the thought made her squirm with longing.

Everyone always knew one kid whose parents left liquor lying around and went away for the weekend. Whether the parents were living some ideology, were just ignorant, or were alcoholics themselves and beyond caring didn't matter. The point was that everyone who was anyone knew the place and the time and would be there.

Since it was only October, maybe the cool kids had been a little more lenient, because Sam saw right away that kids who normally would never have been invited were there. They looked awkward or defiant or afraid, but they were there, clutching beers half of them looked like they didn't know what to do with, watching the other cliques holler and drink and take over the food. The smell of pot hung over the whole house. Sam knew the school's primary aficionado would be set up in the master bedroom, his location of choice, rolling joints for anyone who could pay for them. She bought three.

Between that and the beer pong game and the shots she was encouraged to drink off another girl's bare chest without using her hands, things were definitely blurry by midnight. When someone pulled her into the coat bedroom and told her she was the grand prize in a game of Seven Minutes in Heaven, she just laughed. She was safe around these guys. She knew where to disable a boy who came on too strong. And she was Sam Fielding. No one could make her do what she didn't want to do.

One, two, maybe three guys before him. They'd found the scared ones—a cocky little shit like Dan Kowalczyk wouldn't be nearly as much fun—and they spent their time in the closet getting a Sam Fielding-approved lesson in kissing and not much else. The bravest copped a feel and got kicked out for not asking first.

The last one was different. She knew it from the minute he got pushed into the closet and the door slammed behind him. In the half-light coming through the louvered doors, she recognized him as the gangly kid from the emo crowd. His blond hair had fallen back from his face in the struggle to get him into the closet, and as she stood up from her seated position, Sam thought she could see his eyes were a very light blue.

"Biker boy, right?"

He snorted but looked away from her.

Yeah, he was the kid on the bike. How did he not have someone to drive him? "How do you not have a ride to school?"

"I like the bike," he said in a tight voice. "Not all of us have rich friends with cars, Fielding. You done?"

She wasn't surprised he knew her. Everyone knew her and her crowd. That was part of their status at the school.

But what did he mean, was she done? They were in a closet for seven minutes. Did he not know how this game was played?

Not only did he not seem to know, but he wasn't even looking at her. No clumsy crowding in the small space, no sweaty hands trying to get into a position to kiss her. He looked as if he would rather be anywhere than here.

The hell?

Sam had *never* been rejected before. Then again—and the merest whisper of shame crossed her shoulder blades when she thought this—she hadn't exactly showed him she'd be interested in him.

She squinted at him. "You got pretty hair," she said.

This time he flinched before his lips tightened. He didn't say anything.

"Hey," she said, getting mad even though the pot was trying to teach her peace and love. "I just said you had pretty hair."

"Yeah." He batted at the clothes hanging in the closet. "Thanks."

He was taller than her. God, that was hot. Half the guys she dated were short, intense jocks. Even the basketball players. How skinny was he under that hoodie? Were the baggy jeans to be trendy, or could he not afford ones that fit?

She stood up and moved closer to him. She wasn't going to be thwarted. She had this down to a fine art these days—a tilt of the head, a big smile that said, yes, I am interested; yes, your wildest dreams have come true. She put out a hand and touched his arm.

He looked down at her, frowning. Oh boy, was she going to make his day. It would be a great story for her friends, too—the day she bestowed a favor on the poor geeky bike kid. She slid her hand up his arm, over his shoulder, up to touch the thick blond locks. They felt soft and rough at the same time.

He was standing very still, letting her touch him, still frowning. Sam smiled bigger. He recoiled.

Huh? Recoiled? Didn't he understand what was happening here?

She moved toward his mouth slowly, loving the slow prolonging of that first touch, the power she had to steal the breath of any boy she wanted. And this one didn't move, didn't try to take over the seduction, didn't rush to stick his tongue down her throat, didn't do anything, just waited even though she could feel that she was getting him exactly where she wanted him.

Until he put his hand on her shoulder and pushed her away. Gently, but still.

"What's the matter with you?" she said. "Oh shit!" The rum and Coke she'd had was messing with the pot. She should have realized. "You're gay, aren't you? I'm sorry, I—"

"I'm straight," he said without inflection. "You really think that a guy has to be gay not to want to make out with you?"

Her mouth fell open. No *one* had spoken to her like that. "You–you don't?"

He folded his arms, making her drop hers, and looked into the depths of the closet. She couldn't see his expression.

"Why not?" she demanded. "What's the matter with me, huh?"

He unfolded his arms long enough to pull his phone out of his pocket. "How long do we have to do this?"

"I don't know." She shook her head. He wasn't answering any of her questions. "What's the matter with me?"

Now he did look at her, his face illuminated from below by his phone. "You don't even know. That's what's the matter with you."

"What?"

That vague itchy feeling along her shoulders grew. Okay, so she basically ignored guys like this on any normal day. She'd kind of forgotten that choosing to do that might mean the guy wouldn't be interested in her either.

"Look," she said, immediately annoyed. "You don't have to be rude."

He laughed, and despite her anger, she liked it. Even though he was laughing at her. "Says the girl who turns her nose up at anyone without a flip phone and a roadster."

"I do *not*!"

"I saw you." He waved his phone, a small, old model with a simple screen, at her. "You can't even keep that snotty look off your face."

She gaped at him again. Had she done that? Was she that shallow? She *wasn't*! She didn't care about stuff like that! She was just thinking that he didn't even have a camera phone, and yet–

Oh.

She retreated to the other wall of the closet, leaving at least three feet between them. The emo kid tried to push the door open, but it was held shut from the other side. "Hey," he said. "We're done here."

The boys outside laughed. "Yeah, right!"

"We're not done!" Sam called. "We're *not* done," she repeated furiously to him.

"Make up your minds!" those holding the door closed said. "That was quick, even for you, Cavanaugh!"

Cavanaugh. Right. "Tyler. That's your name."

"Don't wear it out," he said, sounding bored.

Stung, she chanted, "Tyler, Tyler, Tyler, Tyler, Tyler!"

Someone outside said, "Woo! Now he's getting her going!" and Sam felt sick and everything changed.

"Shut the fuck up, Jason!" she shouted.

They jeered but didn't say anything else. A silence fell, during which Sam could only stare at the boy across the unfathomable space from her.

"Okay," she said.

"Okay what?" he replied. "You see how those guys do exactly what you want? Don't you think that's freaking weird?"

"Of course they do," she snapped. "They're—"

She stopped, but he didn't. "They're what, Fielding? Tell me."

She wanted to say "friends," but something about this boy was making her face situations she'd ignored. "I know their secrets," she said truthfully. "They're afraid of me."

"They still threw you in this closet," he said. "That the kind of respect you want?"

"Don't talk to me about respect!" she said hotly. "I *chose* to come in here!"

"I'm not—" He shook those beautiful blond locks. "I'm just telling you. I might be a fucking nobody in this school, but I hear things in the locker room. They don't talk about you any better because you know which ones don't want to come out or haven't lost their virginity yet."

She rolled her shoulders. *Really itchy now.* "I never said you were a nobody."

He laughed again. "You think I need you to walk up to me and say it?"

It was Sam's turn to cross her arms. Against his words. Against her own guilt rising through her gut and clogging her throat. Against his scent, which, unlike the boys outside, was clean and fresh. Because he didn't do sports, probably.

See? She was a good person! She thought this guy everyone said was a dweeb was cute. That meant something, didn't it?

She heard the words in her head, and they made her cringe.

"What?" he said. "You don't like the truth?"

Sam's chest felt like someone was trying to push her through the wall. But his words reawakened her fighting spirit. Not to refute him but to show her that she could take whatever he wanted to say.

Her dad had fudged the truth. He'd lied about the state of the company for years. And he'd died lying. Now her mom was dead, too, after lying about her husband's goodness when Sam wanted to shout at her that he wasn't good at all. If he was, why had he abandoned them?

She was *never* going to be like that. She was Sam Fielding. No one got one over on her. If this guy knew more about her than she did, she could take it. And if she had to face a few actions in her past, she'd handle that, too.

"I like the truth just fine," she said. "Go ahead. Tell me."

Now she'd surprised him. Which was hella satisfying. His eyes widened, and he forgot to scowl at her. "What do you mean?"

"Go ahead," she said. "Tell me. Tell me what I look like from the outside."

This time his mouth dropped open. "I—no. I just—you—"

She'd flustered him. Good. She put a hand on her hip. "Come on, Tyler. The great artist shrink. Tell Sam what she doesn't know about herself."

He'd talked himself into a corner, and his raised eyebrows showed he didn't know how to get out. "I don't want to play this game," he said at last.

"I didn't either, dude, but you started it."

"I—Okay." He scrubbed his hand through his hair, bringing his elbow closer to her. She smelled that clean scent again, and she didn't want to, but she liked it. "Look. I got thrown in here too. I didn't expect to—"

"Don't cop out now, Professor Cavanaugh," she taunted him. "This is your chance." She threw open her arms. One hand hit the door and the other hit the clothes, so it wasn't the grand gesture she'd hoped, but anyway.

"How do I know you won't get your pals outside to beat the shit out of me the second I leave this place?"

"Ugh!" She poked a finger at him. "I would *never* do that! You think I'm some kind of sadistic—oh God. You *do* think that!"

"You ever stop someone from beating up one of my friends?"

"I don't *know* any of your friends."

He raised an eyebrow. "You've been at school with them for three years."

"You know any of *my* friends?" she retorted, hoping the best defense was offense.

"Everyone knows your friends, Sam," he said.

Shit. He had her there. Sam's friends were the kings and queens of the grade. She hadn't let it sink in before that that meant there had to be peasants, and she'd made him into one of them.

"They're not all—" She huffed. Jesus, she was like Clare in *The Breakfast Club*. Was she about to talk about the pressure she was under to be perfect? 'Cause she wasn't. She only had to be herself.

And herself was pretty fucking awful if she were honest.

"Okay. You made your point."

"I..." Now he seemed less sure of himself. "Look, I don't mean to... I wasn't exactly expecting this tonight, you know?"

Neither the hell was she.

"You surprised me. I didn't plan on riding your ass. I mean—"

Sam laughed. He probably blushed, though she couldn't see it in the dim light.

"I mean," he went on, "I know what happened to your parents. That would fuck anyone up."

Chills went all the way from her scalp to her toes. He'd mentioned the thing. The thing no one who knew her dared mention. "It's nothing to do with them," she said through suddenly numb lips.

"If you say so." He seemed to relax a little. "I just wanna say, my dad left us when I was seven. And it sucked. Still does. So I know some of how you feel. Though my dad had a choice and yours didn't."

"My dad did too," she said at once, but the chills went on, rolling over her, over and over. She began to gulp in breaths because her chest was impossibly tight. Where had all the air in this closet gone?

"Hey," he said, coming away from his wall. "You okay?"

"Don't—" She put out her hand, but all that did was make her touch him, and despite his skinny frame, his chest was strong and warm, and her hand clenched involuntarily.

"I'm sorry," he said. "Hey. You wanna get out of here?"

Her eyes were squeezed shut, and she was terrified she was going to cry. For those boys outside to see her like this? "No," she said.

He took her arm, and when she opened her eyes, he was next to her, frowning down at her with impossibly kind eyes. "Maybe sit down for a second, then."

Her knees obeyed him before she knew it, and they both fell in a heap to the floor. Tyler's knees barely missed her chin, and Sam found their legs entangled and Tyler's arms around her. His breath was on her cheek, drying her tears.

They stayed like that while the guys outside the closet laughed at the sudden noise and made rude jokes. Sam couldn't stand it. She couldn't stand herself, her past, her friends, any of it. She shrank into herself. But that only brought her deeper into Tyler's embrace, and he seemed quite happy to hold her. She ducked her head, letting the tears fall off her nose. Tyler's hands began stroking her back. Goddamn him for being nice to her.

"Don't be nice to me," she whispered.

"I'll be whatever I want to be," he replied, but it didn't sound like he was opposing her. After the conversation they'd just had, for him to say that? Sam drew in another shaking breath and found she didn't have the desperate urge to cry anymore.

She liked his hands on her back. His arms were wiry and strong around her. His legs under hers were warm and supportive. She looked up and he looked down, and she only kissed him to say thank you, but the room might have lit up with the charge between them as soon as her lips touched his.

Tyler backed off and stared at her. Sam was about to

apologize—the first time she'd ever done that about one of her kisses—but then he said, "Fuck," and he was kissing her now with abandon, pressing her head against the wall, filling her mouth with his tongue, his lips hot and wet against her. Sam met him kiss for kiss, time and the world outside the closet meaning nothing.

"Time's up!" someone shouted from outside, and Sam didn't even have time to get off his lap before the door opened and four faces grinned down at their dishevelment.

Chapter 12

"Ty."

Her legs had collapsed her onto the leather chair in front of the desk. Cairo immediately pressed to her side at the unexpected movement.

"I didn't forget," she said, holding her head in her hand. "What a goddamn brat I was. God."

"I told you," he said. "No one was their best self in high school."

"*You* were." She looked up at him. "You were thoughtful and kind, and—"

"You can say that after what I said to you in that closet?"

"You told me the truth. That was what I told you to do. All I was, was a freaking bitch to you and everyone you knew."

"You stopped," he said. "I noticed."

What else could she have done after he'd pointed out so clearly what she'd wanted to ignore?

She'd retreated from her friends but couldn't drop them altogether. They'd join her at the lunch table, gossiping, laughing, bitching. They didn't even notice she no longer participated. If she tried to stop them, they laughed at her. And another fact that made her squirm was that she hadn't tried very hard. She didn't know how to be the lone voice of reason after well more than a year of leading the group.

Tyler had fared better. They'd busted on him—and about him—made jokes about how he kissed, guessed at how far he'd gone with the great Sam Fielding, and his stock price had gone up a little. At least Sam knew how to speak up in one respect—she made sure no one touched him or his friends again. That got her a lot more ribbing, but Ty was left alone, so she'd accepted their lame jokes as punishment for her actions.

"I stopped too late," she said. "The damage I did..." She took the end of her ponytail and pulled on it, hurting her scalp on purpose. "I've pushed it away. I graduated, and I literally walked away and have never been back. Until I dropped off Jake and Matt the other day, I... I created a story for myself about that time. And I chose what I wanted to remember about it. And jumping you in that closet wasn't—"

"*You* jumped *me*? You're kidding. *I'm* the one who took advantage of *you*." He leaned against a bookcase and folded his arms. "I knew you were drunk and high, and I kissed you anyway."

"Goddammit, *no*, Ty!" She saw where his thoughts were going. Had gone. "Oh God. Have you been thinking that all these years?" She leaped up from the chair, startling Cairo again, and grabbed his arms. "No one took advantage of me in those years," she said firmly. "No. One. You hear me?"

His lips were soft, his eyes tortured. "How do you know?"

The memories were racing behind her words, all the boys, all the goofy good times. Sam the teacher, Sam the yogi, Sam the mistress. And the bravado that was based on fact, that she might have questionable motivations for being this way, but she was *not* going to be pitied by *anyone*.

"We made out because I wanted to," she said. "I remember it. Believe me. I kissed *you*. And it was exactly what I wanted to do."

Ty looked at her for so long, she wanted to squirm. He even opened and closed his mouth a couple of times. Finally, he said, "If you are telling me that you were in control, I will have to believe you, because I don't think you lie."

"You can believe me," she insisted.

"But if a small part of me thinks that you're saying that to make me feel better, because of all the shit that's been going down the last couple days"—he waved around him—"then I don't know how to shut that up."

"I'm not that nice," she said. "I'm not nice at all, in fact. I do what I want when I want. I feel sorry for your kids, and I feel bad about how I treated you, but I'm not a good person like my sisters. Not enough to lie about this, anyway."

"All right." He moved sideways, away from the bookshelves and away from her. "Then it can stay in the past."

"Absolutely." Except their last kiss hadn't been in a closet in senior year. It had been a couple of hours ago. That wasn't the past at all.

"But we can't travel with you," he said.

"I wouldn't suggest it."

"Good." He began to turn, as though to buy plane tickets then and there.

"If it weren't for Alyssa's face just now," she added.

"Oh God." Ty stopped and pulled his hand through his hair. "What the hell am I supposed to do?"

"Look," she said, coming around to his line of sight. "If you and I have come to a new understanding, then maybe we can be... friends." She swallowed as the memory of that last kiss filled her entire body.

"Friends," he said. His swollen cheek flushed.

"Yes." She pushed the kiss away. It had been a mistake and could not be repeated. "And as *friends*, I want to help your kids get away from this situation. I have a car with plenty of room, a dog who'd love the company, and three days of travel to get through."

He shook his head, but now Sam was picking up steam. "And in case you're worried about the cost, I'll cover the whole thing. Hotel rooms, food. Consider it a graduation gift for Alyssa."

Ty looked at her almost with pity. "I can't let you do that."

She set her jaw, though inside she was screaming, *What are you doing? Drive away from this man immediately!* "What else are friends for?"

"Friends, huh?" He came toward her, and Sam swallowed again at the heat in his eyes. "Sam. What are we going to do about this?"

He took her hand from her side. The frisson that went up her arm made her shoulders shake. Then he brought his other hand to touch the pounding pulse in her neck. Sam closed her eyes and leaned into the touch before she could help herself.

But no. She was always in control. She hadn't needed to keep herself away from a man before, but she could do it now. For Alyssa and Matt's sake. For her own.

She stepped back and shook her head. "We're not going to do anything about this. You'll be with Matt, and I'll be with Alyssa, and we'll be *friends* in between. Because that's the best thing for both of us."

Ty had dropped his hands when she stepped back, and hell if she couldn't feel his very fingerprints on her skin. She lifted her chin and gave him her most determined stare.

"It is," he said. "The best thing."

"Right."

"Because I live here. And you live in New Mexico."

"Exactly."

"And we want completely different things out of life."

"True."

He deflated the way he had when she'd ordered him to let her drive to the airport. As though he'd lost an argument he didn't know he'd been having. "All right then. But only because I can't think of a better way to get the kids out of here. And because of the look on Alyssa's face."

She smiled at that. In the end, what more did he want than to make his kids' lives better? And what else could she do other than everything she could to help him in that?

PART II

Chapter 13

"I feel like a knockoff James Bond," Ty whispered.

"Shh," Sam said. "Let Len do his job."

Ty and the kids had spent the afternoon at his house. They'd gone through the back door because there was still a car parked down the street. The unbroken line of townhouses with their shared backyard meant that the PIs—or whatever they were—couldn't see them. They'd packed, then returned to the Fieldings. Ty had called his mother, who hadn't understood any of his reasons for leaving and was now pissed that she wouldn't see her grandchildren all summer; Noah, who cheered and said he was going to kill the fatted calf; and Lauren, who, to his surprise, agreed that he should go.

"Get away from here. They have the photos for the arraignment. You don't have to be there. It's an abuse case, so it won't seem strange. And this bogus custody filing. Get them out of here while you still have full custody. Just keep in touch."

"Thanks, Lauren. What would I do without you?"

Now it was pitch-dark outside. The lights on the first floor of Cat's house were off. Upstairs, Jake was playing music through his open window. The house looked completely normal for eleven o'clock on a Thursday night. Apart from the four shadows huddled in the window or peeking out of the sidelights in the front door.

Kane had insisted, and Ty was too tired to contradict him. The spying car was still on the street. Being followed out of the state wouldn't exactly help their plans, so after a minute or two, Kane's electric Audi SUV literally purred up to the other car—and died.

Len, the driver, a twenty-seven-year-old old soul, hit the steering wheel so hard the car shook. There was a moment of silence while Len turned around to the occupant of the back seat, and then both doors facing the house opened.

"What the hell do I pay you for?" Kane yelled, throwing his hands up.

"I'm sorry, Mr. Fielding!" Len cried, his voice drenched in fear of retribution. "It's these new technologies!"

"It's your stupid-ass driving!" Kane shouted, looming over the younger man and backing him up so they blocked the spy car's view of the front door. "When did you last get it charged?"

"Now," Ty said, and Sam opened the old front door as quietly as humanly possible. Kane's voice covered the slight creak, and they stayed low as they ran down the porch steps to Sam's SUV. While Kane swore at Len and told him he was trying to save his family from yet another scandal with yet another sister, the Cavanaughs, Sam, and Cairo executed a perfectly pre-choreographed dance—Cairo and the backpacks in the back, kids in the passenger seats, Sam and Ty in the front.

While Kane told the whole street how feckless Sam was and how little she cared about his tenth-generation business and Len swore that he could fix it if he just opened the hood, Sam started the car. That noise couldn't be covered, but Kane's car was in the way, and now the journalists or PIs or whatever they were had jumped out of their car and were swearing at Len themselves. Kane was yelling at them to leave his driver alone, and Sam marveled at his acting abilities while she backed up and squealed around to barrel down the street in the opposite direction from the chaos.

Alyssa was laughing. Ty looked over at Sam, who wasn't. "We're not done yet."

Cat and Megan, who'd begged to be part of the plan, were supposed to wait until Sam had driven away and then block the road further by coming out and yelling at their brother to stop yelling.

They drove for a minute, and then Cat called. "You won't believe it," she said. "Megan's flirting with them."

"Hi, Sam!" Megan's cheerful voice came over the phone. "I'm not flirting! We're just good friends now, right, boys? All good now!"

"Okay, get out of the road," Ty said. Two women were safer than one, but he didn't like what the men would do once Kane drove away.

"We're going," Megan said. "Hey! The car started! Wow, thanks, guys. You must have looked at it and it worked."

"Stop flirting and get out of there!" Sam cried.

"Look who's talking!" Megan laughed. "Good luck! Love you!"

And they were on the highway heading north—Sam's profile determined, and Cairo, his head on the back seat, getting rubs from Alyssa—before Ty could have another coherent thought.

♦

The first hotel was an hour north of town, because Sam said they couldn't be too careful. Ty hated driving away from the direction they should be going, and he already missed home. The kids, too, once the initial excitement had worn off, were morose and not inclined to like anything they saw. In the hotel, Ty closed his and Matt's connecting door with an unbidden sigh of relief.

He took out the little bird he was carving for Alyssa, put on his glasses, and laid a small drop cloth on his lap. While he sanded the bird, Matt lay in bed, wincing and scrolling on his phone.

"Your face feel worse?" Ty said.

"Mm," Matt grunted. His eye certainly looked worse. Ty had never seen so many colors come out on one person's face.

"I'll get you some ice."

So he had to extricate himself from his makeshift workshop and go down the hall. And wouldn't you know it, there was Sam. Already in a tank top and pajama pants, with no bra and her hair in a messy bun on top of her head. He just wouldn't breathe in for the next two minutes and he'd survive this.

"Hey," she said. She was filling her ice bucket already. "How's it going?"

"Matt's eye hurts worse."

Sam nodded. "Alyssa's crying, just FYI."

"Jesus."

"It's okay. It was kinda fun with all the plans and tricks. I think it's just more real now that we're really on the road."

"I'm sorry you have to deal with that. You want me to come—?"

"No." She put her hand on his arm. A quick squeeze and she let go. Okay, maybe he shouldn't breathe for *three* minutes. She smelled like toothpaste. God help him. Toothpaste. "Let them sleep for a few hours. Things'll look better in the morning."

"Is that your general philosophy on life?" Her eyes were bright despite the bruises on her face. She looked as though she could have driven all night and been just as fresh in the morning. Did anything touch her these days?

"No." She sobered. "My general philosophy on life is too depressing."

"What is it?" he asked at once.

"I'll tell you one day. See you tomorrow."

She walked away. Ty wondered if she knew he was watching her. Then he remembered that if she didn't hear the ice machine working, she knew. He rested his head against the cool metal box, his emotions cycling through lust, fear, despair, and guilt while the ice filled the bucket.

◆

Things did not look better in the morning. The kids were grumpy in a way Sam wasn't used to and did not appreciate. Not even Cairo could cheer Alyssa up. Matt's hair was wet and sticking up every which way. His face was swollen and purple on one side. Ty was no better. He hardly looked like he'd slept, with shadowed lines under his eyes, his hair messy and in need of some shampoo. Of course, that just made him look rumpled and irresistible.

Another thing Sam wasn't used to doing. Resisting unattached men who were interested in her. *He's as good as attached,* she reminded herself when he snapped at Matt for complaining about the eggs. *As good as married as far as you're concerned, kiddo.*

She didn't blame them for their crankiness. There were way too many reasons for it. But Sam couldn't help but wonder why she'd signed up for a job she wasn't qualified for. She could love her nieces and nephews and still give them back to their parents at the end of the day. Now she was in a room with two grieving, cranky teenagers and she couldn't get away.

"Can I have coffee?" Alyssa asked.

"No," Ty said shortly.

"Ugh. You know I'm going to be fourteen in two months. I've had caffeine before, Dad."

"Fine." He pushed a cup at her. "You'll hate it. You'll be all jitters, and we're driving for miles today. But go ahead."

"Fine!" She flounced off to the coffeepots. Ty put his face in one hand and rotated his own coffee cup in its saucer.

Sam was useless in this situation. She empathized with both of them so much, it froze her brain. She wanted to keep Alyssa away from her father so they wouldn't have a chance to argue, and she wanted Matt to stay home and play games with his friends to take his mind off his eye—off all of it. But none of those things could happen. All they could do was move forward.

She stood. "I'm gonna get Cairo some food. We'll leave at nine, okay?"

♦

Alyssa came upstairs a few minutes after her, and Sam heard the door close next door, so Matt and Ty had come with her. Alyssa paid more attention to Cairo than to Sam, which was fine by her. They packed up their belongings in silence.

But a couple of minutes later, though muffled enough that they couldn't hear the words, yelling from next door broke through.

Alyssa was opening the connecting door before Sam could hold her back. She hammered her fist on the other door. "Let me in!"

"Fuck off, Lyss," they heard Matt say.

"Hey!" Ty's voice had lowered to an outraged bellow. "What the hell is wrong with you? You don't talk to your sister like—"

"I'm not going to make like this is some kind of nicey-nicey family vacation, and you can't make me!"

There was a pause after that childish outburst. Alyssa was still banging, but now she was crying as well, and her fists on the door seemed almost robotic.

Sam took hold of her hands, drawing Alyssa into her for a hug. The girl slumped into Sam's arms, her energy gone. "It's okay," Sam heard herself saying. "They're just tired. And Matt's in pain; remember that. He doesn't mean it."

It was the wrong thing to say. Alyssa jerked away, and now it was her voice echoing around the room. "That's what Dad always says about Mom! If they don't mean it, then they shouldn't say it!"

Ty opened the door at that moment, presumably because he'd heard his daughter shouting, and Alyssa pushed past him into his room. Sam's eyes met his. *I'm sorry*, she wanted to say, but the bleakness in his eyes stopped her voice in her throat.

Behind him, Matt was throwing more wet towels from the bathroom onto the bedroom floor, where Ty would trip on them if he turned around. It looked as though Matt had used every towel in the place before breakfast.

Matt's rudeness to Alyssa seemed to be forgotten. They stood side by side, arms folded, aiming accusatory glares at Ty.

"Listen," Ty said. "I know you're upset." Lyss rolled her eyes. "I know the last couple of days have been a nightmare," he pressed on. "But we *can't* take it out on each other. Okay? We're all we've got."

"Yippee," said Matt.

"Your dad's trying, Matt," Sam heard herself say.

"Bullshit," Matt snarled.

"Hey." Ty's voice warmed with disapproval.

"Oh, for God's sake, that's what you're going to parent on today? You know who taught me those words?" Sam felt Ty move next to her, as if turning his head away in pain. "Yeah. *Mom*. Great job, there, Dad. I'm *so* glad you're the adult in this family."

"Matt!" Sam exclaimed.

"He should have left her!" Matt shouted, his voice cracking. "He should have left her years ago! You think we can just run away from this? We'll *never* get away from her!"

And the tough, lanky teen broke into tears. Covering his swollen face with both hands, he sank onto one of the beds. Alyssa sat and wrapped her arms around him. She was crying as hard as he was.

Only the children's crying could be heard. Sam didn't dare look at Ty, because while Matt was probably embarrassed to cry in front of her, it was nothing to how Ty would feel if she turned and saw him cry too.

After a minute, Ty said, without looking at her, "Sam, you can go home if you want to."

She did want to. She'd never wanted to be involved with any family's politics, not even her own, and this thinly covered tragedy left her itching to run for New Mexico. She shouldn't have said a damn word just now. Even Cairo would be a better witness to this fight than her. He was already padding into the room and cocking his head at the children. In another few seconds, he'd be putting his head in Alyssa's lap.

She still didn't look at Ty but addressed her words to Matt. "I'll go if it's easier for you all, but don't take this out on your dad. He's doing his best."

Matt snorted.

"You guys are everything to him, don't you see that?" she insisted. "And before you, it was his mom. The whole time I've known him, he's done nothing but look after his family. Has he ever told you about the two jobs he worked in high school?" A silence ensued, swirling around them and making Sam's cheeks flush.

"Thanks for reminding me," Ty said kind of low.

"Well," she said, trying to regain her dignity. "It's nothing to be ashamed of. Hell—I mean, heck—you served half of us pizza and mowed the other half's lawns."

"Yeah. I remember."

Her cheeks wouldn't cool down. "So what I'm saying is, hard work is all your dad knows. And he'll do *anything* to keep you guys safe. Even driving across the country with his high school nemesis."

Ty shifted next to her, so she could see more of him at her side. "It's not like—" But he shook his head. "You don't have to do this," he said instead of whatever he'd started to say.

"It's not for you," she replied, turning her head only slightly toward him. "If you're going to make it through this, I don't want Matt taking out his—very understandable—pain on you, and Alyssa hearing it. You're her big brother." She nodded at Matt. "You need to take care of her. I don't care how pissed off you are."

Matt and Lyss just stared at her, two pairs of blue eyes so like their father's, she flushed.

"Okay, well then." She was running out of steam, and Sam didn't like that feeling. She wanted to be in control of every conversation she had. But they were all looking at her, and the tears were drying on Alyssa's face. She was stroking the top of Cairo's head, which, yes, was in her lap. "So, um," Sam went on. "I'm gonna go down to the lobby. You guys decide what you wanna do. Either way is okay with me."

No, it isn't! her self-preservation chip screamed. *Leave them to it!*

"Cai," she ordered and snapped her fingers. Her dog immediately came to her side, though did she see a reproachful look in his big brown eyes?

♦

It was only another ten minutes before the other three joined her.

Alyssa sat down in the armchair next to her and immediately reached a hand out to Cairo, who happily accepted it. "I'm sorry. We're all sorry. Please don't go home. We need your help," she said in one breath. "I feel safer with you. We all do. Please, Sam. Stay with us?"

Sam dared to look at Ty. His eyes were dark, unreadable, but he said, "I'd appreciate it. For Alyssa's sake."

Who was she kidding? The minute Alyssa had started talking, Sam had known she wouldn't leave them until she had to. "Okay," she said. Alyssa grabbed her hand and bounced up and down in her seat once or twice before remembering she was thirteen and above that kind of display.

Sam made the mistake of looking at Ty. In his rumpled polo shirt and board shorts, he was dressed like any other dad on vacation with his kids. But the heat in his blue eyes when he said thank you made her both long for and regret all of it.

Chapter 14

Ty drove the SUV south and then west. The kids slumped in the back seat, and Cairo lay down in the wayback once they got on the highway. Sam wanted to sleep, too, but Ty hadn't rested and she didn't want to leave him alone to drive. He chose Nickelback and Staind. Sam, who approved, nodded along to the music. They'd planned out the route together, Ty even approving the hotels Sam chose—because she knew he didn't want her spending too much money on them—so there was nothing to do but watch New England fall away behind them and the hills of Pennsylvania appear.

Sam woke the kids up when they crossed the Delaware, and they got out at the visitors center to walk Cairo and stretch their legs. Alyssa and Matt seemed underwhelmed with Pennsylvania so far, and they didn't waste any time moving on. Sam took the wheel; she hoped Ty would rest that beautiful blond head against his window and finally get some rest.

But Alyssa's first words once they were back on the highway woke all of them up. "What did you mean, you were Dad's nemesis in high school?"

Sam got a frisson all over her body. She shouldn't have said that. They'd just reached a truce, and now she was going to expose scars that had been forgotten. Well, maybe not forgotten.

And she wasn't about to share the details of those seven minutes in Heaven.

"Yeah," Matt added. "And when we first met you, Dad said you weren't friends."

"That's right!" Alyssa exclaimed. "So what's going on?" She looked between them.

Ty and Sam exchanged a long, pained look. How was she going to get out of this one? Dammit. Did she adhere to the truth or didn't she? She'd always said the only way out of difficult situations was through. "I wasn't very nice in high school, Lyss," she began.

"Were you a bully?" Alyssa said.

At the same time, Ty said, "Not for all of high school. You were okay until your dad died."

"That's no excuse," Sam repeated.

"And in senior year," he added.

"So you *were* a bully?" Alyssa broke in. Sam hated the horror in her voice.

"No," Ty said.

"Not physically," Sam said. "I was..." She cast her eyes to the ceiling of the SUV, as though that would bring her salvation from this conversation. "I was the mean girl, I guess."

"Did you wear pink on Wednesdays?" Alyssa asked.

Sam winced. She hated that movie. "Nope. I wasn't in a clique like that."

Ty cleared his throat. "Yeah, you kinda were."

Sam flushed. She remembered Janine. All the girls who hung on her exploits, who she knew talked about her behind her back but egged her on when she pretended to consider which member of the basketball team would get her attention next.

She blew out her lips. "Well, I didn't wear pink."

"Why?" Alyssa asked. The warm voice she'd used with Sam since the beginning was gone. "Why were you a bully?"

"Did you bully Dad?" Matt added.

"No," Ty said at once.

She rolled her eyes at him, for all she appreciated his defense. "You don't have to protect me, but thanks." She twisted in her seat to look back at the girl, whose lips were tight and her eyes narrowed, but the steering wheel moved with her, and she had to face front again before she drove them off the highway.

"Her parents died," Ty said, as though she hadn't spoken at all. "She got pretty messed up. She was—"

"Ty," Sam interrupted. "I can explain for myself."

She dared to look at him, but the understanding in his eyes made her glance away again.

"You'll beat yourself up," he said.

"I deserve to be beaten up and you know it!" she snapped. But she didn't want to look at him again. Sam sighed and pulled her hair off her neck with one hand, sending it over the shoulder farthest from Ty. "Look, Alyssa," she said, giving Ty one last glare to make sure he didn't interrupt. "I didn't steal kids' lunch money or beat them up on the way home or anything. But I... I ignored people. It didn't start that way. I just—"

God, she didn't want to say all this out loud. Not in front of two pairs of accusing eyes. "I guess I couldn't—couldn't give anyone anything. And I withdrew, and it turned out that made me mysterious and cool." And boys liked it, which Sam had liked. Treating them poorly seemed to make them flock to her, even before she chose Brennan Caplan and discovered sex. But she wasn't about to tell Ty's kids about that. He knew far too much about it as it was.

"So I was stupid and thoughtless, and I didn't care if... pretending someone wasn't in the room when I went in hurt them or not."

"Dad?" Matt said. "Is she right?"

She shot another look at Ty before she could stop herself. He had been watching her the whole time. Ty regarded her for a moment longer, until Sam rearranged her hands on the steering wheel to attempt to shake off her self-reproach.

"She's not wrong."

Sam laughed, though her shame was making her skin burn. "Now you're telling the truth."

"So what are we doing here?" Matt said. His voice was as heated as Sam's cheeks. "Why are we on this trip with her? And why didn't you tell us this before we decided to keep going this morning?"

"Yeah," Alyssa agreed. Sam couldn't see her face, but her tone made her flinch.

"Because people change, Lyss," Ty said. He twisted in his seat, and

Sam got the scent of wood shavings again. "Does Sam seem to *you* like that girl? She helped us this week. Have you forgotten already?"

"No," he said, less forcefully. "Doesn't make what she did right."

"Of course it doesn't." Sam had to speak for herself. She was letting Ty do too much of the work. "And I know that telling you I'm sorry about it doesn't fix anything. I *am* sorry. There's never an excuse for being shitty—uh, crappy—to other people. My sister Thea went through the same thing, and she didn't turn into me."

"You are nothing like your sister," Ty said. The vibration in his voice drew her eyes to his—the hell with the road in front of her. The intensity in his eyes made her breath catch. "She hid from the world. You went out and punched it in the face."

"You say that like it's a good thing."

"It's the only thing you could have done, Indy," he said. "Being you is your best skill."

Now her skin tingled in a whole new way. Approval from Ty Cavanaugh? Like his kiss, Sam would take the memory of it and lock it away for the future. Lock it from prying eyes and save it for those rare nights when she felt that she'd made all the wrong decisions and would die alone.

"The road," Ty added mildly, and she jerked her head around. They'd drifted over an entire lane. Thank God Northern Pennsylvania was dead right now.

Matt and Alyssa didn't say anything else for a few minutes. Sam was thinking of turning the music back on to drown the silence when Alyssa spoke. "You could, though," she said.

"Could what?" Ty said.

"Could do something to make up for being a mean girl in high school."

"She already has."

"Not to us. I mean, yes, she's made it up to you. I guess she has, anyway, since we're in her car."

"That's not why I agreed to this drive, Alyssa," Sam said at once. "I wanted to help you. This isn't a tit-for-tat scenario. At all."

"Yeah, okay." Sam couldn't tell if Alyssa believed her. But the girl had another point to follow. "I mean, you can apologize to the others. Dad has the app on his phone for the other parents, right, Dad? You could start with the ones who stayed around. And if Dad knows where any of the others are, you can call them."

"Lyss, that's not appropriate," Ty said. "You can't ask—"

"She kind of can, actually," Sam said, while her stomach flipped over at the thought of talking to those people again. Janine was one thing. The kids she knew she'd hurt? Her hands suddenly got slick against the steering wheel.

"Why are you sticking up for her, Dad?" Matt said. "Is it because Mom treated you bad and you think that's okay?"

"Holy cow," Sam said, while Ty said, "Matt!" Ty had gone red right up to his roots.

What was it about children? Sometimes they were wiser than the hills. Sam saw it all now: maybe she'd been the first or maybe she'd been in the middle somewhere, but she'd treated Ty with the disdain the whole school gave his kind, and why would a boy think he deserved more when that was all he'd known? She'd seen his face while Julia had been hitting him. He wasn't scared. But he was resigned. He'd accepted what Julia did. Taken it as if it were his due.

If she hadn't been on a highway with no exit in sight, Sam would have swerved right off the road. As it was, the shoulder looked real tempting right now. She had to handle this cascade of emotions that pinged off her memories, her entire self-image, her self-worth.

"Ty," was all she could say.

"I'm not going to talk about this with you," he said, twisting farther in his seat to look at Matt. "What happened with your mom and me has nothing to do with Sam."

"Why won't you talk about it with us?" Matt insisted. "We're her victims, too. We deserve to know how to avoid women like her in the future."

Ty groaned and rubbed both hands over his face. She couldn't help it. She had to step in. Even if she didn't quite believe Ty when he said she hadn't anything to do with him getting mixed up with Julia.

"He'll tell you. One day. We're talking about my missteps right now." She sighed. She was throwing herself into the lions' den by agreeing to this. "Who will I call first?"

Distraction achieved. She swore Alyssa's glare burned holes through the headrest. "Noah," the girl said.

"You don't have to," Ty said one last time, but she knew she'd won this round. *What do we have for our winner? Five to ten minutes of humiliation and crow-eating, Bob!*

"No, she's right. Can you get him on the phone at this time of day?"

Ty pulled out his phone and hit a couple of buttons. He was also staring at her, but Sam pretended she couldn't see him. She wished Cairo was up front with her so she could bury her hand in his fur and get a hit of his uncomplicated love.

"Dude," she heard Noah's voice say. "Where are you? Change of plans? You flying instead of this crazy road trip with Queen B?"

Now Sam groaned. Ty laughed. "Yeah, about that. She's right here. And she wants to talk to you."

"What?" Noah yelped, but Ty had already hit the speaker button and held the phone up to her.

"You're on speaker," Ty said. "The kids are here, too."

"Uh," Noah said.

Time to pay the piper. "Hello, Noah," Sam said. "Queen B here."

"Uh," Noah said.

Sam was grateful for the road ahead as a place to focus her gaze while she talked. If she looked at Ty or the kids right now, she didn't know if she'd make it. "So, listen, Noah," she began. "I was—I mean, I know I—ugh." She shook her head. "Okay, sorry, Ty, but Noah, I was a shit to you in high school, and I deeply, deeply regret it."

"Oh" was all Noah said.

"I ignored you or dismissed you. You and a bunch of other kids. It's too late to say it now, but you didn't deserve that at all. You were truly talented. I didn't understand then. I didn't have the bigger picture. I focused on what I thought was important and dismissed all the rest. You became part of that. You are way more valuable than I made you feel, and I'm sorry."

There was a long, long pause, during which Sam's nerves began to screech like a wet finger on an out-of-tune glass.

"And," she said, "you could paint your nails way better than I could."

Ty and the kids let out shocked gasps that turned into laughs. Noah said, "Well, um." Ty was looking at his own hands. He'd worn black nail polish too. She'd noticed.

"You noticed more than you let on," Ty said.

"Maybe. Nothing important, though."

"I dunno," Noah said unexpectedly. "My nail game was pretty hot. And it was part of the way we were. So you seeing that means it worked, even with the mean girl."

"It wasn't enough," Sam said.

"No. You were a shit. Sorry, kids."

"You think me and Lyss have never heard the word *shit* before?" Matt said. "Jesus. Adults are stupid."

Ty threw up his hands. Sam felt herself beginning to smile. Which was not appropriate. "I was," she said, fighting the twitch in her lips.

"On the other hand," Noah said. "You helped out my boy, Tyler. And he tells me you've been good to his kids. And you're driving them to me right now, which I've been trying to get Ty to do for years."

"You can't thank me for that," Sam said. She wanted to add "Thank Julia," but not in front of the kids.

"I'll thank you for whatever I like," Noah said, his easy tone at odds with his words. "Not in charge now, Ms. Fielding."

"Dr. Fielding," Ty said.

"F'real?"

"Not the medical kind," Sam clarified.

"Wow. Cool. You were smart. We had to give you that. Okay, so you're not in charge now, *Dr.* Fielding."

"Right," she said. "Sorry."

"Yeah, I think you are." Noah let out an audible breath. "Okay. This how you're gonna spend your drive? You didn't expect that, did ya?"

"No." Now she had to laugh aloud. "I did not. It was Alyssa's idea."

"Way to go, kiddo," Noah said.

"Thanks," Alyssa said. "You're the first person she's called. How's she doing?"

Noah appeared to think about it. "I accept her apology. Honestly, she didn't affect me that much. I knew my safe places, and they weren't anywhere near the Sam Fieldings of this world."

"See that!" Alyssa said accusingly to the back of Sam's head. Sam looked at her in the rearview mirror. "You made people feel unsafe!"

Now Sam really felt like a shit. "I'm sorry, Alyssa." What else could she say? She could have been that. For her siblings, at least. She could have protected Thea from her ex-husband, protected Cat from running the whole family when she'd just gotten married, helped with Megan's schooling. Hell, she didn't know anything about how Megan had handled high school.

Maybe her next calls should be to her family.

It was like a burst dam, flooding a valley and leaving behind all the hurts Sam could have stopped exposed in the soil. Her face began to heat. And Sam *never* blushed.

"She made you feel safe the other day, Lyss," Ty said mildly. "That's why we're here."

Alyssa opened her mouth. Her eyes met Sam's in the rearview mirror. She frowned and folded her arms. "Well, maybe so. It doesn't make up for being a bully."

"She wasn't a bully," Noah said. "If by bully you mean someone who beats kids up or shoves them into their locker. Nah. We had enough of those."

"That's what I said," Ty put in.

Alyssa turned her head to the window, her arms still folded. Why should she sort out her feelings right now? Sam had gone from one personality to the complete opposite with one throwaway sentence. Whatever her dad and Noah said, she was going to be mad at Sam for a while.

"You coming all the way to Taos with them, Sam?" Noah asked.

"Yes. I'll drop them off on my way home."

"Okay. Then maybe we'll figure it out over a smoke—a drink," he corrected quickly. Ty rolled his eyes.

"A drink sounds good," Sam said firmly.

"All righty then," Noah said. "This couldn't have been fun for you. Kudos. Ty, I'll see you in a couple days. Matt, Alyssa, I can't wait to see you. You're gonna love it here."

Ty said goodbye and hung up. Silence fell on them again. Just as Sam had determined she was going to take the very next exit so she could hyperventilate a little, Ty said, "Have you ever run away from a fight, Indy?"

And the admiration in his voice made her want to stay exactly, precisely where she was.

Chapter 15

They spent the next hour making a list of people Sam could and should call. By the time they stopped for lunch, more than two dozen names sat on Ty's phone. His motley crew grabbed fast food together, but Sam told them she wanted a few minutes to herself—with Cairo, of course. Ty knew it was because she didn't want a rejection from Alyssa. What a change in his kid from one conversation. Maybe it was a good lesson for Alyssa. The ole "people aren't black or white" realization. Maybe.

Out of the corner of his eye, he watched Sam walk to a picnic table under a tree. She set out water for Cairo and began to feed him the burger she'd bought for him. Ty watched her shoulders relax and realized how much tension she'd been holding for the last hundred miles. Because of his family.

The kids downed their burgers and fries and began on their sundaes. They were on their phones. Sam was sitting with her face to the sun coming through the branches. As if this were the wooded path by the stream where he'd first met her, not a rest stop on the side of a highway. She amazed him. She could make herself comfortable anywhere.

"I'll be right back," he said.

Matt rolled his eyes, then winced at the pull on his bruised muscles. "Off to make nice with the mean girl again?"

"For crying out loud, Matt," Ty said. "You're being a total brat." And fueled by his own frustration, as well as guilt that he was now snapping the way he'd told his kids not to, he went into the rest stop and ordered another sundae.

Ignoring the narrowed stares of his kids, he walked over to Sam's table. Cairo's tail thumped the floor as he approached.

"Peace offering," Ty said.

Sam lowered her gaze to flick over him and the cup he was holding. "Hot fudge sauce?" she said.

"Yep. And whipped cream."

She took the sundae. "Peace offering accepted."

Ty smiled, and she moved to the side, inviting him to sit on the hard metal bench.

"Where are the kids?" she asked after he'd taken his seat and given Cairo a couple of pats.

"Eating their sundaes. They'll be fine for a couple minutes. You okay?"

"Sure," she answered at once. Sam was always okay.

"I'm sorry about the kids," he said. "I had no idea they'd–"

"Seriously, Ty," she interrupted. "I'm fine. They did exactly what they should have done."

He put down his cup. "Sam," he said seriously, because this was the only reason he'd come over. The only one. "Neither you nor anyone else is responsible for my relationship with Julia."

Sam looked up at the sky and down again. "We're a product of our upbringing, Tyler," she said with a twist to her smile. "You know that. We just talked about it for the last hour."

"Okay, sure. So let's not leave it at high school. Let's go all the way back. My dad left my mom when I was seven. You want abandonment issues? That's where mine started. You want me to tell you that you're the sole reason my marriage was fucked up and my kids are suffering now? Sorry, sweetheart. You don't get that prize."

Her mouth fell open.

"And you, Indy," he continued. "You were raised to be a raving snob."

"I was *not!*" she yelped.

"The kids you looked down on were never the rich ones. And your parents weren't friends with their parents. Did you notice? All the kids on that list were from my side of town. You were friends with *all* the rich kids."

"I wasn't–"

"Think about it. If you didn't like them, you sure made nice with them. Because your parents brought you up to do that. They didn't tell you anything about us. We weren't worth your time."

She looked like he'd slapped her. Her cheeks were going red. "I'm not saying this to get back at you," he went on. "I don't believe you're like that now. I'm saying it so you know that blaming yourself for me and Julia is stupid."

Sam put her plastic spoon back in the ice cream cup. "This why you came over here?"

"To apologize, and yes, to tell you this where the kids won't hear. They don't need any more ammo against you right now."

"This sundae tastes terrible," she said, smiling. "Why don't you eat it?"

He had to grin back at her. He didn't want to be the one to put Sam on the back foot, but he'd had to say his piece. "Just think about it. Or rather, don't think about it."

He licked his lips, wondering how far she'd let him in. He wanted to ask her one more question.

But she asked it for him. "You've been in therapy. And so have the kids."

He nodded. "It's helped. I'm not perfect, as you've seen." God, he wished she hadn't seen him when he'd gotten back from the hospital with Matt. "I recommend it."

Her face darkened. "This is why I don't have kids," she said.

"Huh?"

She frowned. "You and Matt yelling at each other this morning."

"Oh. Yeah. Not my best moment. I'm sorry you saw—"

"Stop. God. You're already damn perfect, Tyler. Don't shake your pretty head at me."

Ty laughed in shock. "My what?"

"You heard me." She lifted her chin, and he saw a challenge—and an invitation, though it was one she was about to revoke—in her eyes. "This is why we're going to be friends and nothing more. Because you'll do anything for your kids, and I'm a selfish bitch who cares about no one but herself—and Cairo. And your kids."

"And your nephews."

"Well, duh. They're totally cool. A chip off the ole auntie." She lifted her hair off her neck and twisted it up before letting it fall.

"And your sisters. And your brother."

"That doesn't count. You have to love your family."

Ty laughed again and shook his head. "Sam Fielding. Frankly, my dear, you *do* give a damn."

"It's not the same. You have to love your kids, don't you? Even when they're being bratty? Because they're family. You don't get a prize for that, *sweetheart*."

He loved that she threw his words back at him. Loved it a little too much. He stood and took his own empty cup. He planned to walk back to Matt and Alyssa, but Sam said, "You wanna walk Cai with me a little?"

He'd thought she was pissed at him. He'd thought he needed to get out of her orbit because she was pulling him in again, even though *she* was the one who'd mentioned that they could only be friends.

"Uh. Sure. If you want."

"Yeah. I want to get it into your thick blond skull that Indiana Jones was a man."

"What difference does that make?" he teased back.

"Up, Cairo," she said and took the dog's leash in her hand. "If you haven't figured out I'm not a man by now, Tyler, we're–"

He was *not* going to look at her body. "I know. Indiana Jones wishes he were as brave as you."

They began to walk away from the building, up the narrow grassy area that ran parallel to the highway. "And your dog is called Cairo," he added. "How Archaeologist Adventurer can you get?"

"I wanted to call him Xochicalco, but no one at the vet could spell it."

Ty laughed so hard, Cairo barked at him.

Chapter 16

Sam called ten people—well, actually twelve, as she had to leave messages for two contacts—before they reached Cleveland. Two hung up as soon as she said who she was.

Ty, remembering the lane drifting she'd done earlier, drove. He gave her his password so she could find the names on his school directory app. And hell if she didn't knock this task out of the park, like she did everything else.

"I wanted to say I'm sorry for that dance, Laura. I should have included you. I knew you were lonely, and I chose to ignore it." A pause. "Yeah. I knew you liked him. I was a shit about that, too."

"I'm sorry I let you struggle in class, Melissa. I could have helped you, but I chose not to." More talking on the other end. "Yeah, I should have been tutoring, not partying. There's nothing I can change about it, but please know that I feel like crap about it."

She knew what she'd done, and she spoke about her crimes honestly and with genuine regret. Ty couldn't believe it. Yet he could.

When she began to move on to the thirteenth schoolmate, Ty grabbed her phone and threw it behind him to land between the kids. "That's enough for now."

"I haven't eaten enough crow yet," she protested. But he could see the exhaustion in her eyes.

"She can keep going," Matt said. "Every day she did this to these kids."

Matt was *not* going to forgive Sam anytime soon. "Not yet. Let's get to the hotel and get some rest," Ty insisted. "You can get out the tar and feathers again tomorrow."

They'd booked a hotel in Cleveland that Sam had stayed in before. It was nicer than Ty wanted, but he knew that staying somewhere safe meant they'd have to pay a premium. He'd hoped to walk around the city a little with his kids—maybe go down to the water, just so they could say they'd seen a Great Lake. Now that he'd finally left his cloistered little town, he was waking up to just how much world there was out there.

But also he was kinda pissed at Matt, and he didn't feel like walking around an unknown town with only Sam as their guide. They ordered room service and settled into awkward silences in their own rooms.

They continued west the next morning. Sam took her turn driving, so there were no phone calls, and they drove for four hours in near silence. "Cairo can wait," she said evenly when Ty asked about him. And certainly the dog seemed to have taken on the atmosphere in the car and stayed with his head on his paws, hidden behind the kids.

They pulled off eventually onto a side road and followed it to a small town with a picture-postcard diner, a regional high school, and not much more. Matt and Alyssa looked around in horror.

"What do people even do around here?" Alyssa breathed.

"Cow tipping?" Matt suggested. "I never believed that was a thing until now."

"Hey," Sam said, surprising Ty, who'd just opened his mouth to reprimand them. "Show a little respect. You don't know anything about these people."

Matt grumbled something like, "I know enough" as he looked out of the window and purposely *not* at his father.

"We're about to eat their food and get gas from them, and you are not allowed to take out your anger at me on them," Sam insisted. Ty had to admire her ability to know what his teenage son was thinking. Julia would never have gotten that subtlety.

"I wasn't gonna!" Matt protested. Sam pulled into a parking space at the diner, and the noise of the engine died, leaving a grumpy, awkward silence in the car.

"I'll take Cairo!" Alyssa finally said, hopping out of the car before Ty could warn her about traffic. Matt got out of the other side and left him alone with Sam for the first time today.

"Thanks," he said. "I was going to say it."

She shrugged. Why did her shoulders always have a kind of golden sheen to them? And why did she have to wear tank tops so he couldn't ignore them? "I didn't plan on saying anything. It just came out. People are interesting all over."

"Have you been here before?"

Sam nodded. "They let Cairo into the diner. That's why I came back."

And he'd thought she'd just made a random decision on the road. He was beginning to learn that Sam didn't do anything randomly. Anomalies like meeting him and his kids, and this trip, did not please her.

"Lunch is on me," he said. Pathetic gesture, but it was all he had.

"Okay." And Sam unfolded herself from the car and stretched her arms above her head before bending at the waist until her hair brushed the ground and her arms stuck out behind. Effortlessly, blood-boilingly beautiful.

Maybe it was a good thing they were all supposed to be cranky and taciturn with each other, because Ty's mouth was filled with cotton and his head with contradictory thoughts.

"Hey!" the waitress who approached them at the silver entrance door said. "You coming back through?"

"Uh-huh," Sam said.

The waitress immediately bent to scratch Cairo's head without being asked. "I remember you, honey," she cooed at him. "But who else did you bring with you?" She gave Ty a look he remembered from a dim and distant past, before he'd started dating Julia. Interest. Maybe even a little admiration.

"This is Ty and his kids, Matt and Alyssa."

"Hi, Ty!" the waitress said. "Hi, kids. Ooh, honey. That's a real shiner. You want a bag of ice for it?" Matt opened and closed his mouth and nodded. "Go ahead and find a seat. I'll be right with you. Y'all want coffee?"

Sam gave an enthusiastic yes, and Ty wasn't going to contradict her. Maybe coffee would help keep his focus on his kids and less on Sam's shorts.

The waitress flirted with him gently every time she came to the table. Ty wished he could reciprocate, but Sam and his situation had muddled his brains. Sam didn't fill the waitress in on why they were together, so the flirting never reached an awkward stage, but in another lifetime, Ty would have enjoyed it. As it was, he just wanted to stop peopling and get back on the road. Once they'd eaten and used the restroom, he got them outta there.

"So much for being respectful," Matt said the moment the silver door had swung shut behind them.

"What?" The coffee had been good, but all Ty felt was a buzzing at his extremities. Sam had just brushed against him while she leashed up Cairo.

"That waitress was giving you the eye, and all you did was grunt at her."

"Ew, Matt," Alyssa said. "Gross."

"Did I?" He looked at Sam, who'd gone two steps ahead with Cai.

"You were fine," Sam said, striding away to the car.

Well, what did that mean? Why wasn't she looking at him? Or was he imagining that she was avoiding him?

"Yeah. You offended her," Matt said.

"She wasn't offended," Sam said unexpectedly. "She wasn't flirting very hard. Just being polite."

She opened the back hatch, and Cairo hopped into the SUV. Finally, she looked at Ty. "She thought you were with me." And she threw him the car keys.

Now Ty was the one to open and close his mouth. That waitress, whose name he didn't even remember, had seen every single thought he'd been trying to hide. The keys fell to the ground in front of him, and Matt and Alyssa stared at him, Alyssa in shock, Matt in accusation.

"You aren't *with* her," Alyssa said at last. "Are you?"

"N-no," he said. Dammit. That hadn't sounded firm enough. "You know I'm not," he added, looking at his daughter with what he hoped to hell was determination. "You've been around her pretty much the whole time I have. You know what this is."

"We're friends," Sam said, as if from very far away. "Just friends, Lyss."

"You better be," Matt said, opening his car door. "We don't need another mean girl mom."

That cut through Ty's stupor. "Matthew!"

Matt slid into his seat and slammed the door on them. The slap of the icepack onto his eye seemed like another accusation.

Ty moved toward the car, but Sam had approached him and now bent to pick up the keys.

"Don't worry about it. He's upset." Her voice was soothing and soft, unlike her usual tough-guy stance.

"He has to stop calling you that."

"Maybe he will. Maybe he won't." She gave him a smile he swore was touched with sadness. "It's okay. Let's just get you guys to Taos in one piece, and I'll be out of your hair." She slapped the keys into his hand and then held out hers. "Your phone?"

"Sam, you really don't have to—"

But that stubborn set to her chin told him she did, in fact, have to.

The tone of her voice on these calls was different today, and it took Ty a while to figure out what it was: Sam was hurt. She could toss her hair over her shoulder and dial the numbers with as much nonchalance as she wanted, but he could tell. After each phone call, he begged her to stop. After the eighth call, even Alyssa piped up, suggesting she could do more tomorrow. But Sam kept on, kept on flaying herself at the altar of Matt and Alyssa's disdain, of her and Ty's history, of the town that would never accept that she'd changed.

Somewhere in Illinois, Sam hung up the phone. She took a deep breath. Just when Ty was wondering if she'd ever let it out, she said, "Pull over."

"What?"

"Pull over."

They were on another empty highway, with little traffic and only fields on either side, separated from the road by a berm of trees. "Where are you planning to go?"

"Pull. Over."

Her lips were so tight he could feel their strain. He avoided a sigh and carefully pulled onto the shoulder. He'd barely stopped before Sam had jumped out of the car and hopped the barrier before taking off across a scrubby unused field.

"Sam!" he shouted through the open door. "You can't just—"

She was running. She wasn't going to hear him.

He was quite capable of imagining an out-of-control semi suddenly showing up on this two-lane highway and plowing them all. Welp, if Sam didn't care about her car, he wasn't going to either. "Kids, get out. Lyss, get out on Matt's side." He went to the back to let out Cairo, who had whimpered as soon as his mistress left the car.

He instructed the kids to climb the barrier and wait on the safe side of it, well away from the traffic.

"What is she doing?" Matt asked.

Hell if Ty knew. He didn't know anything about Sam, if he was honest with himself. Four days in her vicinity did not a relationship make. She sure the hell wasn't confiding anything in him this time. And if jumping out of a car on a major highway hadn't been enough to convince him she wasn't up for sharing, her face at the diner sure had.

She'd reached almost three-quarters of the way across the field now. Cai pulled at his leash and whined again. Another set of trees stood on the far side. Would she stop there? Would she remember that they couldn't wait on the side of the road forever? Or was this really who Sam Fielding was—just as self-centered as he'd thought when he'd seen her again five days ago?

Good thing he was staring after her, because otherwise he would have missed the moment when she disappeared. One second her head was there, moving in the rhythm of her steps, the grass around her hiding the rest of her body—the next it wasn't. Had she fallen? Sat down? What if she'd twisted her ankle or hit her head?

He didn't realize he'd thrown Cairo's leash at Matt and was running after her until he heard Matt yell, "Dad!"

"Stay away from the road!" he shouted over his shoulder. He had to find her. Something was wrong.

Even though he thought he ran in a straight line, he was off course by a few feet, and only when he heard her could he see her. She was cross-legged in a patch of deep grass, her head in her hands, and she was sobbing.

Ty's heart cracked right in two. His mother had cried a few times since his father left, but they'd been quiet tears, quickly stifled when Ty came into the room. Julia's tears had been copious and messy, designed to intrude and then to get her way. He'd never seen anything like this. He and his kids had broken Sam.

The only thing he could think was that he had to hold her together. Literally if necessary.

♦

Sam didn't know he was there until she felt his hand warm her knee. Rain had fallen recently and the grasses were soaking through her shorts, cooling her legs and making her tears disappear into the ground. If she could just disappear, too, that would be *great*.

But Ty bloody Cavanaugh wouldn't let her disappear. His hand kept her there, reminded her of the present, of her situation, of all the phone calls she'd just made and how fucking awful she felt. Her chest hurt from this embarrassing crying. *No one* got to see her cry. *No one*. Except Ty freaking Cavanaugh.

"Get lost, Ty," she croaked. Her body shuddered, and she let out another sob before she could stop herself.

"Sam," he said. And screw him if his voice wasn't as comforting as a warm blanket on her cold legs. "Sweetheart," he added, and Sam sobbed *again*. "You can't do this to yourself," he went on.

"The fuck I can't," she said shakily. Who was he to tell her what she could and couldn't do? Even if that was despising herself and everything she'd decided she stood for? Closing the door on the past, being the badass butt-kicker of the archaeological world, never looking back, never going home, preferring ancient civilizations to the ones she came from? It had worked for so long, and now along came Ty and his kids and dared to show her that there were some things you couldn't walk away from.

She could at least hide her face from him, as blotched and damp as it had to be. She still had some pride left. But Ty sat next to her on the wet ground and stretched his long legs out on either side of her, and she could feel him along her legs and back. And he began to gently rub her back, the bastard, showing her without words that he empathized, that he was there for her, that he was here for this.

"Go away," she whispered one last time.

"Can't," he whispered back. "Sam, has anyone ever just hugged you because you needed a hug?"

"Shut *up*," she said, because the last person to do that had been Ty, in a closet. Eighteen years ago. Like a complete fool, she laughed. Worse still, she leaned into him, and now he'd wrapped his arms around her and was holding her so tight, she couldn't move. His breath was on her neck and his forehead against her hair, and he was whispering things, kind things, warming things, and making her cry and laugh more. The rat bastard.

"You don't know me," she said.

"Sure, I do," he said, his voice not even rising to the tops of the stalks of grass. "You're fearless. You're brave. You're kind. You love endlessly and never look for that love for yourself. You live your life like a grizzly bear"—she laughed again and her body went limp in his arms—"you'll yell when you think you need to, but you'll fight to the death for people you care about." His breath skittered on her neck. "Even people you've just met."

Her face was in his chest now, her whole body given over to leaning sideways into him. If she hadn't been completely exhausted, she would have been disgusted with herself.

"I'm selfish," she said, trying to keep the distance somehow. "I didn't come back because I didn't want to come back. I let my sisters suffer because I wanted to get away so bad."

"You were a kid," he said. "You can't blame yourself for protecting yourself."

"And I'm afraid of *everything*," she went on, shaking her head. "I'm afraid of all the people in town. I'm afraid of anyone finding out who I was, who I really am." More tears fell onto his shirt. "Those phone calls reminded me. I can't get away from it. I shouldn't get away from it."

"I know who you were then," he said into her hair. "And I know who you are now. And I like you just fine."

"Well, don't." She tensed up, but he was rubbing her back again, and she couldn't resist his sympathy.

"I can't help it," he said.

Yeah, well, she couldn't help it either. The longer she spent with Ty, the more she found herself regretting and wishing for the end of this trip. What else could she do? Women like her didn't get to have relationships with men like him. Forget the whole living-in-different-states thing; Sam was a rolling stone, and the *last* thing Ty needed in his life was a woman who might be off on a different dig in a couple years. New zip codes excited Sam; Ty hadn't moved out of his in a decade.

So she should be standing, brushing off her butt, and driving them where they needed to go. But oh, could she just take one more second to love his arms around her? To breathe in the comfort he offered, a comfort beyond anything sexual she'd enjoyed until now? Could she forget that in two days she'd say goodbye to his kids for the last time and might never be allowed to ask after them again? Never help Alyssa through high school the way Sam wished she'd been? Never help Matt with his college choices? Never get inside Ty's head and find out why he smelled like wood shavings when his career seemed to be spent on a computer?

"I guess I can't help it either," she said.

Ty delicately peeled the wet strands of hair from her face, lifting it toward him. Sam resisted, swiping at her wet cheeks, not wanting him to see her ridiculousness. He shook his head and kept hold of her chin. "Whatever we have, Indy," he said softly, "you won't have to hide from me. Of all people, you don't have to hide from me."

"What do we have?" The billion-dollar question. She bit her lip, willing him to have the answer.

"I don't know," he said. "Just... right now, I guess."

And since his hands were already on her face, it was easy to angle her mouth and kiss him, ever so lightly.

The burst of longing made Sam gasp out of proportion to the quick touch of his lips. To have this stalwart man by her side! A man who never asked anything from her, who never wanted to control her but would just be there, standing by her when she needed and waiting for her when she needed that. To have an infinity of those kisses that said so much.

Could they even−?

"God, Dad!"

The voice coincided with a pair of furry paws that tumbled into the two of them and knocked them onto the ground. *Shit.*

"Uh," Ty said. Which sounded about right.

"I knew it!" Matt said. "The mean girl! Again! Jesus Christ, Dad!"

"My fault," Sam said at once, though her voice was a mumble, her lips still numb from Ty's light kiss. "That's on me."

"Stop it, Sam," Ty said. "You don't have to take the blame for everything." He stood and pulled her to her feet. Cairo pulled himself out of Alyssa's hands and gamboled around his mistress, so Sam couldn't focus on what Ty and Matt were saying to each other. But Matt made his point by stalking away from the scene, and Alyssa followed, glancing back only to give Sam one more reproachful look.

"Well, shit," Sam said.

Ty laughed. "I don't even know what we're in trouble for. Specifically."

"Me either." What had they said to each other? Had the kiss just been because of their closeness? Because Sam had been vulnerable? Was Matt pissed because he thought Sam was angling to replace his mother? Or because she wasn't?

"We'd better follow them," Ty said. "Or Matt might play on the highway just to tick me off."

Sam grasped Cairo's leash more tightly and followed him back to the car.

Chapter 17

St. Louis had so much to see, so much history running through it. But Sam didn't even bother suggesting that they do a tour when they arrived that night. She could count the number of words they'd exchanged in the car over the last few hours. They'd booked a motel on the outskirts—a cheaper place than where Sam usually stayed—that took dogs and would get them back on the highway quickly the next morning. Tonight, tomorrow night, and they would be done.

Sam focused on getting Cairo out of the back and over to a patch of grass while the others took out their backpacks. But they were waiting for her at the entrance to the lobby, so she had little time to gather herself before Matt strode through the door.

A woman came out of a room separated from the lobby by a bead curtain. Sam hadn't seen one of those since college, and then only because one of her friends had been trying to relive the '60s. The woman herself was young, wearing cutoffs and a T-shirt that bared her midriff. She had a baby on her hip.

"Hi there!" she said through a wad of gum. The baby looked just like her, blond and big-eyed, though unlike her cheery welcome, it was solemnly gazing at Sam while one chubby hand had half the woman's breast in its grip.

"Hello," Sam said, trying to remember how to be a normal, polite human being. "I called earlier. Fielding? Two twins?"

"Oh sure!" said the woman—actually, the more she talked, the more Sam wondered if she was even twenty-one yet—"so glad you made it!" She sat the baby down on the countertop and pulled a tablet from under it with one hand, keeping one hand on the child's chubby leg as she did so. "I'm Tammy, by the way."

"Nice to meet you. Sam."

"Oh, yeah? That's cool! Guy's name! So yeah, Fielding! Two rooms!"

Yeah! Sam nearly said. *You got it!*

"So do you have your driver's license?"

Finally, a sentence without an exclamation point. "Absolutely," Sam said, giving it to her.

"Hi there!" she sang to the others while she tapped Sam's details into the tablet. "Welcome to the Show-Me State!" She grinned up at Ty for a second and winked at him.

Well, that was uncalled for, Sam thought, irritated. She turned and scowled at Ty. Just because she wanted to.

"How are you?" Ty said to Tammy. Was it her imagination, or was his voice more gravelly and sexy than before?

"Oh, I'm wonderful!"

Sam caught sight of Matt to one side of Ty. He looked a little smacked-by-a-two-by-four. Yes, Tammy was pretty cute. He was probably hoping like hell the baby wasn't hers.

"So where are you all headed?" Tammy asked. With practiced elegance, she braced the baby with one arm, reached behind her with the other, and snagged two keys from the board.

"Colorado," Sam said.

"New Mexico," Alyssa said at exactly the same time. Then her face fell into horror. "I mean, Colorado," she mumbled.

"We're kind of going all over," Sam covered. Poor kid. Lying didn't come naturally to her. And really, was there any point to it?

Tammy looked from one to the other. "Well, that's cool! I've never been anywhere other than Disney, but one day we're going to take Sawyer here, aren't we, sweetie?" And she gave the baby a big smooch on the cheek.

Sam used to do that with Cat's kids, back when they were all living together, before she ran away. The twins were fat little cuties back then. Her eyes cut to Ty. What had his kids been like as babies? He didn't have an ounce of spare flesh on him, that was for certain.

Beyond him, Matt looked disappointed. Sam's mouth twisted in a smile, and he caught it. He knew she knew what he was thinking. He gave her a scowl that was the mirror image of his father's, and then, more troublingly, he smiled. He turned to Tammy. "Hey, uh..."

"Tammy!" she said, looking as though it was the greatest thrill of her life to repeat her name.

"Tammy, hi. Listen, this is my dad and my stepmother."

Sam froze. *His what now?*

"They just got married; isn't that great?"

"For real?" Tammy's eyes were huge circles in her cheerleader-cute face.

"For real," Alyssa joined in, giving Tammy a big smile, which was interesting, seeing as how she'd looked as dreary as the walls when she'd walked in. "It was so cute, you wouldn't believe it!"

Sam was trying not to look as though she was planning new and inventive ways of killing her beloved stepchildren. She had no idea what Ty's expression was.

"And what's even cuter," Alyssa gushed on, "is that they wanted to bring us with them on their honeymoon! Isn't that great?"

"Oh my God!" Tammy echoed. Her blue eyes shimmered with tears. "That's the cutest thing I ever heard! What a great stepmommy you'll be!" She reached the hand that wasn't holding the baby across the desk to grab Sam's arm. "I just knew as soon as I saw you."

Knew what? That these children are getting strangled in their beds tonight? "Well, thanks. Um, can you recommend a place to go for dinner tonight?"

"Sure, I can! Joe Cobra's. It's two blocks that way." She pointed to her left. "Everybody goes there. Get the crab cakes—they're uh-maaazing."

"Thanks." Sam took the keys.

"Yeah, thanks!" Matt said. "It makes it so much better when other people get to share how happy we are, doesn't it?"

"Oh, you are so sweet!" Tammy sighed. "You must be real proud of this one."

"Yep."

Sam finally dared to look at Ty, to whom Tammy had spoken. "He's my joy," he said. "Come on, my joy, let's find your room so I can appreciate you some more." Somehow, he managed to say all this without actually moving his jaw. His eyes were ice-blue pinpricks beneath lowered brows. Matt might have to sleep in the car tonight.

They said goodbye to Tammy and her exclamation points and walked outside. As they walked around to the line of doors to the rooms, Ty said, "What the hell was that?"

Matt and Alyssa exchanged smug looks. "What?" Matt said, turning to his father and blinking innocently. "I was helping. You guys want to take this key, and we'll—"

He reached for the keys in Sam's hand, but she snapped them out of the way. "You're lucky you're not sleeping in the bathtub," she said. "You want to explain to her why a newly married couple booked rooms with twin beds?"

Matt shrugged. "You're kinky that way."

"Ew, Matt, gross," Alyssa interjected.

"Yeah, Matt, gross," Ty squashed the conversation. Well, all right, he didn't have to be that pissed off. The idea of the two of them sharing a twin bed wasn't *gross*. It was... Sam watched him carrying three backpacks easily, his muscles bunching across his shoulders and arms. His hair had been cut recently, so recently that a tan line sat a fraction of an inch below his hairline. Another cord of muscle showed on his neck as he took the weight.

What was the question?

Sam shook her head to clear it. They were all waiting for her to open the doors. She stepped forward to hide the flush on her cheeks and unlocked the first door. Could she pull out her ponytail to hide her face with her hair and not have Ty know why she was doing it? Not really. She willed the color out of her cheeks and went to the second door.

"I call this one!" Alyssa said at once, though from the dingy view she had, Sam couldn't see a difference between the two rooms. "Closer to the vending machine," Alyssa clarified as she passed through and dumped her small backpack on the bed farthest from the door. In seconds, she was hidden behind a book.

Ty brushed past Sam to deposit their backpacks in the room. Sam remained paralyzed in the doorway.

"First in the shower!" Matt called from his and Ty's room.

Ty turned back to her. "You okay? You look like you're planning a murder."

"Aren't you?" she shot back. Her shoulder and—yes, one nipple—were still tingling from the brief contact they'd had with his arm, but she had to gain back some control. "You sure hid your children's sass from me."

He folded his arms. She wished he wouldn't do that. It showed off his rock-hard biceps. "Don't you mean *our* children?"

Her mouth dropped open. "I would never produce children this bratty."

"This smart, you mean? This able to push your buttons?"

"You're fine with this?" Her eyebrows rose.

He shrugged. "At least Matt's regained his sense of humor." One side of his mouth lifted.

"That's what you call it?"

She shook her head, feeling her ponytail swish slowly at her neck. A chill went down her spine that had nothing to do with the room's air conditioner. After what had happened in the field today, was he really going to think this was *funny*?

He turned in the doorway, which hid her from Alyssa's view. "Sam," he said in a low voice. "It's okay. I know it's not what you planned, but it's gonna be okay. Kids do that. They screw with plans. It doesn't really change anything. You and Alyssa can still take one room and Matt and I will have the other."

"That's not the—"

"But also, if you keep standing here arguing, Tammy might remember us more than I'd like her to."

Sam jumped away from the door as though it were electrified. "Fine," she said.

"Idiots," Alyssa said from her book.

◆

However mad at each other they all were, they still had to eat. So at seven o'clock, Ty and Matt knocked on the girls' door; they silently trooped out onto the main road, and as instructed, they walked two blocks to the building with an orange awning that proclaimed it Joe Cobra's.

Inside, it looked like any other bar-restaurant—a long, polished bar along one side with mirrors behind that messed with Sam's sense of perspective, small tables packed into every available square foot of floor space, red glass candleholders offering flickering, uncertain light, and waiters and waitresses wearing black and white squeezing between the chairs. Country music was playing, and the atmosphere was loud and boisterous.

The tables were filled with other families. Ty put Sam's name on the list and went over to the bar to get them a drink while they waited. No sooner had they been led to a table in the middle of the room when a voice said, "Hey! There you are!" as if she'd been watching for them for weeks.

"Hi, Tammy," Sam said. "You're here too?"

"Duh!" Tammy exclaimed happily, hitching Sawyer a little higher on her hip. For the evening, she was wearing one of those banana clips in her hair that had been popular when Sam was very little and a white denim jacket with an American flag on the back. "Glad you found the place all right! We're sitting just over there. Your rooms okay?"

The change in topic threw Sam for a second. "Oh, yes, thanks, they're very nice."

Tammy grinned with pride. "Four stars on TripAdvisor—not many motels can say that! Well, enjoy your meal! Don't forget! Crab cakes!"

After she left, there was a short, rather stunned silence. Finally, Matt said, "Where the hell did they find fresh crab in the middle of the middlest state in the country?"

"Don't say *hell*," Ty said. "And I see your point."

They ordered burgers.

"I hate country music," Alyssa said.

"Early country music was good," Sam said. "Johnny Cash and Patsy Cline and people like that."

"Who?"

"Never mind."

They slumped into silence again.

Thankfully, the burgers were so good, they had to look at each other just to make appreciative noises and roll their eyes in pleasure.

"Is this Patsy Cline?" Alyssa asked. She'd been looking up the names while Sam thought she was sulking into her phone. She held the phone out and Sam took it, holding it close to one ear and trying to shut out the restaurant's noise with her hand over the other.

"Yes, that's her."

"Which one should I listen to next?"

Sam looked at the list. "If you want something fun, try 'I'm Back in Baby's Arms.' If you want a good cry, play 'Crazy.'"

"'Kay." Alyssa took her phone back and somehow managed to shut herself away from the bustle around her. But her body language was different, and Sam warmed to her again, aware of the goofy smile on her own face at the brief connection.

"Dessert?" Ty said.

"Sure."

She ordered key lime pie, the kids got hot fudge sundaes, and Ty had the peach pie. Matt got up to use the bathroom while they waited.

"*I'm crazy for crying, and I'm crazy for lying, and I'm crazy for loving you,*" Alyssa hummed to herself. Apparently, she was still listening to Patsy Cline. Fascinating how long ago that music must seem to kids today.

"Patsy Cline to her must be like... I dunno, Bing Crosby to us?" Ty said.

"That's just what I was thinking!" she said, too surprised to remember to be distant. "Ancient history."

"Duran Duran is ancient history to these kids. Bing Crosby is prehistoric."

She laughed. "How do you know about Bing Crosby, anyway?"

"*White Christmas,*" he said simply.

"You old softy," she teased. "Did you ever watch–?"

But a commotion had started in one corner of the room, and it was getting closer. And louder. And closer.

It was singing.

Happy honeymoon to you,

Happy honeymoon to you.

"Oh, dear God," Ty said.

"Oh shit, no," Sam said.

Happy honeymoon, dear Sam and Ty!

Happy honeymoon to you!

Behind the singing wall of waiters and waitresses, Tammy was bouncing on her toes. Sawyer was asleep on her shoulder. "Surprise!" she yelled.

Their waiter put their desserts on the table. Every one of them had a sparkler stuck in the top, which snapped and, well, sparkled, into the silence at the table. Alyssa took her phone away from her ear and looked up at Matt, whose self-satisfied grin shone out over Ty's shoulder.

Ty's face would have been comical to behold if Sam hadn't been so blindsided herself. In the shifting light from the sparklers, she could see his eyes getting bigger and his mouth getting thinner. He threw a glare at Alyssa, who put her hands out in innocence, indicating her phone as an alibi. So he looked to the crowd surrounding them, searching for his feckless son.

"Smart, huh?" Sam teased.

He gave her a look that could melt glass.

"Kiss!" came an all-too-recognizable voice from the back.

"What?" Sam's teasing smile vanished.

"Kiss!" Tammy called again. Someone else began tapping their fork against their glass.

"Oh shit," Ty muttered.

Now the whole damn restaurant was in on it. Didn't they have anything better to do? Like maybe stick those forks in their own eyes? "Kiss! Kiss! Kiss!" they all chanted.

Matt, apparently figuring he was safe now that everyone was

looking at them, flopped back into his chair. "Yeah, Dad. *Mom.* Kiss," he said.

What would Ty do? Could he really refuse? In front of all these people?

He was coming closer. To keep up the pretense, Sam leaned in as well. She hoped she was smiling a little, as if this were her dearest wish and not incredibly awkward.

Dearest wish... Ty's stubble was blond, but there was a small gray patch near one corner of his mouth that she hadn't noticed before. Or maybe it was the light. His lips were fine and chiseled, and she got an almost overwhelming urge to run her tongue over the curve of his lower lip.

His eyes were impossible to read, hooded and shadowed as they were. But he still came closer and now one hand came up to hold her chin, to hold her still, then to draw her in so that finally, finally, he touched her lips with his.

Fine and chiseled they might be, but his lips gave with a softness that drew a muffled gasp from her. She put up a hand to cover the space left bare at his throat by his button-down shirt, perhaps because she had some vague thought that she should make it a short kiss, that it was all that was required, but her hand slid up his neck of its own accord to run over the short hair at his nape and hold him to her.

She wanted a deeper kiss, a much deeper kiss, one that sent shockwaves down her body to her thighs, and she got it by moving her lips over his, opening her mouth just a little so she could taste him better, getting rewarded for her boldness by feeling a breath escape him and his eyelashes brush her cheeks as he closed his eyes. Sam had closed hers long ago, sometime in the world that existed before he'd kissed her, the world she couldn't understand anymore because kissing him was an absolute requirement of her life, the scent of wood shavings still clinging to him, and Sam was going to run her tongue over that lower lip just as she'd promised herself she might–

And the crowd was whooping and hollering, and Ty had pulled

away, leaving Sam like an idiot still leaning toward him, the sparklers still shooting lights between them.

Chapter 18

To save himself from falling into Sam again, Ty narrowed his eyes at Matt. The boy had no idea what he was doing. Ty had told Sam it wasn't a big deal, but being seen as her husband—even if they only thought of them as together, the way the waitress at the diner had—tolled a bell deep in his soul that he was still shaking from. Matt's joke had turned deadly serious, to Ty at least.

The crowd was cheering, but Ty couldn't hear them. He allowed his hands to fall from Sam, though he thought this might be the last time he was ever allowed to touch her. His kids couldn't see that again. Ty couldn't give them any kind of ambiguity about a woman in his life. He would *have* to stay away from Sam from now on.

Sam looked as shell-shocked as he felt. Ty knew she wasn't faking that kiss, nor the ones they'd shared before. And she'd admitted she liked him. That was all he could expect. All he should expect.

The sparklers were fizzing out, and Matt's smug grin was fading. "Ah, young love!" Tammy sighed, which was rich, given she had to be barely college age. "Congratulations, you guys."

"Let's take our dessert to go," Sam said, her lips stiff.

"Good idea."

Their waiter was still close by, so Ty asked for boxes. While the waiter went off to find them, Tammy exclaimed, "You leaving already?"

"We had a long drive today," Ty said.

"I understand." Tammy nodded, her blue eyes darting between the two of them. "Hey," she said over her shoulder. "You got a bottle of champagne back there for them, Steve?"

"Oh, that's not necessary," Sam tried to protest, but Ty could have told her not to bother. Tammy's baby face hid a spine of steel.

"On us!" she cooed. Ty still didn't know who "us" referred to, but he thanked her, and they bundled themselves out of Joe Cobra's.

"Matthew," Ty said as soon as they were out of earshot, "one more stunt and I'll leave you behind tomorrow."

"Stunt?" Matt echoed, widening his eyes—then wincing and holding a hand up to his black eye. "I thought you'd be glad of the excuse. Apparently, you guys have had something going on this whole—"

"We have *not*," Sam said.

Then how was she going to explain *two* kisses Matt had now witnessed? Ty wasn't that good an actor. Something was definitely going on. What it was, he couldn't say.

"Just... go to bed," he said, not keeping the tiredness out of his voice.

Matt and Alyssa used their keys to enter their rooms, leaving a heartbeat or two for Sam and Ty to follow. He wanted to say something, to... apologize? Tell her those kisses had meant something? Or would she rather they hadn't?

Sam answered the question by collapsing her long limbs into the plastic chair outside her room and holding out the champagne. "They already opened it. Might as well have some."

Ty had to laugh at her resignation. Life was chaos. Drink the champagne.

He went into his room to get the coffee cups next to the tiny machine and joined her, taking his own plastic chair to sit next to her. She poured, and he passed her a plastic cup.

"To Midwestern hospitality," Sam said.

"It's terrifying," Ty said, smiling. Sam blew out a laugh, and they clicked and drank.

"Damn," she said and looked harder at the label. "That's Veuve Clicquot."

It was good. Light, sparkly. Incongruous in the parking lot of a modest hotel and somehow more delicious because of it. "To Tammy," he said, and they toasted their host.

Alyssa came out with Cairo on his leash and began to walk past the cars to the grass. "Thanks, Lyss," Sam called.

"No problem," she called back.

"I'll walk him later," Sam said to Ty. Or to herself. Ty finished his cup and held it out for more. It went down easy, this Veuve Clicquot.

"We should eat our desserts," he reminded her, so they balanced their cardboard boxes on their knees and ate. Alyssa came back, rolled her eyes at them, and took her own box and Matt's. She handed Sam Cairo's leash, and he immediately settled under Sam's chair.

Both kids' doors closed, and there was silence.

Ty's hands began to get itchy to do something. Not with Sam, for once. "You mind if I get my woodwork?" he said.

"Your what?"

"It's my... hobby. Just whittling. Gives me something to do with my hands."

"Let me see."

He had to knock on his door, as Matt had sensibly locked it. He took his glasses, gloves, the kinglet, and another piece of wood he'd begun to shave into a leaf shape and joined Sam again. He handed her the kinglet. "It's for Lyss's birthday next month."

"Holy crap, Tyler." Sam held the little bird in both hands as though it were alive, weighing it, looking at it from all sides, holding it up to the orange sodium light. "This is beautiful."

"Thank you." He hoped the light would hide the heat coming to his cheeks.

"Seriously. Why don't you do this for a living?"

He ducked his head and pulled on his leather finger guards. "Art doesn't pay."

"Didn't you say Noah is an artist? How's he getting by?"

"I'm not sure. I think he has a—a side business. In 'recreational leaf.'"

Sam laughed. "Is that what that is?"

"Not yet. It'll just be one leaf. Kind of a key holder. A thank-you to him for taking us on."

She leaned over, and he smelled that sexy salty scent again. "How do you get the details of the veins in there so perfectly?"

"Different blades." He warmed again at her words. Beautiful. Perfect.

"Well." She leaned back. "Way to hide your light under a bushel, Tyler. I was worried about you. Now I don't have to be."

He cracked a laugh at that. After the week she'd seen him have? "What do you mean? What does whittling have to do with—?"

"Because it's *you*. The artist. You're still letting yourself do what you love." She looked into the darkness beyond their small picnic. "I thought she might have sucked it out of you. But she didn't."

He had no reason to tell her. But why hide it? "Julia hated anything I did that didn't directly involve her."

"I figured." Then she said, "Go ahead. Don't stop. I want to see your process."

He'd put down his piece of wood the moment he'd thought of Julia. Now that Sam was giving him such an open invitation to do this thing that made him happy, he was almost giddy.

Matt would tell him he was still waiting for approval from a woman. Maybe so. But could Ty explain that Sam was just encouraging him to be himself? Not permission. Encouragement. Being anything other than herself was alien to Sam, and she didn't see why he should close down a whole side of his personality to please anyone.

He picked up the leaf again and began to shave and sand it down as thin as possible, with a ring underneath to hold it up. Sam didn't interrupt him, just watched or looked into the dark.

Ty didn't know how long they sat there without speaking. Sam was wearing jeans tonight, having changed out of her grass-dampened shorts when they arrived. The air was warm and smelled of a mixture of car exhaust and barbecue sauce. Sam smelled like sea salt. Occasionally, one or the other of them would refill their cups, and they would drink again. Ty felt the bubbles going to his head, like some teenager.

Or maybe it was his proximity to Sam, to her long legs stretched out next to his. She was so easily beautiful. Yes, it was her genes, but she was breathtaking because of what she did and how she held herself, not just because of what she looked like. Ty had to hold his memory back from thinking about all the good she'd done for his family, had to stop himself from asking her what she did to help Native people recapture their own heritage.

Because he was half in love with her already, he knew, and he did not need to fall the rest of the way.

◆

Sam was contemplating resting her head against the wall behind her chair when the hotel room door opened and Matt came out. Sam and Ty both turned their heads to follow the boy's shadowy form as he quietly stepped around them from one door to the other. Then he winked at his dad and put his finger to his lips. Keeping as quiet as possible, he opened the door to Alyssa's room and stepped inside.

A fart like a gunshot followed by Alyssa's horrified squeal broke the serenity of the evening air. Matt flew out of the room, slamming the door and hightailing it back to lock himself in his own room before Alyssa could catch him.

"You are so disgusting! I can't even believe I'm related to you, you freaking creep! You stink!" she shouted at his door, rattling the door handle. Failing to effect any change on it whatsoever, she kicked it, then turned to Sam and Ty. "Dad!" she yelled, apparently not caring who was trying to sleep around them. "You just let him do that? He's so disgusting! How could you just let him walk into my—"

But Ty was waving her words away with one hand while the other clutched his ribs. His pieces of wood and knives were abandoned in his lap. Sam looked through her own tears of laughter to see his head tilted back against the plastic chair, his face lit up by the sodium light, eyes closed, helpless with laughter.

"Dad!" Alyssa tried again, but Ty was making crying noises now. Sam's cheeks hurt from laughing. "Sam!" Alyssa turned to her instead.

"Ss-sorry, honey!" Sam managed to get out. "We... I didn't—oh, God, the noise you just made!"

"The noise *I* made!"

"Shhh! No—come on, Ty, you have to discipline your—oh, help!"

Because the sounds coming from Ty were setting her off again. He hooted when he laughed. It was the most carefree sound she'd ever heard.

"Adults!" Alyssa said in a voice dripping with disgust and went back into her room.

In her absence, the two so-called adults began to calm down. Sam felt wrung out from the exertion. Ty's legs were a lot closer to hers than before. Not that it was relevant. It was the tiny delight in seeing Ty truly happy for once that made her continue to smile at him, even though she knew any further connection between them was dangerous. Bad enough that he'd trusted her to see the one small thing he kept to himself, the thing he used to show his loved ones that he loved them.

He kept one hand to his chest as he said, "Damn, I needed that." He was still smiling, and it encompassed her by accident, but Sam was grateful for it.

"Extra ice cream for Matt tomorrow, then," she said.

"Yeah, guess so. Ah, the oldies are still the goodies."

"Yeah. Kane did that to us more than once. Pig."

"It's in the boy code."

"Alyssa should have locked her door."

"She was probably keeping it open for you."

"Yeah. She's thoughtful that way, huh."

His body language was different, relaxed and fluid in the chair that was too small for his frame. His shoulders weren't hunched anymore. He wore dark jeans and flip-flops that somehow made him look vulnerable. Perhaps here in this motel in the middle of nowhere, he was finally able to relax.

Sam leaned her own head back and looked away from him, back up to the light pollution and the stars beyond. They sat quietly on, companionable and content.

Chapter 19

Perhaps it was the gunshot fart; perhaps Matt thought he'd paid Sam back sufficiently with the marriage gag, or perhaps they were all exhausted from being mad at each other, but the atmosphere the next morning was friendlier. Cairo even danced around them rather than hiding under the desk while they packed. Tammy had directed them to a premade breakfast next to the lobby, and a couple of muffins and some strong coffee made Sam feel ready to face the rest of this trip.

When they stopped in Kansas City for an early lunch, the kids even wanted to walk around a little and do the tourist thing of standing in two states at once. Alyssa read information out from Wikipedia, and Matt browsed a store full of weird and macabre tchotchkes. They looked like any regular family. When the waitress at their restaurant told them, "Your kids sure took after their father rather than their mother!" nodding to Sam's dark hair, they just agreed. "Funny how those things go," Sam said.

"If you guys are okay with it," she said when they were walking back to their car, "I'd like to take a short detour. Since we're here."

"Are you sure?" Ty asked, which was kind of a weird thing to say.

"I get it if you just want to get on the road. But it's not that far to our next stop, and you'll likely never be here again."

"I want to go!" Alyssa interrupted. "What is it?"

"How about I keep that part a surprise?" Sam said.

"Okay," Alyssa agreed easily and hopped into her seat.

"I thought you didn't like surprises," Ty said to Sam.

She frowned. "What made you think that?" Yeah, how the hell had he known that? That was something she kept well under wraps. It wasn't good for her fly-by-the-seat-of-her-pants reputation.

"Just an impression I got." He cocked his head as though assessing her. "Your very well-trained dog. The fact that you've been to all these places before, and if you haven't, like Tammy's place, you have to straighten your shoulders to go in."

Sam clenched her jaw against the blush of warmth spreading through her. He'd been watching her. The way she watched him. And what was worse—or better—he'd *seen* her. In a way no other man had. A way no one in her family had. He knew her vulnerability, and he was still smiling at her. The truth hadn't fucked up her relationship with a man.

She jerked out of her reverie and opened the car door. Tomorrow night, they'd be in Taos. Not a minute too soon. Because Sam was going to miss Ty and his kids more than she wanted to admit. And *that* was a vulnerability she wasn't about to share.

♦

They drove all morning along the flattest country Ty had ever seen. Only a farm building or a feedstore broke the monotony. Even the sky was dull and cloudy. Thank the gods and all the angels that his kids were in better moods, because even he had to fight a profound boredom. When Sam abruptly said, "It's coming up here," Ty jumped. He wasn't sure if he remembered how to turn the steering wheel.

They took an exit that led to a road between a cornfield and a cemetery. A sign at the entrance read The Geographical Center of the United States.

"There," said Sam. "If you got a flat map of the US and put it on a pin at exactly this spot, the paper would balance."

Their destination was so whimsical, so random and unnecessary yet so perfect for their journey, Ty laughed out loud as he turned onto the road and drove until Sam told him to turn left.

"For real?" Matt said. "That's what we came to see? More land?"

"There's a plaque, too," Sam said seriously. "And a chapel. And a jail. Down that road."

They stepped out and joined a ragtag band of intrepid tourists to look at the small stone monument. Cairo found it the most interesting but thankfully chose not to mark the moment. Matt rolled his eyes at the obligatory selfie photo but stood quietly anyway. And when they got back to the car, temporarily isolated from the crowd, they all turned and looked at the sight.

"We're in the middle of the country," Alyssa said. Ty thought he heard awe in her voice.

"Yep," he said.

"This country is *big*," she said.

"Yep," he agreed. And from where they were standing, it looked as though the land was there just to prove the point of how huge it was and how small they were. They stood in silence for a moment more, then Cairo whined at a passing bird and Sam announced she was going to give him a walk. Since they'd looked at absolutely everything there was to see at the monument, they went with her.

"It's so quiet," Alyssa whispered as they followed a dirt road between the flat fields. "I've never heard it so quiet."

"The colors are different," Matt said. "That gray sky and the green fields. It's weird."

"That sky is pretty gray," Sam said, squinting at it. "We might want to get on the road."

As if it had heard her, a gust of wind whipped up the dirt at their feet and swirled it into their eyes. Since Cairo had made his deposit already, they hustled back to the car.

♦

Sam drove, and as they went south to join up to their original itinerary, the sky got darker and the wind pulled at the SUV. Ty looked at his phone, but there was no signal this far into the countryside. He glanced over at Sam, clenching and unclenching her jaw, and turned on the radio to an AM station that crackled and went in and out but did give accounts of high winds and tornado watches throughout Western Kansas.

"Hopefully, we'll stay east of it," Sam said, but Ty knew she didn't believe her own words. He cursed the lack of rural funding that stopped him from seeing a map on his phone. Even the car's GPS stopped working. "I know where we're going," Sam assured him. "The roads are just grids around here. We keep going south, we'll get to our motel."

But the weather wasn't going to give Sam her carefully thought-out plan. They began to see lightning in the distance, and the sky turned so dark they had to put their lights on. Rain spattered the windshield, making them jump.

"Dad?" Alyssa said.

"We'll be okay," he said automatically. And then the sirens went off.

He hadn't seen the speakers attached to the poles along the highway, but at once it was as though the sound were coming from in the car, in his head, reverberating with a chilling certainty that they were in danger, and right now.

Cars in front of them slowed and stopped, pulling to the side of the road and putting their flashers on. Sam pulled over just as two figures came out of a farm building to their left. "What the hell are they doing?" Ty muttered. Surely, they had a bunker or something to hide in?

The figures ran over a small area of grass, waving their hands. Sam opened her door. "Wait!" Ty said, as though he had any way to stop Sam from doing whatever she wanted to do. But with the door open, under the howling wind, he could hear what the people were saying.

"Bunker!" they yelled, waving their arms back toward the building. "Come on!"

Sam whipped around to the back and got Cairo out. The kids didn't move until Ty said, "Okay," and then they were out with the other people who'd been driving along this stretch, maybe five or seven cars total, now scattered like leaves along the road while their inhabitants fled into the field. Sam let Cai run without a leash, and he got there faster than any of them before turning back to bark at her.

Ty's heart was bursting through his chest, not from the run but from fear. His children. His perfect, precious children. He'd dragged them all the way across the country and put them in mortal danger, just because he didn't want to deal with his ex-wife and whatever she wanted to do to him. He wanted to pick Alyssa up and carry her to the building, as though she were tiny again, but her leg stride almost matched his, and he had to admit his helplessness as they all arrived at the steel doors that leaned into the ground.

"There's room," the person who'd called them over said, and Ty didn't ask for proof. They pelted down the stairs, almost pushed down by the wind, and the next thing he knew, he was in a spacious basement with light, fans, chairs, shelves of food, drink, flashlights, and soft pallets piled up in one corner. About fifteen people of all ages came in behind them. A woman and two small children were already there, handing out blankets. The woman was medium-sized and red-cheeked with short, mousy hair, and she was smiling.

"Hi," she said as everyone came in. "Welcome. Don't worry. You're safe in here. Have a seat."

Her calm hospitality threw Ty, who swore he could feel leaves in his hair from their abrupt dash across the field. "Thank you," he said and directed Matt and Alyssa to seats in a corner.

"Sounds like this happens a lot," Sam said. She hadn't sat down but was crouched near Cairo. "I forgot his leash. He's very well-behaved."

"Not a problem." The woman smiled at Cairo. "You're all welcome."

Maybe a minute had gone by since the warning sirens. The man who'd reached them first ran down the stairs behind the last motorist, and his helper flapped the doors shut behind them.

"Have a blanket," the small child said to Sam who, crouched down as she was, was the same height. "Can I pet your dog?"

"Absolutely. You're very helpful," Sam said, smiling at her. "Have you done this before?"

"Ever' year," the child said matter-of-factly. She couldn't have been more than five. "Sometimes twice."

"Welcome to Tornado Alley," the woman said, shrugging as though death and destruction were just another day at the farm.

Ty felt Alyssa shiver behind him. "We're okay," he reassured her.

"What about Sam's car?" Alyssa whispered.

"Don't worry about my car," Sam said. Ears like a hawk, she had. "The most important things are right here." She sat down next to the girl and put an arm around her. "Okay?"

Alyssa bit her lip but let herself be pulled into Sam's embrace. Ty sat next to Matt, who was on Alyssa's other side, and nudged his shoulder.

"You okay?"

"Peachy," Matt said. His face was pale, or maybe it was the fluorescent lighting in the room. Either way, Ty kept his shoulder touching his son's.

The farmer turned on a shortwave radio and the local weather service crackled out, informing them of damage in towns Ty didn't know. The female farmer offered sodas and water and pointed to a door in the back that led to a couple of composting toilets.

"We're real grateful," a large older man said from his spot next to his wife.

"No problem!" the woman said.

"Isn't she worried about her house?" Alyssa whispered to Sam. Since she was turned toward Ty, he heard her.

Sam shrugged. "Sometimes there's nothing you can do but wait. And hope."

"And pray," the older man's wife said. "Shall we?"

The others bowed their heads, but Sam met Ty's eyes and shook her head with a wry smile. He wasn't a believer either, but somehow the gentle murmur of the prayer the woman led was soothing anyway. Alyssa screwed her eyes up tight. Matt looked down, but Ty could see his eyes were open. All valid responses to what was happening to them.

Something big hit the hatch doors, sending a clang through all their bones. Everyone jumped, and anyone who was still talking stopped. Alyssa gripped Sam more tightly, and Sam now had both arms around her. Ty caught Sam's eye again and saw the fear there.

"We're safe," he said.

"How do you know?" she said, keeping her voice low. She was trying to be flippant, but the words came out as a plea. She hated changes in her plans. Ty had messed with her in the first place, just getting them across the country. Now he'd made it worse. He had to fix it.

"Because we're together," he said. "And these people know what they're up against. Those doors will hold." Did he sound confident? He sure hoped so.

He stretched out an arm behind Matt to touch Sam's shoulder. "Breathe, Indy. It's gonna be okay."

Sam lowered her head to Alyssa's, and Ty saw the shaky breath she let out. Cairo was leaning hard against her leg. The dog couldn't lie down and relax. Like the rest of them.

"I promise," Ty said.

"What about our stuff?" Alyssa said.

"It's just stuff," he said.

"Dad." Matt rolled his head toward him. "Why do you always do that?"

"Do what?"

"Pretend everything's okay."

"Matt," Alyssa begged.

"No, I'm serious." Matt leaned forward and twisted his head to look at his father, blocking Ty's view of Alyssa and Sam. "I think me and Lyss, of all people, know that things can *always* get worse."

He pointed to his eye.

"That was a mistake—" Ty began, but Matt smacked his hand on his seat.

"You're doing it again!" He didn't bother to lower his voice this time, and the rest of the group unabashedly turned to listen. Just like at Alyssa's graduation. "We can stay with Uncle Noah as long as we like, but we're gonna have to go back eventually, and she'll find us again."

Alyssa had moved a little closer to Sam. Ty sighed and rubbed a hand over his face. "She'll find us again anyway, bud. We're not trying to remove ourselves from her life completely; we just need a little space for her to... to get her head on."

"How long do we have to wait for that? Till I'm in college? Till Lyss is in college? Till she finally kills you?"

"Matt!"

Ty's eyes flicked to their neighbors, who immediately looked away. As if they could pretend they hadn't heard in this enclosed space. As if the injuries on their faces weren't telling the story by themselves. There went the Cavanaughs again, living their problems in front of God and everybody.

"I've seen the stories, Dad. You can't protect us from everything. It's usually the guy, but I know how these things end. You're just making her more mad."

"That's not how *this* is going to end," Ty said. "I promise you, Matt. I won't let–"

"*You won't let*," Matt copied, making quotation marks with his fingers. "You can't stop her, Dad. You never could. That's the point."

"He can sure the hell try," Sam said unexpectedly. She turned to Matt a little, shielding Ty from his son's sullen glare. "You know he'll never stop trying, don't you? What he wants is for you to have a relationship with your mom. It would be a lot easier for him if he gave up on that life, don't you see? But he knows how important it is, and he'll keep on trying until... well, until it works."

"Until I'm old enough to get the hell away from her myself, you mean," Matt said, unimpressed.

Ty let out a deep sigh and rested his head against the block wall behind his head. Maybe if he hit it with the back of his head enough times, he'd just disappear through it, like Homer Simpson through the hedge.

"Why does he keep trying?" Matt went on. Alyssa's eyes were dinner plates, but she didn't say anything. Matt was speaking for her too. "She's nuts. There's no way to have a 'relationship' with her. And she scares Lyss. It's bad enough we have to live with the fact that either of us could go crazy any day now, without having to hang out every few days with the one who made us that way."

"Honey," Sam said gently. "Those names won't help anyone. I'm sorry you have to think about that kind of stuff. But don't give your dad a hard time. He's doing what he thinks is best."

"Well, he sucks at it."

"Matt!" she said. Ty was surprised at the maternal authority in her voice.

Matt lowered his eyes and mumbled, "Well, you know what I mean."

Something else hit the storm doors and scraped along them. Whatever it was made two clanging noises before the wind must have dragged it away. "Dad," Alyssa whispered in horror, though she didn't move from Sam's arms.

Ty let his head go back to level. "Move," he said to Matt, tapping the boy's leg. Matt stood without complaint, and Ty swapped places with him so he could get to his daughter. Sam loosened her arms. Ty drew Alyssa to him. God, this beautiful, lanky, smart little girl. She was a teenager, but Ty would always see her as the small blond whirlwind who'd called on him to watch her go down the slide at the park.

"Sweetheart," he said into her hair, and Alyssa gave him her weight the way she'd given it to Sam. "Matt's right that I can't always stop bad things from happening. I'll fight like heck to stop them, but it won't always work. But I *can* promise you that I will *never* leave you. I'll never just decide I don't want to be here, because you kids are the most incredible gifts I was ever given, and a dad doesn't forget that. I'll *always* be here when you need me. If anything ever goes wrong in your life, I want to be your safe place."

He looked around at Matt, whose eyes were wide—well, one eye, anyway. "I told you if you ever got drunk and needed a ride, I'd give you one and I wouldn't punish you. You remember that?" Matt nodded. "I don't want you to drink at all, but kids are kids, and I know I can't always protect you from idiots spiking your drink. But I *can* protect you from getting in a car with someone who's drunk or high. And I won't read you the riot act because I don't want you to hesitate for a *second* on whether or not I'm your safe place. Do you see?"

Matt nodded slowly, and Ty felt Alyssa nod against his chest. She shuddered; he knew she was hiding more tears. He hugged her and kissed the top of her head.

Then, because he wanted to say it, he looked at Sam. "Same goes for you, Indy. If you ever need anything—anything," he repeated, because she'd opened her mouth in surprise, "call me. Whatever you need. Whenever."

Sam looked at him for a long time. Her eyes were so dark he couldn't look away. Could she tell? Could she read him as well as she had before? Did she know he was offering her a phone call because he couldn't offer her his heart? And the only reason he couldn't offer that was because she already had it, and she was about to disappear into the New Mexico mountains and take it with her?

Sam's eyes flicked down to Alyssa and then back to him. "Right back at ya, Tyler."

A beep from inside the room made them all jump again, and Ty lost eye contact with Sam.

"Coffee's ready," the farmer said sheepishly.

Everyone had been listening. The whole time. What could Ty do about it? Not a damn thing.

"I'll take mine black," he said. And a loose line formed at the machine. Sam stayed with the kids, so he got her a coffee, too, as well as a couple of granola bars and dried apple chips. The four of them sat in a chewing silence while the rest of the group returned to their original conversations or sat staring at the ceiling, as though they could tell what the tornado was doing from where they were.

Ty was halfway through his second granola bar when the farmer said, "Warning ran out. We should be good now." Everyone sat up. Real life was back. And the aftermath of being in this bunker might be scarier than staying right here.

The farmer and the man who'd helped him call them to the bunker tried the doors, which opened freely, letting in a shower of debris that rolled down the concrete stairs. The air that came with them was sharp and metallic, charged and uneasy. Like Ty felt around Sam, now that he'd given her everything.

"Yep," the farmer said. Ty was really going to have to ask him his name. "Y'all can come up now."

So like groundhogs blinking from their nests, they crunched over the leaves and dirt under their feet and stepped back into the world.

Chapter 20

"Let me and your dad go first," Sam warned the kids, in case the wind was still blowing branches around. She nodded at Ty, who smiled for some damn reason.

What had that look been, before? And what the hell did he mean, she could always call on him if she needed him? Didn't he know that Sam Fielding didn't need anyone? He might have soothed the kids with that BS, but Sam knew better. Hadn't she told Cat? She didn't need family. Didn't want it. Family meant people relied on you. And you relied on them. And they'd leave you right when you needed them most.

But if that were the case, why hadn't she been able to look away when he'd told her he'd always be there for her? Why had a huge part of her heart reached out to him, begging him to be right, to make it real? To never, ever leave her. In return, she'd...

Ugh. She shook her head and followed him up the stairs. The first thing she saw was her car, on the road where she'd left it. A high-sided Jeep had been blown on its side, but the rest of the vehicles were in good shape. The wind was strong but not uncomfortable, and the rain had disappeared as fast as it had come. To their left, they saw sunshine. The sky on the right was still dead gray and churning as though sharks were feeding above the clouds.

"Midtown's gonna need help," the farmer said, looking in that direction. But Sam was relieved to see that his house looked untouched, apart from a couple of small branches on the roof.

"Joe, get the quad and check the south field," the farmer said, and the other man nodded and jogged to the large barn next to the house. "We'll use the winch on the tractor to get your car up good as new. And y'all are welcome to stay until you feel safe, but if you got a little time, next town over looks like it's gotten hit."

"Of course we'll go help," Sam said at once. "Can we bring anything?"

Inside fifteen minutes, while Joe came back and reported that the tornado had indeed touched down south of the farm, chewing up a planted field, and Sam learned that the farmer and his wife were called Clive and Sue, they all had gloves, shovels, and boxes of garbage bags. Sue and her kids stayed on the porch and waved them off.

Clive led those who could help down the low-lying road into a town that looked exactly like the others they'd driven through today. Or it would have if it weren't for the storm that had just picked up the vulnerable buildings and tossed them about like a waiter showing off with a salad. The outskirts of town were the worst. Mobile homes had their roofs peeled off, and some were no more than matchsticks, their window frames deposited on top of the parked cars. Trees had fallen on several more, and a small farm stand by the road sat next to its display cases, as if it had gotten tired of them and thrown them out through the roof.

"God," Alyssa said. "How are we going to help them?"

"However they ask us to," Sam said.

Since Clive was still moving, Ty didn't stop until they'd arrived at the town's fire station, joining a crowd of pickup trucks and emergency vehicles that came and went in a dizzying ballet of urgency and efficiency. Sam's car was waved into a spot, and a soft-spoken young man with a military haircut and a HiVis vest nodded to them.

"You guys okay?" he asked after they got out of the car.

Belatedly, Sam remembered her scratches, Ty's cheek, and Matt's eye. "Oh, yeah," she said as though bruises and black eyes were everyday occurrences. "These aren't from the tornado. How can we help?"

Rather than helping at the mobile home park, they were sent a few blocks south, where the tornado had skirted the town but hit a development tucked into an old field. The houses were still standing, but debris was everywhere. A man in a T-shirt with a firefighter logo, but nothing else to explain his authority, told them to clear the road. "But don't touch glass or wires, and don't touch nothing without your gloves. You better keep your dog away too."

So Alyssa tied Cairo to a road sign, and Sam gave him an apologetic kiss before they moved away, clearing up the road as they went.

Several people asked them if they were okay, which made Sam realize how isolated they'd been so far on this trip. Hotel staff were too polite to mention their injuries.

With only each other for company and the high emotions that had caused them to leave, it was no wonder Ty had decided she was looking for someone to lean on.

Which, of course, she wasn't. Was she? And if she looked around for Ty several times that afternoon, just to make sure he was safe, that was on his kids' behalf. Right?

The residents of the neighborhood came out of their beaten-up houses and helped, which then led to groups of people going back with them to help clear out broken decks or mangled patio furniture. When Sam next looked up from the pile of brush she was collecting to one side of the road, she couldn't see Ty or the kids.

A shout and a crashing noise came from her left.

She was running before she knew it. Others ran alongside her, but she couldn't see them. "Tyler!" she shouted. "Matt! Lyss!"

A cacophony of sound came from one house that stood in its own small yard. Its front windows were broken, and some strips of roof tile had peeled off and lay drunkenly in the yard. One of the cars in front of the open garage had slid into the other. Sam noted all these things with the detail of an archaeologist's eye, as though she would have to put everything back in place later, but she was mostly just running, running straight for the front door.

"Not in there!" someone yelled. "Windows blew in. Go around!"

Sam made a hard left turn and skirted the house. "Alyssa!" she screamed. "Ty!"

"What?" Alyssa yelled back. She was several feet away, in a copse of trees between houses, away from the damage. Cairo was on his leash, nosing around the underbrush.

Sam took in the scene in a half second and spun around to look at the back of the house. Its deck was leaning off the house, and spindles from the railing lay on the grass. An awning that had been attached to the house lay on top of the remains of the deck. A group of maybe seven men stood around, looking at it. And one of them, with his bright-blond hair, was definitely Ty.

"Tyler!" she yelled again, and he turned around. But Sam was already running up the broken steps, uncaring of the men whose shoulders she bumped as she went up to him and said, "What the hell are you doing up here?"

"I was–"

But she didn't care, she didn't care what his reasons were. She didn't care anything except that she'd thought he'd been crushed to pieces under a wall or something and her heart was pounding through her chest and he was still standing too close to that awning.

She pulled on his arm, and he almost tripped as she yanked him back down the stairs. "You promised!" she shouted. "You promised you'd be there for all of us, and the next thing you're running into collapsed buildings–"

"I didn't–I wasn't–"

"Shut up! You can't *do* that! You can't *do* that to your kids!"

Her breath was hitching; her shoulders were shaking, and she felt like her legs wouldn't hold her up anymore. "Don't you *ever* do that to us again!" she cried. She crossed her arms in front of her so he wouldn't see her shaking. But she was out of words, and everyone was staring.

And then Ty did the opposite of what she thought he'd do. He put his arms around her. He pulled her in. He put his chin over her shoulder and held her, held her until the shakes began to subside and she could feel the tears on her face.

"I'm okay, Indy," he whispered. "I'm fine. I would never have gone inside the house. The awning fell because we pulled it down. We were safe the whole time."

Now she couldn't even talk. She could only dip her head so her wet face was hidden in his shoulder.

"We're safe, sweetheart," he repeated. "We're okay."

"I'm so mad at you," she mumbled into his shoulder.

"Yeah. I get that. Listen, why don't you go get Cairo and Lyss and find that coffee tent I saw at the end of the street?"

"Is Sam okay?"

Damn. It was Alyssa. She'd heard Sam's ridiculous, embarrassing outburst. Of course Ty had been fine. Sam had gone into full-blown panic based on no information whatsoever. As her heart rate slowed, she thought of how she looked and what she'd said. Now she never wanted to take her face out of Ty's shoulder again.

"She's fine," Ty told Alyssa. "Just tired. Why don't you guys get something to eat? We've only had granola bars since Kansas City."

"Okay."

Sam took a tiny peek over Ty's shoulder at his daughter, who was looking at her and biting her lip. Sam's face got even hotter. So much for being the big heroine.

"Sorry you got triggered," Alyssa said, patting her arm. "Is this how your dad—is this how you lost your dad?"

Damn Ty's kids and their generation for understanding what was still difficult for Sam to voice. And damn Ty for not telling her she was overreacting and to pull herself together. What defense did she have against a man who saw exactly who she was and liked her anyway?

Not a whole lot. That was what.

She backed up from Ty's comfort and swiped at her eyes. "I'm fine," she said to Alyssa. "Just hungry. You want us to bring you back something?" she asked Ty.

"Coffee. And whatever they have to eat."

"Come on, Sam," Alyssa said. She pulled Sam's hand the way Sam had pulled Ty's. Sam followed her the way he had Sam, stumbling and confused.

"Do you get hangry?" Alyssa said as they walked back. "Matt does."

"Your dad doesn't?" Her voice still sounded faint.

"Nah. Matt must have gotten it from our mom."

Sam slowed. Alyssa frowned at her. "Lyss," Sam said. "I haven't asked you about your mom on this trip. I didn't want to upset you."

"I know." The girl looked as though Sam was stating the wildly obvious.

"Right. Well, I just wanted you to know that I do want to talk if you need to. Your dad talked about being there for you, and I want you to know that—" She glanced away as though she needed to keep track of Cairo, but that wasn't why. She needed a moment before she made a commitment she'd always sworn she wasn't the type to give. "I'll always be on the end of the phone if you need me."

"I know," Alyssa said again, as though she'd always known she could rely on Sam, even if Sam didn't. "And I know you're telling me this because you don't want to talk about your dad. That's okay too."

And then the rotten kid hugged her from the side, and Sam wanted to cry all over again.

◆

They helped until the road was clear and the sun touched the endless horizon. Townspeople who hadn't lost power brought over huge pans of lasagna, and everyone ate, sitting on a cleared piece of grass. Everyone was chatting and laughing, grateful that the town had taken only a glancing blow. They told Sam that a second crew had gone with heavy machinery to help clean up the trailer park, and those who had power were housing those who'd lost their homes. The sense of community was overwhelming.

"You guys have a place to stay?" Clive, who'd come and gone several times over the afternoon, asked. Alyssa and Matt had gone back for more dessert, and Cairo was finishing up his own bowl of hamburger. "You're welcome to come back to the farm for the night."

"We appreciate it," Ty said. "We're going to keep on moving. We can get a few hours of driving in before we have to turn in."

"If you're sure." Clive looked troubled. "You've been working hard. Don't drive tired."

"We won't," Sam said. "Ty wouldn't allow it."

"You two make a good team," Clive said. "If you don't mind my saying so, it sounds like those kids have been through some stuff. They're lucky to have you for a stepmother."

"I—" Sam said. "Thanks."

She wasn't going to tell Clive the truth. It would take too much explanation. And Ty might think she was pulling away from him and his family.

Not that she shouldn't be doing that immediately. How could she lean into this warm comfort, this—dare she say—safety she felt around him? That wasn't how the world worked. Not for Sam anyway.

"We should get moving," Ty said, and they shook hands with or hugged everyone in sight, gathered up the kids and Cairo, and walked back to Sam's car.

They talked about where they'd stay as Ty drove out of town, and Sam pulled out the map. "You know, it's only eight hours to Taos from here."

Ty looked over at her before turning his attention back to the road. She couldn't read his expression. "You want to drive through?"

Sam bit her lip. She wanted to give this family to Noah. She wanted to start missing them, because it was going to hurt like fuck, and she wanted to rip off the Band-Aid quickly. She wanted to leave Ty in Taos and dream about him for a while before getting back to her normal life. Because that was the only way this could end.

"If you're up for it," she said. "We'll swap the driving every two hours. I've done it before." Though not since college.

Ty drove along the dead flat road. The sun was blazing as it set under the clouds to their left. He looked at it, then over to Sam's right, as though scanning the horizon for danger. Or saying goodbye.

"Sure," he said. "Kids, you okay with sleeping in the car? We'll take a couple of pit stops and be with Noah by morning."

Sam looked around. Both children had dark eyes—Matt's black eye notwithstanding—and pale faces. They were done.

"That's fine by me," Alyssa said and leaned her head against a hoodie she'd positioned at the window as a pillow.

"Sure," Matt said, closing his eyes and letting his head fall back on its rest. "Don't crash and kill us all," he added as if he barely cared if they did.

So they drove. The sky went from orange to purple to black. There were no streetlights, no looming hills, no nothing. Just them and the car's lights, picking through the high plains like ants on a bedsheet.

Ty's phone began pinging like crazy, so he and Sam swapped driving, then he listened to voicemail after voicemail. His face darkened.

"What is it?" Sam said.

"Not a problem," he said, though he sure the hell looked like it was. He called Noah and told him they'd be there in the morning instead of the afternoon. Noah's enthusiasm was loud enough for Sam to hear it, and she had to laugh. But as soon as Ty hung up, his face fell back into lines of worry.

They found a diner around midnight, ordered breakfast, and used the bathrooms. Sam used the excuse of safety in numbers to grab Ty while she walked Cairo. The kids, two bundles of sweatshirts and messy hair, stayed to eat their pancakes.

"So what is it?" she said almost before the door had swung closed.

Chapter 21

Ty sighed and scrubbed his hand down his face. "They bailed her out again. Said she knew she needed help and they were taking her to a hospital. Instead, they took her home, and her parents let her leave again. They've lost track of her."

"Jesus, Ty."

He shook his head. "Amazing how you can just lose someone in this age of technology."

"Does she know where we're going?"

He shrugged. "She might guess. Julia visited my mom first, but she'd never say."

"So she might not even know you left town. Your car is still in the driveway."

"You forget those private investigators she set on us."

Sam stopped dead. "Shit. I did forget. They didn't follow us though, did they?"

"But she can find out where *you* live. And she might guess that we're going to Noah if we left with you. They only have to do a quick internet search to find you, right?"

They were under a streetlight. The air smelled of gasoline from the gas station across the street. It seemed to be an omen, somehow, of the danger close by.

"Sam," he said. "Don't go home yet. Not until we know where she is."

"I have to," she said at once. "I have work on Monday, and I have to get my stuff together and move back to my trailer."

"Indy," he said.

"No. You should come to *my* house. She's expecting you to go to your friend. You can come to mine and bypass her altogether. If she shows up at Noah's, he can have her arrested."

"Indy," he repeated and put out a hand. He stroked her arm. "If anything were to happen to you because of me, I couldn't stand it."

Sam caught her breath. "I'll be fine. She's too chicken to fight a woman." And she tried to smile.

Ty sighed again. "Fine. I don't know where she'll be, so let's just get the kids to Noah's. They know now not to trust her, so even if I have to go back to Massachusetts, they'll be safe with him."

"Okay." She hated not knowing the right answer. She hated that Ty didn't know the right answer and had to make do with the one they had. "Come here."

She wrapped her arms around him. Not to kiss him. But she couldn't do nothing when he was standing there looking more alone than ever. She'd brought him all this way only to have Julia loom as large as ever over their heads.

This time Ty dropped his head to her shoulder. "Sam," he said.

"Uh-oh," she joked. "When you don't call me Indy, things are serious."

He laughed, which was all she wanted. "Do you mind?"

"I got used to it. Yeah, kinda like it. Damn you."

He adjusted his position so he could hold her more tightly. "Sam," he said again.

She couldn't see his face, but she could feel his thoughts. "I'm right here," she murmured. "I'm right here."

"I know. You've been right here for us all week."

"And I always will be. Whatever happens."

Whatever happened. She could love him from afar, right? That would be better than loving him up close and running the risk of losing him right in front of her face.

She shook a little and breathed in his hair.

"I know you will," he said. "I don't think I've ever trusted anyone as much as I trust you."

"Ditto."

They stood there for a minute more, exchanging soundless emotions, their bodies touching from head to knees. The cool desert air pimpled Sam's arms, but she wasn't letting go until he did. This might be her only chance to love him, and she wasn't going to waste it.

Cairo twitched on the end of his leash and whined, and the moment had to pass. Sam looked up from Ty's shoulder and saw a figure walking another dog across the street. Cairo was only doing his job. "Good boy," she said.

"Thank you," Ty said. She heard the smile in his voice and smiled back at him. Sighing, she outlined his lips with her spare hand, then kissed them. *One more time.* She loved his lips, loved their softness. Loved how they yielded to her but were well able to control the kiss when she let him.

She let him.

Who cared if they kissed on a nameless road in a nameless zip code mere hours from their destination? Who cared if Ty pulled out her ponytail and gathered her hair in his hand as though they were alone and he'd be taking off the rest of her clothes as slow or as fast as he liked? Who cared if Sam moaned into his mouth, not holding the sound back this time, and grabbed the muscles of his back as though she were going to push him back against a wall and climb him like a tree?

This may be the last time I get to kiss him.

So she made it count.

"Get a room!"

The shout came from the gas station, whose light was probably helping them put on quite a show. They broke apart and laughed. Sam waved at the heckler and smoothed her hair. Ty straightened his shirt and bent to pet Cairo, who'd waited patiently for their PDA to end.

"Let's get you to Noah's," Sam said. She entangled her free hand in his, and they stayed that way until they got to the lights of the diner.

Back inside, Matt and Alyssa still looked mostly asleep. The detritus of their dinner/breakfast was all over the table.

"We're at five thousand feet elevation," Lyss said, looking at her phone with her head in both hands. "In Kansas we were only at two thousand."

"Impressive," Sam murmured. "Good thing we're driving instead of climbing."

Alyssa wrinkled her nose. She was all done with driving. Yet onward they had to go. *Our last meal together*, Sam couldn't help but think. *Maybe the last time we get gas.* Stupid, pathetic, teenage thoughts. She should have spent the full seven minutes in Heaven kissing Ty. She'd wasted so much time avoiding intimacy with men, when the perfect man had been right in front of her all along.

Eventually, the towns became more numerous, the roads more winding. Ty and Sam continued to alternate shifts, and the children slept. When Sam was driving, she spent her time either looking over at Ty, who was also asleep, and *not* looking over at him. She'd gotten so used to him, to having a teammate by her side whom she knew would always have her best interests at heart.

To be loved by Ty would be intoxicating.

And there was the kissing. She clenched things when she thought about the kissing and what it might have led to. Ty's mouth was relaxed in sleep, his lips slightly parted. His blond hair seemed to catch specks of light that didn't exist outside the car. Sam wanted to stroke his head. She wanted to kiss the pants off him. Literally.

She shook herself and focused on the road. In the rearview mirror, she noticed a tiny crack of dark-gray frosting along the quiet, flat landscape. Day was coming. After another few minutes, the crack became a seam, which became a thread, which became a ribbon. And in front of Sam—was that a mountain? An actual honest-to-goodness rock formation that wasn't a flat field or a small stand of trees?

"Wake up, baby," she whispered before she could stop herself. And she put her hand on Ty's knee.

He stretched and opened his eyes. His hand squeezed hers. "Time already?" he said.

"No. Just... look ahead. The mountains. We're nearly there."

He squinted. The mountains were still a dark-gray mass against a dark-blue sky, but they were there. "Wow," he said. Sam felt the breath leave him. "We made it."

"Of course we did." But she'd wondered too.

Together they watched the sun light up the mountains from behind them, turning them orange the way it had turned Kansas orange the night before. The mountains weren't just ahead of them; they were all around them, in a U-shape that felt like a hug, like congratulations for getting the children here at last.

In all that time, Ty didn't let go of Sam's hand.

And Sam didn't want him to.

The dawn was still moving when Ty turned to Sam. "Do you want to swap?"

She looked at him, then looked away. Yes. She wanted to swap her life for a woman who could hold his hand forever.

A wave of grief hit her. She took her hand away.

"What's wrong?" he said.

"Nothing. Not a damn thing. Hey, kids." She reached a hand back to tap Matt and Alyssa's knees. "Wake up and look at the mountains."

"Sam," Ty admonished, but she sniffed and ignored him. So she was a coward. So what?

In all too short a time, they were heading off the main road and up a narrow street that opened into dirt yards with a few chickens and horses behind railroad-tie fences. The GPS took Sam's SUV up to a house that was half log cabin, half raised ranch and dominated by a peaked roof over a deep, cool porch. Trees surrounded the lot on three sides. A red-brown horse with a small head and kind eyes ambled over to the fence when they pulled into the driveway. Noah was on the porch and running down the steps at once, followed by two small brown dogs—part Jack Russell, part Chihuahua, maybe—who set up a yapping welcome that made Cairo let out an aggrieved bark.

Sam, Ty, the kids, and Cairo got out of the car slowly—Sam hadn't realized how stiff the long ride had made her—and greeted Noah in a flurry of hugs and hellos and relieved smiles.

"You guys must be wiped!" he said, his big face split in a warm grin. He wore a shirt that looked homemade, and his hair was at least a foot longer than Sam remembered. He hugged her just as hard as he hugged Ty.

"Dudes, you gotta tell me everything," he said, smacking Matt on the shoulder. "Coffee's on."

"Is that your horse?" Alyssa said. "Can I pet him?"

"He is, and of course you can," Noah said. "His name's Jimmy."

"I can't believe you have a horse." Ty shook his head while Alyssa left their little group and ran to Jimmy, who was looking at them with his huge eyes over the fence.

"Got my eye on one the kids can share while they're here," Noah said. "Might hafta go bigger. You kids've got long legs. Anyway, let's get you around a cup o' joe."

"Mom!" Alyssa screamed.

Sam spun around. From the trees they'd just driven past, along Jimmy's fence line, Julia was walking as though she hiked this way all the time. At first, Sam could only see her straight pale hair, blown back by the breeze. Against the natural russet of the land around her, she seemed impossibly artificial and out of place. Then she turned the corner, and Sam saw that she was carrying a pitchfork. A goddamn pitchfork. She must have taken it from the stable.

"Kids, get in the house," Ty said at once. He beckoned to Alyssa without taking his eyes off Julia.

"No, Dad," Matt said. "I–"

"Matthew. Get in the house." Ty's voice was ice and allowed for no argument. "Take your sister."

Matt snapped his mouth closed. He'd protect his sister no matter what. He and Alyssa disappeared into the house. Sam knew they'd only find the closest window and watch anyway, but at least they might not hear whatever Julia had come to say.

Sam took a stance that would be hard to unbalance, with one foot in front of the other and her flank turned to Julia. Ty stood square on. She couldn't see Noah and didn't dare turn her head.

Noah's little dogs were barking at Julia from several feet away. She gripped the handle of the pitchfork and poked the business end toward one of them. She didn't make contact, but the dog jumped back anyway.

"Hey!" Noah said. He was behind Sam and to her right, forming a triangle with her and Ty.

"What are you doing here, Julia?" Ty said in an exhausted tone.

"You left town without saying goodbye," she replied. Her voice was trying to sound light and unconcerned, but her smile was rigid, her muscles tense.

"For God's sake," Ty said. Sam wanted to hold him. But she wouldn't relax her position. "You're not allowed to be here. I thought you were going to get help."

Julia showed all her teeth. "My 'help' is being with my kids." Then she struck a pose. "Pissing you off is also very good for my mental health."

"Julia." Ty shook his head slowly. "You could have been with the kids all you liked. But you blew it. Every time."

"Only because you made them hate me." Her smile slipped at the word *hate*.

Ty, for once, didn't contradict her. "Why do you want to see them anyway? You don't even like being with them."

"Because they're *mine*, you bastard. Mine! I made them. They're mine. And *you* don't want me to have them. And that's reason enough in itself."

So she didn't even care about the kids for themselves. They were just pawns. Sam wanted to knock her through the fence and into the road.

"How did you get here?" Ty said.

His phone began ringing. He ignored it, but Julia said, "Go ahead, Tyler. I got all day."

He took the phone out of his pocket, glanced at the screen, and said to Sam, "It's Lauren."

"Oooh, Lauren!" Julia mocked. "Lovely lawyer Lauren! Did you sleep with her, too, while we were married?"

Sam didn't need to ask to know that Ty hadn't slept with anyone but Julia when they were married. And he, again, had given up explaining himself. He hit the button. Sam didn't take her eyes off Julia.

"Hi," he said. "Okay. Oh, Newark. Yeah. No. Dallas is a hub. She probably got a driver here from Santa Fe. Yeah, she's right here." He paused. "Yeah."

He pressed the button again. "You can't be here," he reiterated.

"And yet!" she exclaimed, widening her eyes as if in shock. "Here I am! Hi, Noah!" She waved her fingers at Noah.

"Wish I could say it's a pleasure," Noah grunted. So much anger in one simple sentence.

Julia hefted the pitchfork and looked at it. "Thanks for the pitchfork." Like a baton, she twirled it at arm's length for a couple of turns before pointing it at them. "'Cause I heard you were with him, Sam Fielding."

"I am," Sam had to say.

"Well, I see that." Julia rolled her eyes as though Sam were an idiot. "Not gonna let you touch me today."

"And I," Sam said in a conversational tone, "am not going to let you touch Ty today."

Julia curled her lip. The pitchfork swung around her again and pointed at the other small dog. It barked at her and jumped forward and back on its little legs. She ran forward and jabbed at it. Noah shouted something, but the dog was too smart to get within reach of the tines. It backed up to Jimmy's fence and set up a warning cascade of barks that rang in Sam's ears and made her wince.

"You're not mad at the dogs," Ty said. "Don't take it out on them."

"You're so right." Julia moved forward. Sam held her breath. Would she really use that fork against people? Was she really that unhinged? Was Matt right?

"What are you going to do?" Ty said, as though reading Sam's mind. "You won't get out of jail this time if you attack us. You can't say it was a second of madness this time. You've had a day and a night to think this over."

"I have." Julia stopped maybe ten feet away from the three of them. She held up the pitchfork like a staff and looked at its tips as though they were old friends. "The pitchfork was a bonus, I must say. But generally, yeah. I know what I want to say to you, Tyler."

"Then say it." Ty seemed to deliberately relax, folding his arms and moving his feet. "And let's make this the last time we talk, huh?"

"Ha!" Julia took a firmer grip on the fork. "You wish. I'm not going to let you take those kids from me. You can hide them in that house as long as you like, but you'll have to go back to Massachusetts eventually. And I'll be there."

"You won't," Sam said. "You'll be in jail. You jumped bail." Something loosened in her. She was all in, and there was no reason not to tell this woman what she thought of her. "You're such an idiot, Julia. You think any judge would let you near Matt and Lyss after you pulled this stunt? It's over. Can't you see that?"

Julia's eyes widened, and she bared her teeth again. "Shut up. You don't know anything about it."

"I know *all* about it," Sam said.

"You think you'd be a better mother than me?" Julia sneered. "You don't have kids of your own, so you want mine?"

"At least I'll never leave them at a movie theater because I got bored."

Julia's eyes snapped to Ty. "You *told* her about that? You rat bastard!"

"Sticks and stones, Julia," Sam said. "We're all done here. Come on, Ty."

She knew she was baiting Julia by saying this, but she wanted the painful tension in the yard to cease. She knew that by turning her back on Julia, she was going to drive her to the edge one way or the other, but then the game would be done and Ty could get on with his life.

But everything happened in the half-second she turned her back.

Cairo, about whom she'd completely forgotten, took her movement toward him as a sign to put himself into the fray. He'd been behind her, but now he dashed around and began barking at Julia, his deep bark a sharp contrast to Noah's little defenders.

Sam yelled, "No!" but Julia was already moving, the tines of the fork glinting in the corner of Sam's eye as she spun around. She saw the pitchfork angle down and swing at her beautiful, brave dog, and she screamed.

But Ty dove in front of Cairo, putting out his arm to protect the dog. The fork caught against his forearm, and he yelled in pain and fell to his knees.

Sam's vision filled with red. She didn't give a shit about the pitchfork or the law or anything. She flew at Julia, but Cairo got there first. Darting under the length of the pitchfork, which clattered to the floor next to Ty, he went for Julia's legs—not biting but hitting her with his head, making her stagger, which gave Sam enough time to barrel into her and knock her to the ground, hard.

Julia fell sideways. Sam forced her onto her front and sat on her feet. Julia was the one screaming now, but Sam didn't care. She shifted up to Julia's legs and then her hips. A small voice told Sam not to sit on her back because she'd break it, but since Julia was now trying to buck Sam off, Sam thought about it. When Julia got one arm free and began grabbing for Sam, Sam used her knee to pin it down.

Julia might not have been able to move, but she sure could shout, and Sam's ears were ringing worse than ever. Oh, no. That was sirens. And the blissful view of flashing lights on a patrol car. Thank God Noah didn't live out in the country. Thank God Lauren had called just when she had. Thank God one of the kids had the wherewithal to dial 911. A cop got out and ran over to them.

Putting the cuffs on Julia didn't stop her screaming obscenities at anyone within reach, but Sam was able to get off her.

"You might need two—" Sam said. And sure enough, Julia twisted out of the officer's hands and began running to the side, away from the horse paddock, her hands behind her back and the stilettos making her steps awkward. But another officer was there, and this one was twice as wide as Julia and stopped her by the simple virtue of whipping a hand around her waist and lifting her off her feet. Between him and the first police officer, they at least had her where she couldn't move, and Sam was able to scramble over to Ty.

The stab of the fork hadn't been so bad. It was the drag of the tines falling out again that had driven Ty to his knees. Two large punctures in his inner arm started to bleed profusely. Someone had stolen his voice, so he couldn't tell Sam that she should get off Julia, that, even unarmed, she was dangerous. That he didn't mind the injury—all the injuries—as long as Sam and their kids were safe.

One side of him might have started slipping toward the blissful, welcoming ground. Oh, all of him. Sam was popping up and down in his vision, sitting on Julia. Then the cops came, and Noah was crouched next to him, saying, "You okay, dude?" and he heard Noah's shirt tear. He wanted to tell him it wasn't worth Noah's cool shirt, but Sam was there now, and anyway, he had no voice.

She dropped to the ground, sending a cloud of dust into his face. "Ty," she said.

He fought unconsciousness. She wasn't strong enough to take his entire weight, and he should stand or something. As he floated a little, he could hear her crying.

"'m okay," he said, though all his blood was on fire. Was this just from the injury? Or had Julia finally given him an aneurysm?

"Ty..." She was crying. "Oh, Ty. You saved Cairo. I can't believe it. You saved Cairo."

"'Course I did," he mumbled. "Love that guy." Keeping his eyes open took too much effort.

"Ty. Stay awake. Don't you dare. Don't you dare leave me now." Her arms were around his waist, her head next to his. She'd pulled him to a seated position. She was strong enough, after all. Of course she was.

"You're mine now," she said. "I won't let anything bad happen to you. Not ever again."

"'Course you won't," he said.

Another scream from Julia. He gained enough strength to turn his head to see what had made her so mad. Ah. It was him again, of course. Or rather, if the words she shrieked could sink in, it was

Sam's proprietary way of holding him that made Julia incoherent with rage. Luckily, both cops now had her firmly in their grasp.

Sam settled her arms around him even more closely, and he heard her say, "That's right, lady. And don't you forget it." Julia couldn't hear her because she hadn't stopped her rant, but Ty appreciated it all the same.

He was so tired. "Let me lie down," he murmured.

"No, no, honey, come on, don't go to sleep. Just a couple more minutes till they get here." She was holding his arm too tightly. He murmured at the pain. "Noah, get that tourniquet going. Come on, baby, stay with me. I love you. Stay awake with me."

Funny. She was actually holding him up now. "Love you too," he said, drifting. "My arm hurts."

"I know, baby," she said. "But it can't be worse than seven minutes of Heaven with Sam Fielding, can it?"

He laughed and passed out.

Chapter 22

"We're going to stay here," Ty said.

They were in bed, as they had been a lot in the last week while Ty convalesced. Noah had been true to his word and given the kids so much to do, they fell into bed at night completely exhausted. Leaving Sam and Ty plenty of time to catch up.

Sam sat up and let the sheet fall off her as she twisted to look at him. "What?" she said, but a shiver of hope went up her spine.

"The kids and I talked," he said. God, he was so beautiful, blond and tan against Noah's cream-colored sheets. One arm was above his head, a bandage hiding the angry red marks where Julia's pitchfork had pierced his skin. The crook of his elbow still showed the puncture wound where he'd received three units of blood. Sam hated to see it.

"We're going to find a place halfway between here and Albuquerque so we can visit Noah and you both. Maybe Santa Fe."

"But... your job." Since her embarrassing meltdown at his side, Sam had told herself *not* to make plans, to hope, to even daydream. Loving Ty wasn't the same as sharing her life with him and Matt and Alyssa. Massachusetts was just as far away from New Mexico as it had ever been, and Sam's skills weren't needed there.

"I can work remotely for now," he said. "Maybe make a couple of trips north to finish out my projects. I'll sell my house. Then I'll look for work here. And do my woodwork. Sell it at Noah's gallery. He's right. The cost of living here is way less than Massachusetts. I can give myself time to work on my comic book stuff."

"Graphic novel." She smiled. "And don't tell me you can draw as well as you carve wood."

He shrugged in his typical modesty.

"Seriously, Ty," she said, leaning on one hand and looking down at him. "Do the kids know what they're agreeing to? They're willing to give up their lives in Massachusetts to come here?"

He brushed her hair out of her face. "There are too many memories up there for them. Their friends can come visit, but after what happened at Alyssa's graduation, they're ready to start over. Matt says he'll have the best college essay in the state."

She snort-laughed.

"Plus"—he stroked her jaw—"you live here."

"Ty."

"If you'll let us," he said, "we'll find a way to be with you as much as we can." His hand stilled. "Sam, I don't want you to feel like you have to be with us. I know your independence is important to you. I come with a ton of baggage, and I know that scares you."

"Ty, you—"

He talked over her, as though she were about to argue and he had to finish his speech or she'd walk away. "I want to be by your side your whole life. But however you want me. And"—he looked away from her to the rough-hewn headboard Noah had made by hand—"if you don't want to, we'll still—"

"I want to," she said over him. "I want to, you complete fool." She kissed him. "You've spent a week with me. You knew me at my worst. If you're still willing to let me around your kids—"

Her throat was closing up in some embarrassing way, so she threw herself down on him, making him *oof* at her weight.

"I love you," he said, and Sam's throat closed up even more. "Please make our family whole again."

"Damn you, Tyler," she said. "Stop making me cry!"

He was already wiping the tears from her cheeks. "It's okay, Indy. I won't tell anyone."

Epilogue

Six Weeks Later

"I still can't believe we have to start school in August," Matt said.

"I don't mind," Alyssa said, swinging her new handmade crossbody bag onto her shoulder, its beads and fringes catching the morning light. "Anyway, at least we get to take the bus together."

"If you think I'm gonna talk to my pipsqueak freshman sister on the bus, you can—"

"I don't need you! I got *friends* I can talk to!"

"All right, you two," Sam interrupted. "Come eat your breakfast or you'll miss the bus altogether."

"You could drive us," Alyssa said with a big grin.

Sam waved the spatula at her. "Nuh-uh. Start as you mean to go on. 'Sides, until my contract runs out, I won't be here most mornings. So don't get used to this." She indicated the spread in front of them.

"Don't remind me." Ty came down the stairs of his new townhouse, one of a community made out of adobe that couldn't be more different from what they'd left behind in Massachusetts. Outside, the sky was an almost painful blue against the russet red of the buildings and the green of the small trees in the courtyard. They'd chosen it together, renting while Ty sold his other house and Sam wrapped up in Albuquerque. The Puebloans around Santa Fe had hired Sam the second she reached out.

He kissed the side of Sam's head, real quick, then stole a piece of bacon from the plate and blew on it before throwing it to Cairo.

"Don't spoil him!" Sam exclaimed. "He'll stop listening to me."

"No one stops listening to you," Ty said seriously, putting his arm around her. Sam humphed and relaxed into him.

"I'm tryna eat!" Matt protested.

"I don't care!" Ty parroted in the same tone. "When does the bus come again?" And he kissed Sam, who angled her face up to meet him.

"Ew!" Matt said. "God, you two are gross."

"Thank you." Sam curtseyed. "You want juice?"

Matt held up his glass in answer, because his mouth was full of eggs.

Ten minutes later, Alyssa's friends from the complex arrived and whisked her and Matt to the bus. Sam hugged them and promised she'd be back on the weekend—"Yes, with Cairo." She laughed when Alyssa asked. "Honestly, I don't think you'd agree to any of this unless Cairo was in the picture."

Alyssa took her seriously. "You know that's not true," she said, her heart-shaped face falling.

"I know it, sweetie," Sam said, hugging her close. "I love you too. Now get. I'll see you Friday."

Cairo whined when the door slammed behind the children. Ty put his arms around Sam. "I hate this part."

She kissed him, trying to make it quick, but as usual, it went on low and slow and Sam's shirt was fully unbuttoned before she could push Ty away. "It's only until October," she reminded him.

"Three months. What do I do with all my weekdays for three months?"

Sam knew the real answer. He would be figuring out his and his children's new lives. Settling them into school, keeping up their therapy appointments. Finding work. Negotiating the part of their lives that included Julia being in prison for real. One day, when the kids were ready, he'd take them to visit their mom. Sam wasn't holding her breath.

But he looked so bereft, she didn't give him the real answer. Where was the fun in that when she could say, "You're gonna spend them remembering this," let her unbuttoned shirt fall off her shoulders, and wrap herself around him instead?

The End

Preview of Rise

Want to see more of Megan and find out who could take care of her the way Ty does Sam? Have a sneak peak at RISE, available now!

Chapter 1

Megan Fielding was *fine*.

"Hey, hey, hey!" she said to the early-morning concierge in her building.

"Morning, Ms. Fielding!" He smiled back. "Happy New Year! How was the wedding?"

"Beautiful. You wouldn't believe the mountains. And my sister's clients gave her a handmade animal-hide wedding dress. I've never seen anything like it."

"You've always told me she was unique."

Megan nodded. "Made sense she'd have a wedding like no one else."

Made sense her favorite sister would find a husband in Massachusetts but somehow, they'd both end up settling two thousand miles away from her family. From Megan.

But Megan was fine with it. *Fine*.

"You're up early," the concierge said.

"Yeah. Gotta get back to real life."

"Well, we missed your smiling face around here."

Good. That was what Megan did. Made other people's days better. She adjusted her scarf, ready to face the January air. "Have a great day!"

"You too."

One human interaction down. A few dozen to go.

Not that she didn't *like* people. They just needed... *handling*.

At least she was up so early, there wouldn't be many of them at her favorite coffee shop. Oh Beans! had been a staple of her day since she'd first started at Fielding Paper ten years ago. As she moved through the departments of the family business, learning so she'd take over one day, the grumpy owner and crew of baristas at Oh Beans! was the one group she didn't have to impress. She'd won their affection through sheer longevity.

Her sturdy boots, new ones bought in Taos, were thick and warm and complemented her calf-length shearling coat perfectly. She was ready for her world. Everything was as it should be.

Megan put her hand on the horizontal bar that opened the door as though greeting an old friend.

But the moment she entered, she could tell the atmosphere was off.

It still smelled heavenly, with freshly ground coffee and Roman's Danishes sweetening the air. The morning baristas who'd worked there when she left for New Mexico were still behind the counter—well, two of them. One was sitting at a table at the back of the otherwise deserted room with a man Megan could hardly make out. This was unusual. Sophia was usually full-stretch into the morning routine. Was the stranger a relative? But then why was the atmosphere so charged?

A dark scruff of stubble all but hid half the man's face. He wore a baseball cap and hoodie parka pulled up, despite being in the warmth. He wore heavy-rimmed glasses and didn't look up like the others did when Megan came in.

"Hey, stranger!" Grace called to her from the espresso machine.

"There she is," Roman, the owner, said in a growl that somehow still carried over the noise of the steamer.

"Hey, guys." Since they were trying to be normal, Megan would as well. It was none of her business who the other guy was. She loosened her collar and scarf and walked up to the counter. "How've you been?"

"You're in early," Roman said. It sounded like an accusation.

"I just couldn't wait to see your sunny self again, Roman." She smiled. Okay, maybe she had to work a little to get these guys to like her. Not having people like her was anathema to Megan. And since no one ever walked up to her and said, "I like you; you can relax," Megan kept on working.

"How was New Mexico?" Sophia asked, standing. The stranger was hidden from view behind her back.

"Incredible," Megan enthused, while Grace went straight into making her drink. A large café au lait with a caramel shot, extra froth. Roman's pick of the Danishes. "You should've seen the mountains in the snow."

"Your Instagram has been hopping," Grace said. "Your family is disgustingly beautiful."

Megan usually saved her account for photos of events that supported her brother's foundation, but she hadn't been able to resist posting photos of Sam and Ty's wedding. "Thanks. I think."

"Pecan," a voice said suddenly from behind Sophia as Roman reached for the bakery shelf. "Don't give her the cherry, Roman. She likes the pecan better."

Megan's thoughts screeched from Taos back to the room in front of her. She recognized that voice. For the last five years, the whole world had recognized that voice. Smooth, Italian. Consonants hidden behind his teeth. Pronounced "Roman" with a rolled R.

"Hello, Megan," the voice said, then, "It's okay, Sophia," and Sophia stood to one side so Megan could get a good look at the stranger.

He rose from his shadowy corner and tipped up the baseball cap, letting the hood fall behind him. His hair was shaggy and unkempt, and not in a styled way. The effect was heightened by his stubble. Megan had always seen him clean-shaven.

His piercing gray eyes held hers. No mistaking the man with those eyes.

"Alessandro!" she exclaimed. The anonymity, the quiet early morning store, the hoodie and the ballcap all clicked into place. "Well," she went on more quietly. "This is a surprise. You guys must be thrilled to see him again."

Sophia grimaced, Roman rolled his eyes, and Grace said, "You're kidding, right?"

"What?" How could anyone not be happy to see Alessandro

Rosselli, former barista of this corner of Boston, now the hottest actor in Hollywood? Not to mention the most beautiful man Megan had ever seen. Which was beside the point, but she couldn't help it. He was taller than her, unless she wore her heels, which she almost always did. Even those thick glasses couldn't hide his silver-gray eyes.

She hadn't been this close to him in so many years, she wanted to turn away to compose herself. When he'd been her barista, there had been a counter between them, which had been a good thing. His charisma radiated off him, even now when he wasn't smiling.

With five years of morning small talk, she'd learned about the highs and lows of his auditions and his introductions to the American movie industry. She'd known he'd be discovered one day and whisked away from them to the bright lights of LA. She'd been so very right. Five years ago, she'd walked into the shop and Grace had told her he'd gotten his big break. He was off to Hollywood and would never come back.

Which had been *fine.*

"Don't you ever go on the internet?" Sophia said.

"I was traveling all day yesterday," she said. "I've only been posting photos from the trip. What's going on?"

"Our sweet little Alessandro," Grace said, barely containing her obvious relish, "got himself arrested the other day."

"Sweet?" Alessandro asked the air. "Little?"

"Um," Megan said. Those were the words he chose to focus on? He was supposed to be living his best life over there on the West Coast. "Arrested?"

Alessandro grimaced but didn't say anything else, so Grace helped him out. "He and Nicola Kulik partied hard over New Year's. Got into a leeeetle scuffle with a photographer. Right, 'Sandro?"

"Something like that."

"And now his manager has told him to lie low until it blows over. So of course he comes to the safest place in the world, with his best pals."

"Who he's ignored for five years," Roman growled even lower than Alessandro had.

"That's not true," Sophia said. "Remember all that traffic we got after his first big interview? When he mentioned us?"

Megan remembered that, too. The place had been mobbed for weeks. People's memories were short, though, and they'd soon gone back to more convenient coffee shops, leaving Oh Beans! to the Waterfront regulars.

"So you're back in town for a while?" she asked Alessandro.

"For a while, yes," he said. He'd looked at her throughout this exchange, and now he took off his glasses. Those pewter eyes pinned her in place.

"Well," she said, trying to lighten the atmosphere and clear her deer-in-headlights feeling. "You might want to take a box of Roman's coffee to go, because you won't be able to set foot in here after seven a.m. You remember."

"I do."

She didn't know why this thought made her want to touch her throat. Of course he remembered the crowds. It was just... with the way he was looking at her... and the way he'd told Roman what her favorite Danish was... he seemed to be remembering more than just a bunch of customers.

"So how are you, Megan?" he asked.

"Oh! I'm fine! You know me," she said like a complete fool through her skipping heartbeat. Now she wanted to reach for the ends of her hair. "Running my brother's PR takes up all my time right now."

"Are there any departments left for you to move to?"

He remembered that she'd been moving from department to department, learning everything she could about the company before getting an office on the executive floor.

"Yep. Just manufacturing. Then it's the C-suite all the way, baby! I can't wait to steal my brother's coffee mug every day."

"You won't be sad?" Grace said. "Seems like PR is a good fit for you."

"Oh, well." She smiled big. Her personal feelings didn't matter on this one. She was moving in a month, and that was that. "Let's get back to you, Alessandro! Are you really in trouble? And where's Nicola?"

According to the fashion blogs Megan followed, Nicola was his girlfriend. As blond and bubbly as Alessandro was dark and brooding, they made a great couple on the red carpet.

"She went home, too. Back to Poland."

"That's a shame." Why hadn't they holed up in some random city together? Why hadn't he gone to his native Italy? Why wasn't he with his family if he couldn't be with Nicola?

Why had he come back to Boston?

"It's not a big deal," he said. "It will blow over."

Megan frowned for a second but cleared her expression. It was none of her business, no matter how hard he was staring at her. That was just his movie-star quality shining through his no-good, very bad day. Making her feel like she was the only person in the room. He'd always been like that. No one could say "mocha latte extra foam" like he could. Like it was a love language. A promise. Three-quarters of the people who came into the shop had to have been in love with him.

"Here's your coffee, Megan," Grace said.

What? What was coffee? "Oh, yes." She came back to herself, gave Alessandro the big smile she used to disarm any hint of confusion, and turned away to pick up the cup and the bag containing her Danish. The mixed scents of coffee and caramel made her mouth water. "Life-giving elixir," she said, bringing the cup to her nose and taking a deep sniff. "Well, guess I'd better get to work."

"And I should go," Alessandro said, looking at the huge clock installation on the wall beside him. "Before the crowds descend."

"You were very well camouflaged, by the way," she said. She kept the cup by her face, as though it could stop him from noticing that she had trouble looking away from him. "I would never have known it was you until you spoke."

"Noted," he said. "It was good to see you."

"Um," she said. "Yep! You too!"

And she walked out without saying goodbye to any of the others.

♦

Want more? Get RISE at your favourite bookstore now! https://books2read.com/u/3nBXQe

Acknowledgements

First, and least importantly, I'd like to thank Google. One day I'll do Sam and Ty's trip myself for real, but boy oh boy isn't Google Maps handy when you can't.

Thanks to Victoria Farhat and Lena Pinto for taking time out of their schedules to read this all in a hurry instead of at our weekly critique group because I'd run out of time. You are the most fabulous plotters I know, and I'm glad to have you in my life.

Thanks to the rest of my critique group: Noreen Lekhak, Kim Katil, Margaret Dudonis, Delores Stewart, Michael DeMarco, and Maria Imbalzano, who read the other bits of this and helped me corral it from its disparate parts into some kind of comprehensive whole. Sam couldn't have got her HEA without you.

Thanks again to Laura Quinn, who barely knew me from Adam, but jumped to help me with the sensitive parts of this story. Any fudge-ups are my own.

To my fantastic editing team: Julie Sturgeon and Kimberly Dawn. And of course the über-talented Lyndsey Lewellen, who knocked it out of the park AGAIN with the cover. You all make me look better than I deserve.

And finally and most importantly to my family, who put up with me in general. Wind beneath wings, and all that crap. Love you!

About the Author

Kimberley Ash is a British expat who has lived in and loved New Jersey for almost 30 years. She writes fish-out-of-water stories about people who find home where they least expect it. When not writing contemporary romance or romantic women's fiction, she can usually be found cleaning up after her two big furry dogs and slightly less furry children.

Other Books by Kimberley Ash

The Fieldings
Breathe
Hold
Rise
The Van Allen Brothers
Forgive Me
Forget Me
Free Me

Connect with Kimberley

If you've enjoyed Sam and Ty's story, and are looking forward to Megan's, join my Facebook Group, Read Your Ash Off, sign up for my newsletter, and follow me to get the latest info on my new releases and events. I look forward to meeting you!

Website: www.kimberleyash.com

Bookbub: @KimberleyAsh

Instagram: @KAshAuthor

Goodreads: Kimberley Ash

Facebook Page: Kimberley Ash Books

TikTok: @kimberleyashauthor

Twitter: @KAshAuthor

www.ingramcontent.com/pod-product-compliance
Lightning Source LLC
Chambersburg PA
CBHW030623190726
48286CB00008B/2371